ROGER ELWOOD

Creation House
Lake Mary, Florida

Creation House
Strang Communications Company
600 Rinehart Road
Lake Mary, FL 32746
(407) 333-0600

First printing, June 1990
Second printing, September 1990

For Murray Fisher—

there when he was needed most,
with the prayer that I can be
the same when he needs me.

─────── ACKNOWLEDGEMENTS ───────

THREE OF THE MOST PROFOUNDLY INFLUENTIAL individuals in the creation of *Dwellers* have been Clyde and Ruth Narramore and Harold Lindsell. They encouraged me in more ways than one, and I am deeply indebted to them all.

I am also grateful to Stephen and Joy Strang; they are examples of Christian love being shown to someone who isn't always lovable.

And there is Carl Dunn, who brought Creation House and me together; I owe him a great deal, too.

But then our Savior, Jesus Christ, is the principal architect of all this, and to Him I pledge my dedication to His honor and glory forever and ever.

...SATAN'S PALACE WAS ON THE PRIMAL EARTH
...one of Satan's main titles concerns itself with his principality over this particular world. Now, it is most important that we determine where Satan was at the moment of his rebellion. Most commentators have assumed that he was somewhere in heaven, that his fall took place there, and that he was cast down to earth. However, we find no evidence for such a position. Rather do we find the Bible specifically teaching that his rebellion took place on earth....

Donald Grey Barnhouse
from *The Invisible War*

IT HAPPENED IN THE EARLY MORNING NEAR Nocales, New Mexico. Visitors with arthritis and various other ailments had been soaking in the hot springs on the outskirts of town, enjoying the supposed therapeutic value of the soothing waters, a natural phenomenon that drew people from all over the United States.

"An earthquake!" one of the men yelled.

The ground shook, the springs rolling like water in a glass.

And then nothing.

"A short one," a woman sighed in relief.

Several minutes passed.

The people went back to enjoying the soothing warmth.

"Look!" somebody yelled suddenly.

At first the rest didn't see anything.

Until—

The shape stood before them, its body shaking slightly as though trying to steady itself. Then it turned and saw the springs.

"We've got to get out of here!" one of the women shouted.

"Quiet, big mouth. Maybe it won't see through all this steam."

But "it" did and, limping slightly, walked slowly to the edge.

The being was less than six feet tall and quite broad.

"Like something out of one of those prehistoric movies," a witness would later describe it.

It said nothing but just stood there, looking at them, its expression apprehensive.

They are scared of me. They seem unwilling to trust me. What can I do to communicate past their fear?

Then suddenly it took off its foot coverings, rolled up its lower garment and sat on the edge of the springs, dangling its legs over into the hot waters.

All but one of the people were terrified, that sole exception being a twelve-year-old boy who broke away from his parents and waded toward the creature.

"Jonathan! No!" his mother shouted.

Jonathan was quite pale, his blood thinned dangerously by a rare disease that was a biological cousin of leukemia. The heat of the springs seemed to revive him.

The little one is not so afraid. He seems weak. I can almost feel his pain in my own body. He hides the full truth of it from the others.

Jonathan stopped in front of the creature, the two of them momentarily studying one another, the boy a quite pitiful sight, frail-looking, his eyes perpetually bloodshot, his skin stretched thin over a bony frame. He had no hair on his head, radiation treatments having taken their toll.

The creature had hair everywhere, flowing down in a thick golden mane from its head, protruding from under the sleeves of its garment, up over the edge of the collar.

Jonathan touched his hand—the hair on the back of it.

"Soft," the boy whispered, "so soft...."

Just as he was saying that, his mother reached him and started to pull him back.

The female must be his kindred. She is afraid that I will harm him. Perhaps if I spoke, that would reassure them all.

"Yes, it is soft."

Words. In perfect English. With only the slightest hint of an accent to mark them.

The mother's eyes opened wide.

The creature reached into a pocket of its garb, brought out a little leather-like pouch, took a tiny white pill from inside and handed it to the boy.

Yes! Perhaps the pills we use could benefit the young one.

Jonathan grabbed it and swallowed it before his mother could stop him.

"Jonathan."

The creature spoke his name once.

Even the mother hesitated. In that tone, that deep, almost baritone voice was a note of tenderness so profound that it brought tears to her eyes.

"We could have—," it started to say, then switched to thought only.

Taresa and I might have parented such a child.

The mother noticed that the creature's eyes were now moist.

"Who are you?" she said, suddenly losing her fear. "Where did you come from?"

Turning its attention to her, it seemed transfixed by the golden color of her own

10

hair. He started to touch one strand with his right hand. Her husband spoke up with intense alarm, but she waved him to silence.

"Your eyes," she said softly, looking up directly into its own. "I have never seen ones as sad as—"

"So much like her," it interrupted, its mind far away from that spot, and she could feel its overwhelming sorrow.

Indeed she is. Taresa's eyes—

Suddenly it turned and climbed out of the springs.

"Don't go," Jonathan begged.

I must. Memories force me to flee, little one.

It left them, disappearing first through the steam that rose from the heated water and then into the desert.

For an instant, before it was no longer in sight, they all thought they heard it say just one time in a low, mournful voice a single name strange to their ears.

"Taresa...."

THE MAIN STREET OF NOCALES WAS AS YET
unpaved, pockets of dust stirred up by passing feet, clouds of it by the wheels of
cars. The place was blessed in that it hadn't become a thriving tourist mecca; not
everyone knew about the springs, and fewer still believed that they were anything
out of the ordinary.

Horses outnumbered cars. And one of the unwritten requirements was that visitors
as well as residents dress in the fashion of the Old West. This was partly to maintain
the aura of another time and place. Also, cowboys had dressed that way in the first
place because their clothes helped keep them cooler in the midst of the dry but intense heat that baked that entire region much of each year.

Rev. Matthew Kindred had stopped in Nocales for a couple of days before moving
on. The springs provided him with some relief for muscles tight with the tension of
his life.

Before moving on.

He wasn't sure of any specific destination, hadn't been for a very long time, only
that he would be better off staying as mobile as possible. At one point he was successful in deluding himself that he was merely putting himself in the Lord's hands and,
accordingly, that the Lord would guide him to the appropriate destination.

The modest hotel where he had been staying in Nocales was Western in style—its
bellboys and maids dressed in the requisite boots-and-leather outfits, their manner
genuinely friendly. It was satisfyingly Western in service as well, featuring hearty
breakfasts and superb fresh steaks for dinner. Under other circumstances he might
have remained there for a longer period of time.

The accident. It had occurred a few months earlier. He had been driving home after church one evening with his wife, Mary, and their son, David. Someone sped past a stop sign and hit the car on the passenger's side.

It's not your fault. It's not....

That didn't help afterward. Mary was dead. David was paralyzed. He dragged them both from the wreckage before the car burst into flames.

The guy was on drugs, the police said.

Yes, but I should have been more alert. If I had....

No one could help him through the awful guilt that followed. Friends tried; friends were there when he needed them, but that need was infinitely greater than they could ever satisfy. Repeatedly drowning out their well-meant advice were the incessantly recalled moments directly after the impact of the two cars, like an accusing harridan shrieking at him while waving a finger obscenely.

Mary's body was covered with blood. One arm had been bent completely back. She had cuts all over her face.

David had survived but with no feeling in his legs.

"Dad, they've been cut off!" he screamed. "I've lost my legs!"

He hadn't, but Kindred knew that his son's spinal cord must have been badly injured or perhaps severed below the neck, his arms and hands alone still functioning.

He had been thinking about a sermon with all the old force and conviction and inherent truth when the accident happened: A new heresy is abroad in the body of Christ. It equates Christianity with a fat pocketbook or a fulfilled wish list. Name your desire and claim the reality of it.

If only my mind had been more on my driving....

Kindred had the duty of officiating at his wife's burial. Other ministers wanted to help out, to take some of the chores off his shoulders. But he refused their offers.

Penance. A Baptist doing penance.

The irony of that behavior wasn't lost on him. But the trouble was that nothing alleviated the deep-down guilt that continued to smother him. He managed to get through the ceremony, managed to keep from collapsing as he stood before Mary's coffin, but crushing him as well was the knowledge that David couldn't attend his mother's funeral. The youngster was trapped in a hospital bed, his body in traction, completely immobilized. He would be there for several weeks, a chance for as much of his body to heal as possible.

Later, when Kindred was alone in the parsonage that Mary and David and he had shared for half a dozen years, he screamed out loud to the walls and the furniture, let loose a gusher of pain and shock and rage.

There was never any doubt about one terrible fact from the moment of the accident and beyond: David would be confined to a wheelchair or crutches for the rest of his life!

13

Kindred was unable to face, squarely, the double tragedy. And he was forced to admit that Mary had been more a source of his strength over the years than he cared to admit.

With her by my side, I could have gone on in the midst of anything, faced any other tragedy.

There was an irony in the circumstances, he knew—he who had been able to comfort hundreds of others in the past, helping them to talk about their guilt and encouraging them, usually with success, to place it at the feet of Christ so that His blood could wash it away forever. God's only Son had paid the price not only for their forgiveness but also for their cleansing, with guilt having no place as a result. This man was as yet incapable of claiming that forgiveness for himself.

So he ran. Perhaps it could be expressed more elegantly, but that is what he did, in a moment of spiritual cowardice. It lasted more than a moment, of course; it was months of fleeing—this in itself another reason for his guilt—as he was haunted by that last look at David struggling to use a wheelchair properly, when just a short time earlier the two of them had been playing basketball together.

He had not had a single moment of contact with David in the interim. And so the flight from guilt cured nothing but added to the reservoir itself, driving him deeper and deeper into a pervasive pit of self-pity.

So much he had encountered ahead of him reminded him of what was behind—happy children in a playground, jumping and running as David would never be able to do again; families sharing the love that was obvious between them; this and much more.

It had all been left there in his wake—David, the deacons, the choir, the committee chairmen involved with him in the pastorate, the congregation—left without warning. He waited until David was in bed, packed a few clothes and odds and ends, and then he was gone.

He told no one. He wanted no one to find him. Someday he might get his life together again, but the longer he was on the road, fleeing, the less he believed that would ever happen.

He worked as a cook, a runner, any and every job he could grab for a week or a month, here and there, and then on the road once again, periodically tracked down by someone at church and, once, by Mary's mother.

She had found him just one day earlier, in fact, at Nocales. She had called him in the middle of the night and begged him to return. And he had told her that he couldn't, he couldn't face David, face that wheelchair, face the memories that would be sharper and even more accusing in those familiar surroundings.

And as he hung up on her, his hands were shaking, and the tears streamed down his cheeks, and he wanted so much to say to her that he would be back, that he would beg David's forgiveness and try to make a life for the two of them. But his strength was diminished to the point of abject cowardice. Having to admit this to himself drove him further away from doing something concrete about it.

This is how it must be with drug addicts, he mused to himself. *They are killing themselves by addiction to the very thing they loathe, but they are unable to extricate themselves from it.*

Once, at night, he had returned, with no one else around, and stood at Mary's grave. Though he knew it was only her body there, he asked his beloved for forgiveness, and then he was gone again.

Nocales was only a few miles behind him that morning when the second earthquake hit. His car swerved as he tried to control it, and rolled over once, twice, a third time, landing in a ditch beside the road, the wheels spinning, darkness wiping the vision from his eyes....

Sheila and Max Forester were waiting impatiently as the local doctor examined their son, Jonathan.

The floor shook only once, but for several seconds.

"Another quake!" Sheila shouted as the lights in the reception area flickered.

The receptionist was nearly knocked off her feet as she was standing before a metal file cabinet.

"Worse than the first one!" she exclaimed nervously.

In a minute or two the doctor opened up the door to his inner office and told them that they could come inside.

Glass was all over the floor, along with bottles, some of which had broken, their contents tumbling out. A window had cracked.

But for the Foresters nothing mattered except the favorable diagnosis they were being given.

"Thank God!" Max exclaimed.

The three of them were smiling as they went back to the hotel, washed, changed their clothes and went downstairs for dinner. Any damage there was minor, and debris had been cleaned up.

After giving the menu a cursory look, they each ordered the thickest sirloin steak offered by the restaurant.

"We should report what happened," Max suggested.

"My guess is that we won't be the only ones," Sheila said, pointing to the green-uniformed soldier who approached a couple at one of the other tables.

"They were with us at the springs," Max recalled.

"I noticed."

Sheila's attention drifted about the dining hall. She had never been enamored of Western styles either in furniture or in dress, but somehow it all came together properly at Nocales, and the room in which they sat had just the right feel.

The soldier left, followed by the other couple.

Then another soldier came in, walking toward their table.

"Mr. and Mrs. Forester?" he asked.

"Yes," they both answered.

Suddenly Jonathan stood up, gripping his stomach.

"Mom, Dad, the pain!"

He fell forward onto the table, which toppled over. The soldier rushed to help.

Jonathan rolled off the top of the table and onto the floor. He was spitting up blood.

"Don't move," the soldier said as he bent down beside the boy, and then, looking up, with urgency on his face: "In the lobby, please, have one of the others radio for a helicopter. We need to get him to the base hospital, quick!"

Less than an hour later, the Foresters had been taken to the Nocales Army Base.

The initial reaction of the army doctors was that Jonathan had had a severe attack of his leukemia-type disease. But later they ruled that out.

"It's showing some different symptoms, whatever it is," the one in charge observed. "We just can't—"

Whatever it is.

"You don't know, you—," Max interrupted.

The creature had reached into a pocket of its garb, brought out a little leather-like pouch and taken a tiny white pill from inside and handed it to the boy.

Max told the doctor about what had happened.

"Why didn't you stop it, Mr. Forester? An apparent alien life form gives your son a pill and you do nothing?"

"Alien life form?" Sheila asked. "Are you saying that that thing was actually a—"

The thought choked off any other words.

The doctor urged them to go back to their hotel room.

"We'll phone you instantly when we have made some headway."

At first they were reluctant but decided they couldn't do Jonathan any good by pacing the corridors of the base. So they were escorted to the same helicopter that brought them there.

In a short while they were sitting on the edge of the bed in their room.

17

"We came here to help our son and look at what's happened," Max said. "All because of that thing."

He stood up suddenly and went to a long, narrow case leaning against the dresser to the left of the bed.

"I was hoping to take Jonathan hunting near here," he said.

"Max, what are you doing?" Sheila asked, her voice loud with alarm.

He unzipped the case and took out a hunting rifle.

"This'll do it," he said, glancing over the rifle. "This'll do it real well."

"No, not out there, alone," his wife pleaded.

"Wanna bet, Sheila? Whatever it is deliberately poisoned our son. I'm not going to wait for the bureaucratic military to do something about it."

She tried to pull the rifle out of his hands, but he was too strong and determined.

"I'll be fine," he told her. "It looked kind of dumb, more like an animal of some sort. No match for a man and this here rifle."

"Not alone," she begged. "You don't know the area. Please, wait until tomorrow. Let's see how Jonathan is then."

He looked at her intently and then put the rifle back.

The next morning, when Sheila Forester awoke, she found her husband gone, along with the rifle. Just as she was reaching frantically for the telephone, it rang, startling her.

"Yes...," she answered hesitantly.

"Your son," the voice at the other end said, "he—"

Mᴀᴛᴛʜᴇᴡ ᴋɪɴᴅʀᴇᴅ ᴋɴᴇᴡ ʜᴇ ᴡᴀs ᴀᴡᴀᴋᴇ. ᴛʜᴇ pain in his head could not have been from a dream. But when he opened his eyes, or thought he did, he could see nothing.

Blind!

Could he be blind?

He remembered losing control of the car. And yet he wasn't in the wreckage—he knew that much.

A hospital?

"Is anyone there? Doctor! Nurse! What's going on?"

No answer.

He moved his left hand.

Hard.

He felt something very hard, not the soft mattress of a bed.

I'm lying down, he told himself. *I've got to stand.*

Pain. In his back.

I'm not paralyzed like David.

He indeed could move his arms and legs.

But I'm blind....

He sank backward and let out a yell of pain.

Something sharp in his back.

Rock, uneven, edges jutting outward.

He stood then, falteringly, and raised his arms upward, felt a jagged rock "ceiling."

A cave!

He was in a cave. Somehow he had gotten out of the wreckage and crawled blindly away. Or...

The thought that followed made him tremble.

...he had been taken to the cave.

But who? And where are they now?

He felt quite dizzy at that moment and had to lean back to steady himself.

How much of a mess it all was...*in a strange place...knowing no one... while his son waited for him to return...this time the father the prodigal in a far land.*

He smelled something. It had come in on a vagrant breeze.

A breeze, yes! I must be near the mouth of the cave.

The odor of cooking meat....

He groped ahead toward the smells that touched his nostrils. Finally he fell forward onto warm desert sand.

"I am glad to see that you have regained consciousness," a voice said.

"Where are you?" he asked, confused.

"About ten yards directly in front of you."

"What's going on?"

"I pulled you out of the wreckage of your vehicle, or what was left of it. A very short time later it burst into flames."

Kindred's mind was spinning. He had almost been killed!

"Let me bring you to the fire," the voice added. "We can eat together, you and I."

He felt a rather large hand take his own and guide him gently forward. Flickering heat touched his cheeks.

He was helped into a sitting position.

"I...I can't see," Kindred said inanely.

"I know," his benefactor commented. "You will regain your sight soon."

"But how do you know?" Kindred asked, a sense of panic nibbling at him. "How can you be so sure?"

"I gave you some medicine."

"To cure blindness?"

"It is only due to nerve shock. I have encountered it myself. In the caverns, a spitting dragon's venom."

"Caverns? Spitting dragon? What—"

"I am sorry to give such information so quickly. There is much that we both need to absorb from one another but more slowly. Please forgive me."

"Of course," Kindred replied, feeling relieved that whoever it was seemed to have

20

a note of authority in his voice when he spoke of sight returning.

"Here, eat this."

Kindred was hungry. He took what the other handed him and started to bite into it...a semi-sweet taste...not too bad.

"What is this?" he asked.

"It was on the ground, crawling, a green color. I killed it and cooked it."

On the ground, crawling, a green color.

Kindred knew he should have been sick to his stomach but he wasn't. Hunger overrode all of that.

He blinked his eyes.

A faint form had appeared in the fading darkness.

"You should have some sight returning about now," Kindred was told.

"A little, yes."

"Good!"

"Who are you?" Kindred asked. "Where do you live?"

"Here. Now."

"I mean, where do you come from?"

"A very long distance away."

"What state?"

"Not a state."

"What country then?"

"Not a country."

Kindred choked on what he was eating.

Have I run across someone escaped...

"Deep within the planet."

...from a sanitarium?

Kindred got to his feet.

"Please," the voice said. "I should not have told you yet. But you will see me soon anyway. You will see that I am similar to your race but also very different."

The image became clearer.

Kindred saw golden hair, an extended forehead, pronounced cheekbones, a flat, wide lower jaw and a mouth containing teeth twice as wide as any...

...human teeth!

The clothes were leather-like, grayish in color.

So broad. The frame of a professional wrestler. Heavy.

"No!" Kindred screamed as he turned and ran.

His eyesight was nearly normal but not quite. And the relative darkness of nighttime under a full moon made him trip over something in his path, something that produced a low but insistent rattle.

He felt the fangs pierce his flesh, and his veins were on fire.

He could have been dying. He knew that was a distinct possibility, at one point perhaps probable.

"I killed the creature that attacked you."

The voice echoed as though down a long tunnel.

"You must take more of the pills."

Someone was holding him.

For an instant he saw that face again, like a prehistoric man's, and yet he couldn't acknowledge it as human.

Kindred struggled, tried to get away, but he was unable...too weak...that creature stronger.

"You are shivering despite the fire. Let my warmth become your own."

No!

He had to escape, get help. He—

Another pill.

"Let me tell you about my world."

The words were spoken softly, a soothing edge in the tone.

"It is very dark, and often cold and damp. We have been there for millions of years."

Every muscle in his body seemed to be exploding, fire coursing along his veins.

"Only a few of us have ventured above ground. I came to search once again for my beloved."

"Why don't you keep quiet? Can't you see that I'm dying? Have you no pity?"

"You are not dying, my friend. You will live. This is a period of purging the poison from your system. It feels like death rushing in on you, but it is not."

My friend.

How could that...that creature be a friend?

Later he discovered the pain was beginning to dissipate.

"You're saving...my *life!*"

The realization of that singular fact hit Kindred broadside. Whatever or whoever it was had fed him medicine and was now trying to keep him warm, holding him tightly, communicating with words that knew no emotional barrier.

"I lost a female whom I loved very much. She disappeared some time ago. Every so often I go above to look and then return below in sorrow."

He, too, had suffered a great loss!

"To not know whether she is alive or dead, to wonder where she is...."

How much time? Hours more than likely. The fire within him extinguished. He was able to drift toward sleep without a struggle, held so gently by the arms of one who called him friend.

Kindred opened his eyes and saw a being with golden hair and protruding forehead and cheeks and flattened jaw...sobbing.

KINDRED DID GET THROUGH THE NIGHT. WHEN he awoke, the sun was already rising, casting a glow over the sand as far as he could see. And the desert heat was coming back strong, held at bay only for a few hours.

He looked at himself, his clothes dirty and torn, spots of blood here and there. *What a mess,* he said to himself, *and so weak.*

He started to wobble as flashes of memory from his accident trickled back to the surface of his mind.

"Here," a now-familiar voice said. "Lean on me."

The hulking being was by his right side, and he leaned against that strong body.

"Do you have a name?" Kindred asked, trying to shake the last vestiges of discomfort about being so close to something from which, only hours earlier, he had recoiled in shock and fear.

"I was very close to asking you the same question. My name is Klatu."

"Mine is Matthew...Matthew Kindred."

"Whether we are entirely comfortable with the situation or not, Matthew Kindred, you and I *have* become friends."

Kindred looked at Klatu, studying him, and realized to his amazement that he was not altogether uncomfortable with the notion of friendship.

"We have been here for a very long time," Klatu was saying as they sat around a campfire inside the cave, warming themselves against the desert chill of evening. *We could have been here for a very long time.*

24

Trapped in a prison of earth and stone and also thought, assuming that their destiny would never be different, wallowing as nihilistic humanity did, in an abyss that seemed endless and inescapable.

"You've not spoken of God as yet," Kindred observed. "Is there no thought given to a Supreme Being?"

"Exactly the opposite, Matthew Kindred," Klatu said cryptically.

"I don't understand."

"We give daily thought to Him who has been punishing us all this time."

"But God isn't vengeful in the way that you suppose. He has established a channel of forgiveness."

"We hunger for that, but it cannot be appropriated for us."

"Not so, Klatu. No sin is beyond the reach of His Son's sacrifice at Calvary."

"We know about Calvary. We have been there."

Kindred could hardly speak.

"You have seen—"

"That is enough for now, my friend," Klatu said as he stood abruptly. "I need to go outside just now, to get some fresh air."

And he headed toward the cave mouth.

Left alone, Kindred drank more water from a little stream nearby, and then splashed some of it over his face.

Seconds later he heard the sound of gunfire.

STILL WEAK, KINDRED FELL SEVERAL TIMES AS he hurried from far inside to the mouth of the cave.

Klatu had been shot in the shoulder by a burly-looking man who was now clubbing him with the butt of a rifle.

"What in heaven's name are you *doing?*" Kindred yelled.

"I'm gonna kill this...this...whatever the devil it is," the man growled.

Klatu was trying to fight back, but the pain from the bullet wound had weakened him, as well as the accelerating loss of blood.

Kindred rushed forward, remembering a maneuver from his college football days. The man was knocked off his feet, the rifle flung from his grasp. But Kindred was no match for him. The man tossed him to one side, stood and ran for the rifle. Grabbing it, he turned and took aim at Klatu.

"Max! Don't!" a voice shouted. "Jonathan's been healed. That pill cured him!"

Out of the corner of his eye, he saw a familiar figure running toward him.

"Sheila?" he said, hesitating.

She was only a few feet away.

"Yes. It's true. Jonathan's going to be fine in *every* way."

Max turned his head and saw her smiling and crying at the same time.

"I got someone to lend me their car," she yelled. "I had to find you...before it was too late."

He dropped the rifle.

"The doctors back home said he had less than a year. You're saying that's not true?"

"It *was* true," she said, standing in front of him. "It *isn't* now. His blood's *completely* back to normal."

"He's—?" he started to say.

"Yes," she smiled through a cascade of tears. "Yes, yes, yes!"

Max turned to Klatu and then to Kindred, who had gotten to his feet and was hurrying to the prostrate form.

"Dear God," he said, "what have I done?"

"Forget that," Kindred pleaded. "I need help."

Kindred and Max carried Klatu back into the cave.

"Is there anything in that car that could hold water?" Kindred asked.

Sheila told him there was a thermos on the back seat and immediately rushed out of the cave to get it.

"Why did you do this?" Kindred asked.

Max told him.

"I guess I can understand how you felt, but praise God that you found out in time."

"You're a preacher, aren't you?"

"How did you know?"

"It shows."

Klatu was groaning.

He was standing on the edge of an abyss, *tottering, fearing the fall forward, the sound of voices calling him from below, faces appearing out of the darkness and then gone....*

"I've got a knife," Max said. "Let's build a fire, sterilize it. I've been a hunter for a long time. Every so often one of us is shot accidentally. I've done this sort of thing before. I can handle it, Reverend."

Kindred had had no such experience.

"Do it," he said.

Sheila Forester brought back the thermos and some clean towels she found, as well as a bottle of whiskey.

"Does using that bother you?" Max asked. "It'll help clean out the wound. But he should also drink some."

"It's medicine at that point, nothing more," Kindred said without hesitation.

Max Forester was hardly a trained surgeon, but he got the job done. Klatu had become quite drunk from the whiskey, unaccustomed to its potency, and he didn't feel the pain nearly as much as otherwise would have been the case.

The wound itself wasn't so serious, but Klatu's loss of blood was, and the battering Max had given him inflicted other damage.

27

Klatu went in and out of delirium every few minutes for a couple of hours. Much of what he mumbled was not clear enough, yet the three of them gained *some* interesting insights.

"...we...we had ghastly masters...they...they tried to—!"

"Who the devil are these...these mysterious things?" Max asked.

"Listen!" Kindred said.

"They were upon us, spectral beings, their manifested shape bent and ugly, with cloven feet and wings!"

Kindred and Max looked at one another.

"But if they have no shape," Max said, groping with unfamiliar patterns of thought, "how could they—"

"Demons have no actual physical substance. Yet when they manifest themselves, they have the ability to do so with the illusion of a body that seems quite real even though it is not."

"Klatu's people were once ruled by demons; is that what you're saying?" Sheila asked, holding herself tightly.

"Perhaps."

That thought forced the three of them into silence. Max Forester was far from being a stupid man, but neither was he a soaring intellectual. He had been oriented toward physical action the greater part of his life, both in school athletics as well as the customary rigors of his trucking business. What he preferred was living from day to day without ambiguities, everything clear-cut and upfront, as the expression goes. Facing the reality Klatu represented was a struggle for Max, but to his credit he was honestly trying to come to terms with it.

Sheila was the dreamer of the two, losing patience every so often with her husband's outlook. It had gotten them into trouble more than once over the years. Yet she knew how much he loved their son. And now, an irony that hadn't escaped her, they were trying to save the life of someone who violated more than one of Max's preconceptions!

Klatu survived, tentatively at first, throwing up every hour or so, chills gripping his body. But it was survival in any event.

Sheila and Max Forester stayed by his side, as did Matthew Kindred, for the rest of that day and into the evening.

"We're so ashamed, so sorry," Sheila told him. "You were only trying to help. You *did* help. Our son's blood is whole and normal. The doctors are astonished."

"My Taresa and I were not so different from you both," Klatu responded. "She was expecting our child. If someone had appeared to be threatening him, we would have responded the same way."

"You seem so much like us," she said, her voice breaking.

"According to my friend, Matthew Kindred, God created us both in His image."

"You know," Max said, "I've seen lots of science fiction films over the years. Life on other planets, I mean, green-eyed monsters, creatures with tentacles, giant insects, you name it. Or creatures living below. How far off-base they are!"

"True," Kindred agreed. "Man is responsible for those images, which makes them suspect from the start unless Christ is given some place in it all and—"

The sounds of commotion directly outside the cave cut off his words.

"I'll go," Max volunteered. "Stay here."

After a short while they could hear him shouting, and then he came rushing back inside.

"Helicopters, jeeps, soldiers!" he said breathlessly.

"They want Klatu?" Kindred asked.

"You got it."

"What did you tell them?"

"I don't like lying any more than you do, I guess. I said he was inside with my wife, and if they acted hastily, I couldn't tell what he might do to her."

Max looked back into the inner part of the cave.

"How far back? Can you tell?" he asked.

"Not really. It may be only a few hundred yards or maybe miles. We've only gone as far as a little spring."

"Pray that it's miles. You and Klatu have to make it as far inside this cave as you can. And pray for something else."

"That there's an opening far away from here."

Max stood in front of Klatu.

"Can you do this?" he asked.

"Can I not do it?" Klatu replied.

Kindred and Max helped him stand.

"I'll go outside," Max told him, "and delay them as long as I can. As they start to enter, Sheila will begin screaming. That should make them hesitate a bit, for her own 'safety.' "

"And by then we could be safely hiding ourselves."

"You'll have to, Reverend. The alternative is for the military guys to get their hands on him."

Quite to his surprise, Kindred found himself caring very much about what happened to Klatu.

Even as they penetrated deeper within the cave, Klatu seemed to gain strength by the minute, especially after Kindred gave him another of the tiny white pills.

In the background, fading quickly, were chaotic sounds arising from the confrontation the Foresters were having with the military.

Lord, how amazing! Kindred prayed silently as the two of them hurried along. *Max Forester was bent on killing Klatu, and now he is putting himself at risk to save him. And here I am, heading where I can't possibly guess in order to help someone from another world survive. Lord, I certainly don't have the stuff to be any kind of prophet.*

"What is a prophet?" Klatu asked, and Kindred realized that he had, in part, spoken out loud.

"Someone who can tell the future."

"Do many have this ability?"

"Not very many, even if you consider the false ones around whom whole religions have sprung up, but especially so if you are talking about only those directed by God Himself to show humankind the future."

"We must talk further about this God of yours."

Kindred nodded, grateful for that opening.

"Matthew Kindred, I am feeling suddenly very faint."

And with that Klatu passed out, falling to the ground.

They were hardly beyond the reach of their pursuers. Klatu outweighed him by perhaps a hundred pounds, which meant that Kindred was not strong enough to drag him very far.

He closed his eyes and bowed his head.

Lord, I don't know what to do just now. Please help us. Please....

Klatu was groaning.

Kindred bent down beside the large body at his feet, lifting it up as Klatu had done with him after the encounter with the rattlesnake, and held it in his arms.

Klatu's eyes were half-closed, perspiration matting his hair and standing out in thick beads on his forehead and cheeks.

"Matthew Kindred, if Taresa is dead, how...how could I ever face such a reality? To know that she has gone over into the abyss."

"God gives us much more hope than that. He—"

30

Kindred wasn't able to finish. Something was moving directly ahead.

"Ahead, Klatu. Look!"

Klatu turned as best he could, and they both saw shapes in the darkness ahead of them, not from behind, which would have meant the soldiers.

"Can you help us?" Kindred called out to them. "Can you please help us?"

One by one they came closer, Kindred gasping at the sight of the four of them, foreheads and cheeks pronounced, chins flattened, hair a light gold in color and, truly, perhaps not more than six feet tall—quite identical to Klatu.

T HREE OF THE FIGURES LIFTED KLATU GENTLY
and carried him back in the direction from which they had come. The fourth
accompanied Kindred, who was having to fight lingering weakness of his own.

The group went on for some distance. Kindred caught glimpses of shapes hovering
in the darkness, to one side or another. Whispering sounds could be heard, in obvious
reaction to the presence of the intruders.

The tunnel narrowed dramatically at one point.

"Where are we going?" Kindred asked, not really expecting a reply.

"To the main cavern. Our leader, Miath, has requested your presence."

Kindred stopped instantly.

"You speak English."

"Just like Klatu, we can speak English and many other languages with fluency,
I assure you," his companion said. "Please, let us continue."

Ahead Kindred could see an opening, and when they had passed through it, he
marveled at the size of the cavern in which they found themselves.

It was three or four stories high and nearly the size of a football field in length
and width. What it contained was equally extraordinary.

An entire community in miniature. Portions of the surrounding rock walls had
been excavated, beginning a foot or so above the ground level and continuing all
the way to the top, hundreds of cubicles, each an apartment of sorts, with barely
adequate room for sleeping and other limited purposes.

Most of the cavern inhabitants' time was apparently spent on the main floor. Kindred
and Klatu happened to arrive when they were having a communal meal, all sitting
down on their haunches and eating from clay bowls.

A collective murmur arose, with echoes of it spreading throughout the huge cavern. It wasn't a reaction to Klatu, of course; they had seen Kindred.

Scores of them gathered around him.

"So much like us!" one exclaimed.

"And yet so *big*," another added.

Kindred was at first flustered and then as awestruck about them as they were about him. From what he could see, the race greeting him so kindly and with so much excitement was at an almost aborigine level, not much beyond what prehistoric man was supposed to have achieved.

Yes! Kindred exclaimed to himself. *They look very much like Cro-Magnon man, including their relative shortness of stature. The evolutionists claimed that this ancestor of modern humankind represented an advanced stage in the evolutionary scale from the apes to the present. But they never found the link, that biological "jump" from cave-dweller to what humanity is today, the so-called "missing link."*

Kindred was stunned by the implications of what was transpiring around him.

Kindred was introduced to the settlement's leader, someone named Miath, who took his first glimpse of Kindred with a bit less emotion than the others. Kindred, though, had the suspicion that the veneer of control was just that—thin and easily peeled off.

Klatu was given hot broth of some sort and allowed to sleep. In a few hours his strength was returning quite rapidly.

In the meantime, Kindred and Miath were able to converse.

"We are glad that he feels better," said Miath, obviously pleased at the recovery. "He is our finest young one, a credit to all of us. But we are also glad to have you here, Matthew Kindred."

"There is obviously much that we have to learn from one another," the minister agreed.

"I think you will find a session with the council illuminating."

"The council?"

"Please forgive me," Miath apologized. "I was referring to the Council of Many. They are our elders, wise beyond comprehension, for reasons you will understand fully later."

At the start of what must have been evening, Kindred and Klatu gathered around a large fire in the center of the cavern, which had been precisely placed below a natural air duct in the ceiling.

The sight of the "banquet" made Kindred gag, but he fought desperately not to show it. The main course was a large earthen pot of slug-like creatures, quite slimy-looking.

That group of underground beings took thin, pointed sticks, jabbed them into the pot and pulled out slugs or whatever they were, still alive and squirmy. Then they held the things over the fire and roasted them on the spot.

"Make sure they are dead," Miath said helpfully. "If not, they do something quite unpleasant in the stomach."

Kindred followed instructions but a bit ineptly. He thought his "dinner" was dead, but just as he was about to put it in his mouth and swallow it, the thing squirmed off the stick and fell on the ground. Miath, who was sitting to the right of Kindred, reached over, jabbed his own stick into it, wiped it off on the sleeve of his garment and then held it over the fire a bit longer, finally handing it back to the minister.

"It is fine now," he said simply.

"Oh...."

So Kindred swallowed it and tried to keep from passing out.

Next were the side dishes, identified by Miath as, respectively, ant soup and raw wasp larvae.

"The main course is usually so filling that we don't have room for much else," Miath informed the two of them.

"What will you have tomorrow?" Klatu asked innocently.

"Fried bat. It's a delicacy, because they are very hard to catch."

Kindred pretended to eat more than he had but consumed just enough to know, in any event, that he was not in for a good night's sleep.

"Would I offend anyone if I went to sleep early?" he asked. "It really has been an extraordinary day."

"Go right ahead," Miath assured him. "No one will find that offensive."

As Kindred was standing, he thought to ask Miath one question.

"What do you call yourselves, by the way?"

"*We are known as the Dwellers.*"

That night Klatu did not sleep well. Neither did Kindred, but for him it was purely the food or the thought of the food he had eaten.

We are known as the Dwellers....

Hours later, after both had awakened, though in truth they had been awake off and on all night, Kindred asked Klatu about that reference.

"It is a very long story, Matthew Kindred, not to be told at present."
Klatu's expression left no doubt that the subject was closed for now.

Breakfast consisted of eggs and long shiny strips of meat.
"Klatu?" Kindred leaned over to him as they were eating the food.
"Yes?"
"What laid these eggs?"
"My advice is that it is best for you not to ask."
Later, Miath took Kindred on a tour of the settlement, and Klatu asked to join them. As it turned out, the settlement consisted not only of that huge cavern and its cubicles but also of smaller caverns spread out in an astonishing network of tunnels.
Kindred began picking up various details of what life was like for the Dwellers. There seemed to be a perpetual odor of mustiness.
"That is quite true," Miath explained, after Kindred had commented about it. "We are living within the bowels of an ancient planet. On the surface the elements bring renewal, purging. But not so down here, at least not to the extent above ground. We have no wind. There is no rain or snow. The air hangs heavy, with only the smallest of vents, I suppose you might call them, enough to keep us from suffocating but never sufficient to refresh the air really, to cleanse it. Our light, as pitiful as it is, comes only from luminescent algae, which are what you might call natural batteries. And there is quite another element of this existence of ours that you will have to face."
"What is that, Miath?"
"The way time is experienced down here. Our bodies are used to it. Yours is not.
"You mean what chronobiology talks about?"
"I will have to take your word for that, Matthew Kindred."
"Yes, of course, sorry. Chronobiology teaches that each individual has what might be called a 'body clock.' Proponents of the theory suggest that the body itself is a kind of timepiece that marches to its own internal rhythms and cycles."
"Your clock will be malfunctioning almost immediately," Miath said, with a friendly and knowing chuckle.
"In what respect?" Kindred asked.
"How long did you sleep?"
"Oh, a few hours, I suppose."
Miath was smiling from ear to ear.
"Quite wrong, Matthew Kindred."
"How many then? A dozen hours? I wouldn't be surprised actually if you said—"

35

"We suspect that it was more than thirty hours, according to above ground measure," Miath interrupted.

"More than thirty hours?" Kindred repeated disbelievingly.

"Indeed."

"How could that be?"

"Time as measured by watches and clocks is suspended here. There is no sunrise or sunset as far as we are concerned. The seasons do not exist. This is total isolation, Matthew Kindred."

"And you have been here for how long?"

"Ten million years."

Kindred stopped short.

"Ten—"

"You heard correctly, Matthew Kindred. It has been indeed a very long imprisonment."

"People have seen you, though."

"Yes, from time to time certain members of my kind penetrate the surface, gather information and then return."

"Has this happened in what we call the Rockies?"

"I believe so," Miath replied.

"And the Himalayas?"

"Yes."

Kindred's eyes widened.

"You are correct, Matthew Kindred," Miath said, sensing his thoughts. "But reports are greatly exaggerated in terms of our size."

The three of them continued walking. Kindred happened to peer in at one cavern which was empty then but had seats fashioned out of rocks arranged in several rows, one level above another.

"The Council of Many holds forth there," Miath said before Kindred asked. "They are resting now in a special place reserved just for them, isolated from the rest of us."

"What is the function of the Council of Many?" Klatu asked.

"You will find out in time."

Miath's manner suggested that that time could not be rushed.

Later, Kindred and Klatu attended a town meeting of sorts that took place in the main cavern.

Grievances and various concerns were aired, ranging from family disputes to the quality of the food to a variety of other problems.

"There really is no privacy, is there?" Kindred asked during a break.

"We have no doors," Miath said without guile.

The most intimate sort of details were discussed, even those within marital relationships, from impotence to infidelity.

"The group decides," Miath told Kindred. "Whatever affects the individual affects all of us since the group is nothing more than the assembling of ourselves as individuals together."

Kindred noticed an air of melancholy about the Dwellers he saw. They didn't hang their heads and stoop over in despair, but neither did they throw their heads back with any confidence and smile very much or laugh or show any joy.

Kindred spoke his observation aloud to Klatu. "Why is that so?" he asked when there was another break in the "town meeting."

"I think it may be derived from the circumstances of our life here. After millions of years, we can be excused, I suppose, for letting a sense of hopelessness overtake us."

After millions of years....

That was what he was told, of course; but it would mean the Dwellers had existed back in prehistoric times.

Once more the missing link!

Kindred brushed it out of his mind again, not willing to concede anything to the evolutionists.

"But is that all?" Kindred continued.

"Are you asking if there is something else that makes us hopeless, Matthew Kindred?"

"Is there?"

Klatu hesitated, as though something deep within himself had been tapped.

"Yes, there is another element in this almost palpable despair that you perceive."

Their dialogue was cut short by an announcement from Miath to the multitude there.

"We have a visitor, as you all know by now. Let me introduce him to you."

Miath leaned over and whispered, "You can talk as long as you want."

"About anything?"

"Yes, my kind are very patient," he said sardonically.

Kindred stood on a raised platform of rock, not unlike a natural podium. Spread out before him, sitting on their haunches, were hundreds of Dwellers, all of them seemingly attentive.

It wasn't so easy, Kindred discovered. Over the years he had stood before his various congregations hundreds of times, not counting civic meetings, convention appearances and so on. He lost the feeling of intimidation a long time ago.

But not before this gathering.

What could he possibly say? How could he possibly *know*?

They were a group of primitive creatures, and yet they spoke, by and large, with coherence and intelligence. Miath had explained that they picked up language usage and such during their forays above ground over the centuries, adding that it was possible to learn much about many languages through the course of millions of years.

Kindred knew he had to resist the inclination to talk down to them, to treat them as some sort of savages.

"It's safe to say that, as recently as a few days ago, I had no idea that I would be here now," he began, the crowd laughing in appreciation at that. "To go where no man has gone before...."

"*Star Trek!*" one of them shouted.

"Yes," he said, taken aback.

"They have had a broad tapestry of exposure to your culture," Miath whispered into his ear.

Smiling, Kindred felt himself loosening up.

"I remember, as a child, thrilling to the idea of discovery. I wanted to go into the central Mexican jungles and explore those ancient Aztec ruins."

One of the Dwellers stood and started speaking in a tongue unknown to Kindred.

"His ancestors witnessed the Aztecs in the full flowering of their civilization," Miath explained, whispering again. "That language he is using has been passed down through the generations to him. He is named Nahuatl, after the extinct dialect spoken by the Aztecs. And he is doing so as purely as they did in their day, uncorrupted by the passage of time."

Kindred's sense of anticipation was growing rapidly.

"But I know at least a little about the Aztecs, the Mayans, the Incas. Yet even though you all have been down here for millions of years, none of us amateur archaeologists has ever suspected your existence, not even those who have studied ancient civilizations most of their lives. I have read nothing about your society and—"

"Atlantis!" someone from the crowd shouted.

"Oh, yes, it's a fascinating story," Kindred agreed, humoring the individual and not showing any irritation over their tendency to interrupt—which reminded him somewhat of a participatory service in a Mormon tabernacle that a friend had told him about.

"It is more than a story, Matthew Kindred," Miath said. "Ask Wurken to come forward. He has something for you."

Kindred motioned the Dweller to approach him.

Wurken handed him a coin.

Fascinated, Kindred examined it front and back: shiny, gold, with an inscription in a language he didn't recognize.

"It says: 'To the great cosmic forces of the Pyramid,' " Wurken said, seeing his puzzlement.

"Where did you find it?"

"Out there." Wurken waved his arm toward the back of the cavern.

Kindred turned toward Miath.

"Later," Miath said. "We will show you."

Kindred nodded and thanked Wurken.

"So much to discover," he continued. "So many treasures of knowledge unknown to my people. And you have it here, in your minds."

Kindred felt motivated to change the emphasis.

"How many of you believe in God?" he asked. "Raise your hand."

No hand was left unraised; all had indicated affirmation.

"How many accept Jesus Christ as Savior and Lord? Or are willing to do so?"

Once again everyone assented.

"That is more wonderful to know than you can imagine."

And indeed the sight was overwhelming, a "backward" tributary of the human river, so to speak, had collectively and individually welcomed Christ into their lives.

But then the huge cavern became totally quiet at that point. The mood seemed to have changed instantly. Kindred glanced about.

"There is nothing but pain and despair for us, who are the cursed ones of planet Earth...."

A kind of song started in the crowd and spread throughout it, a mournful dirge, hummed as much as spoken, in waves from the far end to the front.

Kindred turned to Miath.

"What is this?" he asked.

"Now is not the time for questions," Miath told him. "Please believe that, Matthew Kindred. Simply listen and try to get the sense of what is coming from inside each one here."

Kindred respected Miath's advice.

The humming sound rose in volume and intensity. The Dwellers were swaying back and forth.

And suddenly Kindred caught something inside himself, a dark feeling of sorrow, probably generated by the humming, which had become increasingly oppressive.

In a minute or so, after reaching a crescendo, it stopped altogether. The Dwellers acted as though they were coming out of a trance.

Miath spoke abruptly.

"We have been oppressed by this world of ours for a very long time," he said. "There are moments when the sorrow that eats at us brings us together in the kind of dirge you have witnessed."

"But in the midst of salvation, Miath? How could it be so? Every last one has acknowledged Jesus Christ as Savior and Lord."

"It has always been so, because there is no salvation for us, Matthew Kindred— only the delusion of the same for those who achieve some sort of surface peace by mouthing the words. Yet it is an exercise only, a ceremony that is repeated but without substance, without conviction."

"But—"

"You are a very cherished guest here, my friend, and we are honored to have you join us. But please show my people and me the courtesy of letting us determine when and how much we reveal to you about our past and present way of life."

Kindred and Klatu soon left the gathering and headed back to their own cubicle at the end of another tunnel.

"What did he mean, 'only the delusion of the same'?" Kindred asked. "It is almost as though that song was one they had repeated so much over the centuries that it has become a dead exercise, nothing more."

"My friend, you are like a tourist here, in a way," Klatu replied. "We go through the ceremony for your benefit, period. And that is not meant in any unkind manner."

As soon as they had reached their cubicle and sat down on the hard floor, Kindred asked Klatu about Taresa.

Klatu leaned back against the rock wall, sighing.

"I loved her so very much," he said softly. "She was with child, as I said before, when she disappeared. We both were looking forward to the birth. And we planned so much as parents. We...."

He started crying.

"Forgive me," he said. "Forgive me for being so weak."

"Tears are a release," Kindred hastened to reply. "They do not show weakness. Let them come without shame."

"We were above ground when it happened, you know."

"Could she have become lost?"

"It is possible. But—"

"But what, my friend?"

"I was tired and fell asleep. I knew Taresa was going off on her own. There was no reason to be concerned. She and I had gone above before; that was one of our duties as scouts, like the others appointed in times past, to learn, to bring back information.

"When I awoke, she hadn't returned. I went looking for her and kept doing so for a very long time. I found only the sand disturbed at one spot as though there had been a struggle, and what you call tire tracks. But nothing more. And I do not know if any of that involved my beloved Taresa."

Klatu lapsed into silence and was soon sound asleep.

Kindred wasn't tired as yet.

I'm restless, he told himself. *I'm going to walk the tunnels a bit.*

Kindred left the cubicle and strolled down the tunnel outside and turned right.

To face a sight he could not have anticipated.

Row after row of holes excavated out of the walls, reaching up to the ceiling. Inside each was a shape barely discernible in the darkness.

And a single Dweller in that large cave, kneeling.

Kindred's presence was detected immediately. This Dweller acted quite differently from the others—and looked less well-scrubbed.

"I have heard about you, foolish one," the Dweller said mockingly.

"Why do you call me foolish?" Kindred responded, trying to hold his temper.

"Because you are foolish and stupid. You talk of Christ as Savior and Lord."

"Yes, I do. He accepted me the moment I did so with Him. And He will do so with any human being."

The Dweller started laughing hysterically.

"Is that what you think? You talk of Him as though He has put His arms around us and taken us in as members of His precious flock."

"That is what I believe."

"Your belief is as dead and aimless as I shall be soon."

"You are dying?"

"Because of them!"

He pointed to the ceiling of the tunnel in which they were standing.

"What have they done?"

"They have poisoned my lungs with their fallout. They have doomed thousands like me over the past quarter-century of pain and despair."

"You mean my race, my people?"

"Good for you. And they take us and use us in their laboratories, trying to... to...."

He suddenly became weak and fell back against the stone wall of the tunnel.

Kindred went to his side.

"Is there anything I can do?" he asked with genuine concern. "Call one of the others for help?"

"No, no," the Dweller said, his manner softening. "Nothing will help. The pain spreads, through my veins, my bones, through every muscle in my body. Death will be merciful."

He grabbed Kindred by the arm.

"Klatu is young. Make sure, as his human friend, that he lives this life as well as he can. Forget heaven. And hell. For us neither exists. Only this world matters— please, please believe that. I speak the truth."

"But your truth contradicts the Bible, which assures us that—"

"Not us, Matthew Kindred. Never us!"

He became quite nervous then, his eyes darting from side to side.

"I go now. Do not hate me. Think me crazy. But do not hate me. There is already too much of that, you know."

And he was gone, disappearing down the tunnel and around the corner of another.

Kindred walked up to several of the excavations.

So very old.

He had seen Egyptian mummies. Some from the Mayan and other cultures. But these....

All of those he could see seemed to have died in agony, few stretched out as though they had simply drifted off into death. Rather their bodies were contorted, hands sometimes raised upward.

He noticed one in particular. The head was turned toward him, the mouth opened wide as though screaming.

Oppression.

It hit Kindred then, a feeling of unspeakable heaviness in that place, a sensation of utter doom.

He turned quickly and hurried out into the tunnel and found his way back to the right cubicle. Klatu was asleep. Kindred lay down on the soft bed of leaves that formed a mattress for each of the Dwellers and now for himself.

Kindred dreamed that night, of being inside a tomb.

"IT ENDED SO SOLEMNLY YESTERDAY," MIATH told them. "I thought we would go on a little adventure this time. I've asked Klatu to join us."

They followed him down a section of tunnels neither remembered being in before. And then they had an encounter that could never be forgotten.

Kindred stood on the edge of a body of water of such purity and clarity that he could see deep within it, a sight so breathtaking that he could not speak, could scarcely comprehend the magnitude of it.

"Yes," commented Miath, "it truly *is* amazing the first time or even the hundredth time. The wonder of a world those above ground know little or nothing of, and this is just a small part of that world, our world."

The wonder of a world.

And even those words merely hinted at the sight of layers of tunnels fanning out from the rock walls that contained the water before them, dozens of these tunnels, going off, it seemed, in as many directions.

"Where do they lead?" Kindred eventually found the energy to ask.

"All around planet Earth."

Kindred turned, startled, to look at Miath and then at Klatu, with an uncomprehending, even disbelieving expression.

"It is true, Matthew Kindred," Klatu assured him.

"Surely you mean in *many* parts of the world, but not *everywhere*."

"But that was precisely the meaning," Miath said.

Kindred returned to gazing through the water at the rock walls acting as a kind of giant cup for it.

"A network of these, crisscrossing the globe?"

"And our people use them as what you might call an underwater subway system," Miath said.

"But how? You aren't amphibious. You simply can't stay underwater indefinitely."

"Ah, but we can. And so can you..."

Kindred was about to protest when Miath bent down and held up in his left hand a cluster of something green and wet-looking. It seemed no more unusual than a piece of seaweed.

"...by using these plants as we do."

He then engaged in an elaborate process of fastening the stuff over his body, with one tube-like protruberance fitting into his mouth. While they stood by and observed, he began to breathe into it. The plant puffed up dramatically.

"Protects from the pressure," Miath managed to say, his voice barely recognizable.

With that he suddenly jumped into the water, diving down to a third layer of tunnels and disappearing through one of them.

Kindred glanced at his watch.

A minute.

Two minutes.

Three.

Four.

Eventually a total of nine minutes had passed before Miath reappeared through another tunnel altogether and surfaced again in front of them.

"It really does work, my friend."

"But how?" Kindred asked, fascinated.

"Certain plants are used in your world in aquariums, is that not so?"

"Yes, but—"

"And these prove invaluable by contributing oxygen to the water?"

"That's right, but—"

"This plant is an adaptation of a variety of strains. Its 'job,' you might say, is to—"

"—give oxygen directly to those who 'wear' it," Klatu finished the sentence for him.

How stunning, Kindred thought, *and yet how logical. It was a natural oxygen tank, and it would never run empty as long as it was submerged in water.*

"We cannot explain all the mysteries of its service to us," Miath said, "but I should add that, wearing it, we are immune to the pressure at great depths if we do not remain for excessive periods of time."

Kindred was speechless.

"Will you join me now?" Miath asked.

Anticipation sent tingles through Kindred's entire nervous system. He could scarcely wait until Miath had connected the plant, one tube-like portion of it to be held in his mouth. The taste was unusual but not unpleasant, perhaps a bit like spinach or asparagus.

"These are for your eyes."

Miath handed them each something that looked like a pair of eye-shaped, hollowed-out crystals tied together by leather strands.

"And this is all that is necessary?" Kindred was skeptical even though he had so recently seen Miath don the same outfit.

Miath nodded with the manner of a patient teacher who had been entrusted with a cautious child.

"Since it is quite easy to become lost if you are not familiar with the tunnels, please stay close behind me," Miath instructed both of them. "Other than that, there is little danger, really."

Miath dived back in, followed by Kindred, and then Klatu.

And a wondrous journey it was. Periodically the tunnels would widen substantially, and the three of them would surface again, meeting other colonies of Dwellers. Mile after mile, as he saw portions of each tunnel linking in with other tunnels, Kindred had growing appreciation for what Miath had said about becoming lost. Furthermore, the minister could find no hitch in his "equipment." The plant mass functioned better than any scuba diving gear he had ever used.

The Dwellers had developed a way of preserving food that eliminated the necessity of freezing their supplies.

"We have deep sea food storage," Miath commented. "It works extraordinarily well, I assure you."

Kindred remembered reading about foods (protein, starches and fruit) recovered from a sunken vessel after ten months at a depth of nearly one mile; all were well-preserved!

"The combination of low temperature and high pressure slows down organic decay," Miath pointed out. "At a mile or more below the surface, the temperature is usually thirty-eight degrees, the pressure a hundred and fifty times what is normal at sea level. This produces a rate of deterioration for food supplies that is ten to a hundred times slower than on land. In addition, the water itself acts as a kind of pickling agent."

He showed them containers of rodents and other "food."

"They've been here for many weeks, and they will *remain* edible for many more!"

"I am thinking of the whole notion among my people of using the oceans as places in which to dispose of wastes," Kindred said. "What you have discovered would tend to have the same effect there as well, so wastes could be a problem for a long time to come."

The idea was hardly encouraging.

According to his senses, several hours had passed, but he wasn't tired since they did stop every so often at various settlements, catch their breath and eat, the food brought to them by hospitable Dwellers.

It was approximately six hours into their odyssey that the three of them were confronted by a most awesome creature.

And Kindred somehow wasn't surprised when Miath identified it.

"You seem to know," Miath said appreciatively. "You seem to know that this is your legendary Nessie."

They came upon the creature as the rather narrow tunnel through which they had been swimming opened up into a huge cavern that was easily a dozen times larger than any of the others.

The prehistoric amphibious reptile was resting momentarily on the edge of an out-cropping of rock. Nessie spotted them well-nigh as soon as they entered the cavern and roared so loudly that the walls vibrated to the sound.

Kindred, floating on the water, turning with amazement, reacted by turning virtually as white as Miath and Klatu were normally.

Miath started laughing.

"Your Nessie is vegetarian. She would find you both quite indigestible. Besides, she is utterly harmless; indeed she is more than a little friendly."

Kindred's mind initially was blank. The shock engendered by what he was seeing drove out all thought and froze his vocal cords into speechlessness. All the while, Nessie simply sat there on her rocky perch, stuffing plants into her mouth.

"My kind grow her diet for her," Miath told them. "She stops at our colonies all over the world. That is why she is seen so seldom at the lake in Scotland."

Words finally came to Kindred.

"But why does she go back there at all?" he asked.

"Because that is where she gave birth to her little one, as her mate remained nearby, guarding them both. I know this is true because several of my kind witnessed the event."

No more! Kindred couldn't cope with such infusion of knowledge, knowledge beyond the wildest fantasies of even the most fanciful dreamers.

"Three such creatures?" the minister said inanely.

"Indeed. Their child didn't survive, however."

Nessie had abruptly finished her meal and decided to take a swim. She approached the three intruders, picking Kindred to show her friendliness to by lowering her body below the water directly in front of him.

"She will surface directly behind you," Miath said quickly. "Wrap your arms around her—"

Nessie indeed surfaced exactly in that manner.

"—neck!" Miath shouted.

Which Kindred did, finding himself in the rather astonishing position of sliding down an ancient creature's very long neck until he landed on her back.

Kindred looked helplessly at Miath, hoping for some clue as to what would happen next. But he found out quickly enough. Nessie turned slowly over on her back, causing Kindred to follow this movement until he ended up on her stomach. The creature's head, tiny in relation to her body but large by any other yardstick, poked up through the water, and she let out a low sound that was a combination of pig's grunt and cat's purr.

"She wants you to scratch her stomach for a bit," came Miath's words in the midst of Kindred's amazed torpor.

Kindred proceeded to do what the Dweller had suggested. And Nessie's flippers vibrated with obvious pleasure.

A number of minutes passed. But Kindred actually didn't mind at all. He was hypnotized by the events of the past hours, and now this! How he would have reacted a few weeks earlier if someone had come up to him and predicted that he would soon be scratching the midriff of the Loch Ness monster—that last word hardly apt as it turned out!

But eventually Nessie became bored and signaled this by gently righting herself, letting Kindred slowly back into the water. It was as she was doing so that the minister noticed a ghastly scar on her left side. When he had rejoined Klatu and Miath, he asked the latter about this.

"From what I hear, in bits and pieces gathered from my kind over the years, her child died when attacked by a group of great white sharks. It is believed the mate perished the same way. And those scars suggest Nessie was attacked similarly but survived."

A creature long regarded as a myth, as the plaything of overactive imaginations or as outright hoax, that creature returned to Loch Ness from time to time. Perhaps, in her reptilian ignorance, she thought she would find her "family" there somehow.

The three watched as Nessie continued on in her own odyssey, disappearing through a large tunnel at the opposite side of the huge cavern.

The NEXT EPISODE WAS IN STARK CONTRAST, showing an undersea world that was anything but whimsical and pleasant.

Pollution.

It was in a section of ocean designated as a dumping site for urban wastes, masses of sewage that had been treated and supposedly rendered harmless to marine life.

Lobsters cowering under outcroppings of rock, their hard shells turning black, collapsing; dolphins drowning because they lacked the strength to swim to the surface for air; even a shark whose lower jaw had partially rotted away, unable to eat, just swimming around in circles and then going through convulsions, spinning over and over until it hit the ocean floor.

And then one of the most pathetic sights of all.

A huge shape loomed in the near distance, fully thirty to forty feet long. It had been sinking slowly, not quite dead as yet but not really alive. Following behind it was a smaller figure, not more than ten feet in length.

A sperm whale and her offspring!

Kindred, Klatu and Miath looked with awe and immense sorrow as the mother whale finally hit the ocean floor, oxygen bubbles still escaping from the hole in the top of her body. The baby kept swimming around her, again and again, nudging her gently with what they sensed to be accelerating confusion and alarm.

The mother was only seconds away from death, but she summoned her remaining strength to send a "call" to her child that carried with it such waves of love that the three onlookers were themselves overwhelmed with emotion.

And then she was gone. The baby, of course, did not understand what had happened except that the sensations of love and warmth and caring given freely and with profound devotion were now no longer felt, no longer reaching out to envelop and reassure and remove from life the fears and uncertainties that would assault in this severe underwater world of survival of the fittest.

Almost as though on cue the predators came, and Kindred, Klatu and Miath had to pull back considerably to a much safer distance.

Sharks.

The water was churning with their attack, teeth tearing into the dead mother's body, bits and pieces of flesh floating this way or that, until devoured by eating machines.

The baby tried frantically to help the mother, with no conception that this was pathetically futile, and sacrificed itself in the process, no match for the sharks. It, too, became their prey, dying even more horribly than the mother, first with loud cries of pain, then mournful whimpers, and then nothing.

Finally, temporarily satiated, the sharks left, in their wake two ravaged and ugly carcasses with plenty of meat still available for the smaller, more timid scavengers. In a short while only the bones would be left, and eventually these would be covered by sand, nothing at all remaining of a devoted mother and her valiant child, destroyed ignominiously by excrement and chemicals and soda pop bottles and other wastes rendered "harmless," or so the story was told by propaganda purveyors above ground.

THEY MET OTHER LIFE FORMS THROUGHOUT their travels in the tunnels: prehistoric fish thought long extinct; a species of pink-skinned octopi of which Kindred had heard or read nothing.

He was transfixed by the sight of these many-tentacled creatures. They existed in an area that Kindred guessed was in the Gulf of Mexico, a spot surrounded on two sides by submerged volcanic rock, probably hidden for innumerable centuries; he conjectured that the octopi never ventured from this one spot, at least not very far and not enough afield ever to have been discovered by humans.

Astonishing, he remarked to himself. *They are—*

His words were cut short by a group of the octopi performing what seemed to be very much like an underwater ballet, indeed dancing through the water with a natural grace comparable in its own way to the Bolshoi.

As the dance intensified, the color of the octopi's skin changed gradually to a vibrant red, and as it slowed, faded back to the original pink. When it was over, and they were obviously tired, the creatures swam into niches in the rock partially surrounding them. One, however, remained outside, perhaps on sentry duty, ready for unfriendly intruders.

Miath, Kindred and Klatu swam into its line of sight, slowly, without seeming at all threatening. The octopus emitted a very thin stream of blackish liquid, then stopped, the stuff dissipating quickly in the water. It approached Kindred, first stretching out one tentacle, then another, touching the plant around his face, then his shoulder, then the top of his head. It did precisely the same to Miath and Klatu. Finally it pulled back a bit, motionless in the water for a few seconds.

One by one its tentacles started vibrating. And one by one others of its kind came out from their niches and surrounded the three intruders. None of the creatures was more than three or four feet in height, some as small as two feet perhaps.

Kindred did not feel in danger, curiously enough. He reached into the leather shorts a Dweller had made for him, taking out a greenish vegetable that he had been given as a sort of snack and broke off about half of it, holding it in the palm of his outstretched hand.

One of the octopi came slowly, gracefully toward him almost immediately, wrapping a tentacle around the piece of vegetable and then swimming back a few feet. The tentacle bent around toward the center of the creature, and Kindred could see what must have been its mouth open and swallow this new food.

Within just a few minutes, the octopi had been fed all of the food Kindred, Klatu and Miath had left!

Then something even more amusing and gratifying happened.

A school of multicolored fish swam into the vicinity. Four of the octopi left the group and headed toward them. It took only seconds for them to trap several of the fish—which they brought back and offered to the now-welcome intruders!

The three made gestures that they hoped would be taken as appreciative. And apparently that was the case. Satisfied, not feeling threatened, all but the one octopus returned to their niches.

Kindred felt momentarily sad as they left that place. Dumb creatures had shown instinctive hospitality. How little human beings had learned over the centuries.

OFTEN, TO GET THEIR GEOGRAPHIC BEARINGS, they would penetrate the surface and find themselves near New Orleans or Jacksonville or Atlanta. Then they went back down again into a world of which no one above ground had any conception—an odyssey that took many months but was continually fascinating, invigorating, the passage of time actually seeming quite swift.

While the regions on the surface often reflected different cultures, there was no such delineation with the Dweller settlements. The Cajun influence in Louisiana, for example, may have been different from that of other parts of the United States, but not so underground. Dwellers in that area were the same as those under Oregon or Texas or Washington, D.C.

"We keep our identity, our culture," Miath confirmed. "It is not a thing lost on the shores of another."

The three of them did not linger long at each settlement, just enough to rest and get nourishment, then off they went. At least this was their intention, so great was their expectancy about what remained ahead of them. And yet the rigors of the journey took their toll on them, though a bit less so with Miath, who had learned to pace himself during similar journeys over the years.

The primitiveness of each Dweller settlement, unadorned by what were called "modern conveniences" above ground, struck Kindred again and again. These people indeed seemed not much above the "caveman" level in many respects. And yet, counterpointing that were the remarkable senses they had developed, not the least of which was the inherited memory in each settlement of the Council of Many, a group larger or smaller according to the number of inhabitants themselves. All members of the council were treated with utmost respect and accorded what was as close to a life of ease as anyone could have in such a spartan society.

As they traveled in tunnels under the surface of the Atlantic Ocean, Kindred, Klatu and Miath encountered the most intriguing discovery of all.

Yet another civilization.

But this one had long since died, at least the physical part of it.

The tunnel they were in at that moment opened out onto the ocean itself. And directly in front of them, in surprisingly shallow water in view of the fact that no one above ground had discovered it, were the remains of what could only be an ancient temple, some columns partially standing, others tumbled over onto their sides. Beyond that one structure were others, stretching on for perhaps a mile in all directions, though the visibility factor in the water limited their direct view to a few hundred feet.

Is it possible, Kindred thought, his body taut with the potential reality that faced him, a reality that once seemed only myth, *is it possible that this is...*

Atlantis!

The three of them swam in and around the destroyed city, exploring what were once streets and the interiors of buildings, examining artifacts, gazing at inscriptions whose content they couldn't even guess, startled as they came upon piles of bones here and there.

Klatu found a bizarre stone image about a foot in length, examined it curiously and then handed it to Kindred.

It was blatantly erotic, reminding him a bit of the images discovered in the ruins of Pompeii, a city destroyed by the eruption of Mount Vesuvius.

Kindred tossed it to one side.

Miath found another image carved from stone. This one was quite different. The face was reptilian, the body human. There was a long tail extending from the rear, coming to a triangular point.

Kindred felt especially uncomfortable as he examined that one. It looked like some representation of evil he had seen in paintings, even a bit like one or more of the woodcuts of Gustave Dore.

They entered a giant enclosure more intact than most of the others. The ceiling was curved, supported by Greek- or Roman-like columns on either side. There were no walls, the sides open through the pillars. In the middle of the enclosure was a round excavation. On top and all around it were plankton-covered bones.

An altar of human sacrifice! Kindred exclaimed to himself.

He reached down and found a long, carved stone dagger still sticking in the rib cage of a skeleton there. Increasingly uncomfortable, he waved his hand to indicate that they should leave. Klatu and Miath agreed with him and started to swim away. It wasn't long before they found themselves pursued by two deep water sharks entering the enclosure.

The creatures were only a dozen or so yards away.

Miath fell instantly, flattening himself against the ocean floor. Kindred and Klatu followed suit. The sharks went by just above them and then turned and headed back toward them. But the seconds this took were valuable for Kindred, Klatu and Miath as they started to swim frenziedly away.

The sharks followed.

Eluding these experienced hunters was a formidable challenge at which many divers over the years had failed.

Then Miath did something that seemed utterly unfathomable.

He stopped swimming away from the large sharks and remained in one spot as they headed toward him. His eyes were closed, on his forehead a deep frown, as though he were waiting for that awful moment when they would be upon him.

Kindred wanted to shout but, of course, he would never be heard. And then he found out the reason for his friend's behavior.

Dozens of dolphins. Swimming at a depth not typical for these mammals and which must have involved extraordinary effort for them. Coming in from the north and from the south. More than Kindred had seen together at any one moment in his life!

They headed straight for the sharks, hitting the larger creatures head-on with their snouts. So many dolphins battered them virtually all at the same time that the sharks were tumbled over and over. Finally they steadied themselves and fought back. Several dolphins were injured as giant teeth ripped at them. But in a matter of three or four minutes the sharks were driven off, and all but six of the dolphins had gone away. Two of the injured dolphins had not joined the rest, because they were obviously dying. Their companions hovered nearby, as though waiting patiently.

Miath swam over to the two dying ones. He suspended himself in front of them, reached out a hand to each and gently touched the snout of first the one, then the other.

Then he stepped back a bit as their comrades came and nudged them away with what Kindred sensed to be infinite tenderness. To be "buried"? To be given some sort of primitive ceremony? Whatever it was, the minister felt a touch of the special bond experts had long been claiming could occur between humans and those remarkable creatures.

They went through other sections of the submerged metropolis. A feeling of oppressiveness encircled them, born not of the depth or the resulting pressure of the water, but of seeing evidence of what may have been visited on this place: tiny skeletons, perfectly formed, obviously of infants or very small children; more erotic stone carvings; and then a huge statue, now lying on its side, perhaps three stories tall, with the face of a devil!

Less than a hundred yards beyond that, Kindred found the first remains of an airplane. Most of it was little more than flimsy pieces of metal by now. He approached the cockpit and pulled back. The bodies of the two pilots were still there, their skeletons partially covered by the military outfits they had been wearing.

Kindred turned away and then saw other wreckage in varying degrees of intactness. Six. Seven. A dozen. More. Spreading out in all directions. Some planes. Some boats. Several helicopters. Vast numbers altogether.

And in the distance, near enough to give some clue of itself but far enough away not to be totally clear, he saw, briefly, the shape of a pyramid.

But it was not the outline that fascinated Kindred. Something else, so intriguing and yet so terrifying that he wanted to swim away from that spot and never, never look back.

Beams of light emitted from the structure, and he could see, for an instant, that the pyramid was essentially a gigantic, nearly transparent crystal!

Suddenly Kindred went through convulsions, spitting out the tube in his mouth, taking in water very rapidly. He could feel himself starting to lose consciousness until Klatu and Miath were able to get the tube back into his mouth.

In a short while they were back into the tunnel from which they had earlier emerged, and a few minutes later had found an outcropping of rock on which they could rest.

"What happened, my friend?" Klatu asked with the utmost concern.

Kindred looked at them both, an expression of gradually dissipating panic on his face.

"I don't *know* whether that was Atlantis," he said, his voice trembling, "but I suspect that it was and that it was destroyed for the same reasons that brought the doom of Sodom and Gomorrah."

"But what happened to you there?" Klatu probed.

"I came face-to-face with the rankest, darkest sensation of evil I have ever known, as if I were standing right at the door to hell itself."

"But why did you feel it and not either of us?" Klatu asked.

"I don't know. All of us should have been touched by that—"

He shivered at the thought.

Miath interrupted just then.

"There are answers yet remaining, my new friend," he said. "I know a little of that which you find puzzling, but now is not the time, I can assure you."

"Something else," Kindred said, "I also sensed back there, in my spirit's mind, I guess, something of Noah's time that makes me think Atlantis was part of the antediluvian creation and that it was destroyed because it had become an instigator of the rampant evil of that time."

Miath bowed his head.

"You are correct," he said. "Those who lived there, it is said, were our kinsmen."

"Would the council be able to tell us more?"

"There is one member with whom we have seldom talked. His recollections are especially horrible. We allow ourselves bits and pieces of his memories, but that is all any of us can endure. What he says suggests you may be right!"

"I'm *not* crazy."

"No, and in the time of tribulation, Satan will cause Atlantis somehow to rise again and reclaim its dominion of evil."

Kindred shivered.

"He certainly does that even now, with hints of the terror to come. He uses the—"

"Bermuda Triangle," Miath interjected.

"And now triangular or pyramid shapes have been mass-produced by the New Age movement as part of it."

"Let me add this, Matthew Kindred. In the midst of Atlantis, we are told, there is a giant pyramid-shaped crystal the light of which has not died for countless thousands of years."

A gigantic, nearly transparent crystal—the one he saw!

He had separated himself from them when he happened upon it. When they found him, he must have drifted some distance away, because it was apparent that they had not seen what he did.

Suddenly Kindred's mind was reeling from a staggering truth.

"It is that which destroys, at will, Satan's will, any planes or boats that venture into the Bermuda Triangle!"

Miath nodded, adding, "Evil that is so strong—!"

"And that's what I felt out there!" Kindred interrupted.

"But there is more," Miath offered.

"Please tell me."

"You know of Stonehenge? And the other stone gatherings nearby? The huge statues at Easter Island? And other mysterious, shall we say, 'monuments.' "

"I do know of them, Miath. Fascinating, to be sure."

"They are all connected."

"What?"

"They are part of a vast network constructed by Satan and ready to be activated in the end times."

Miath saw the surprise on Kindred's face and added, "We have considerable biblical knowledge, you know, because it is certainly as much a part of the history recounted to us by the Council of Many as anything else over the centuries."

A vast network constructed by Satan....

Atlantis. Stonehenge. And the New Age movement. All pulled by strings controlled by puppeteer Satan!

And that couldn't have been the entire picture, either. What about drug abuse, which the Bible called sorcery? And such notions as good witches and bad witches to confuse the unwary? Astrology? The whole evil basket of damnation!

"Let's leave this place," Kindred said abruptly.

Both Miath and Klatu nodded, as they shared the melancholy that had swept over the minister like a mournful tidal wave.

THEY VISITED OTHER SPOTS, SOME QUITE
wondrous, such as a series of caverns inhabited only by underwater bees.

"It's really remarkable," Miath told his two companions. "They get juice from
underwater plants and take it to places such as these."

"Why has no one ever come upon them before?" Kindred asked.

"You mean of your kind?"

"Yes. Why?"

"Because this is their world and ours. Water covers a majority of the earth's surface, the land masses only a fraction of it. You have not explored all of the latter
as yet; whole sections of the Arctic, for example, are unknown to your scientists.
Should it be so surprising that even less is known about a species *down here* as small,
as elusive as these bees?"

The cavern they were in was literally abuzz with the creatures.

"They show no interest in attacking us," Kindred observed.

"Because they have nothing to fear, for that is what causes most of nature's
inhabitants above ground to lash out, you know—fear of humanity that has been
learned over many, many centuries."

What a sight it was in that cavern and others they encountered. The hard rock
walls were covered with honeycombed hives; the nectar was constantly seeping out,
like water from a leaky roof.

"It tends to be yellow or light green," Kindred noted.

"As it should be. The honey with which you are familiar varies in shade from
dark amber to very light and occasionally what is called water white. That is because
the juice is sucked out of orange blossoms, sage, clover, often buckwheat and tulip

trees. But down here it is different—they suck from what you call seaweed, living coral, underwater ferns and other such plants and animals.

"The bees here, just like their cousins above ground, have inside themselves a honey bag of sorts, in which the juice or nectar is stored as they swim from plants to the caves, which serve as hives into which they emerge from the water. While the fluid is in that bag, something happens to change its flavor and color. It becomes naturally sweet and rather thick, and it hardens as it is sprayed on the cave walls.

"We eat much honey, my kind and I. It gives us energy and provides nourishment for our young especially, since it contains mineral salts and other material needed by our bodies.

"In ancient times any household in the Middle East that possessed a great deal of honey was considered quite wealthy, you know, hence the promise of a land flowing with milk and honey was a great enticement then. The Egyptians even used it as part of the embalming process. When we want to keep meat nearby for a time, without having to swim out to our underwater storage areas, we soak it in honey and let the honey become quite dry to retard the spoiling process. It has a pleasant flavor as well."

"Honey-dipped bat?" Kindred said, grimacing.

"We've been eating it for millions of years, Matthew Kindred."

Kindred sampled some of the green-tinged honey by stepping near one portion of hives where it seemed to be leaking more steadily than from others, holding his hand underneath and letting it accumulate in his palm.

"How wonderful," Kindred commented. "I have never tasted anything as fine as this."

Kindred was indeed astonished. It wasn't as sweet as the other honey he had enjoyed over the years, but it had a taste that was altogether delicious.

A few minutes later, he experienced an unexpected burst of energy.

"I was feeling quite tired, Miath," he admitted. "But now—"

"I know what you mean, my friend. It's marvelous."

It was just what he needed to lift his spirits after the encounter with Atlantis.

They left that cavern with some reluctance, but knowing that if they stayed any longer he might be tempted to eat enough of the greenish honey to become sick.

Soon the odyssey neared an end. Miath indicated that he should be returning to his settlement soon. Kindred and Klatu concurred.

"We can go out again, if you like," Miath told them.

Kindred couldn't understand until later the thin edge of sadness that surfaced in his mind then and that would remain for some time to come.

KINDRED FOUND A DWELLER NAMED PARANE
especially interesting. This one was not as socially oriented as the others. He preferred
staying by himself, off in a little cavern of his own. That was fine with the rest of
the Dwellers; they seemed quite democratic in the way they approached whatever
informal government had been instituted over the centuries.

Parane spent most of his free time painting. Initially his canvases were the walls
of his own cavern. But he also was then allowed to paint the corridors and other
places throughout the region occupied by this particular group of Dwellers.

Kindred was impressed by the gentleness of most of the images—scenes of Dwellers'
family life: a number of portraits of little ones not more than a few years old, male
and female Dwellers holding one another tenderly, elderly Dwellers. It was artwork
of sensitivity.

Parane seemed delighted to take Kindred and Klatu on a tour of his "gallery."

"My own favorite, if you won't consider me arrogant for saying that, is this one,"
he said as they approached a scene larger than most of the others.

What Kindred saw was astonishing, a mixture of Dore and Da Vinci. In this wall
painting there were essentially two portions. The one on the left was quite bizarre,
in a sense, showing a single Dweller surrounded by deformed and frightening creatures,
their faces shrunken, boil-ridden, long teeth protruding from thick, blood-red lips.
Their talon-like hands were reaching out for the Dweller, whose body was covered
with heavy beads of perspiration.

The portion on the right was the opposite in tone, showing the same Dweller looking up at the sky, which was brightly lit; within the light could be seen winged angels
coming forth in a continuous stream toward the Dweller, who had reached out his

hands for them, an expression of sublime hope on his face.

"Our two natures," he said simply.

"The sin nature versus the redeemed one," Kindred said.

Parane turned to him, their eyes meeting.

"No, Matthew Kindred. It is much more, yes, truly much deeper than you know."

"What are you saying?"

"Something you will find out when you meet the council."

"The Council of Many?"

"That is correct. You will learn from them a great deal more than you could ever have imagined."

Again that mysterious Council of Many. Again unanswered questions.

They spent more time with Parane. The scope of his ability was frequently staggering. Interestingly, he painted the ceiling of one chamber with scenes depicting a moment in the history of his race.

"It's huge!" exclaimed Kindred.

"This is where the Council of Many meets," Parane commented. "During Awake-time, they come here to meditate."

"In my society," Kindred pointed out, "meditation is not often used in a way that honors God. It has been usurped by movements that are anything but divinely oriented."

"Here, Matthew Kindred, that isn't the case at all. We talk to God all the time even though He never—"

Parane cut himself off.

"What were you about to say?" Kindred pressed a bit.

Parane had obviously closed off the topic to any further discussion and could not be budged.

Instead he guided the attention of his two guests to the cavern itself.

"This was not its original size. Over the years we have enlarged it more and more, as the size of the council has increased. And other settlements elsewhere have done the same thing."

"There are places like this all over the world?" Kindred asked.

"Wherever there are Dwellers living together in large numbers, yes."

"What is it that makes the Council of Many so special, Parane?"

"You will be shown very shortly, I am told."

They left the cavern and re-entered the corridor outside.

"Ah, a messenger!" Parane exclaimed.

Another Dweller approached them literally at a gallop.

Parane reached into his garb and pulled out a small fragment of leather, with some letters on one side. He handed it to the messenger, who went right on past them, not breaking stride for an instant.

Parane could see that Kindred had some questions.

"What you might call our Pony Express."

"That was a letter?" Kindred asked.

"To a very dear friend—a female—whom I indeed have come to love very much."

"Why isn't she here with you?"

"We have never met."

"Only through letters?"

"Yes, Matthew Kindred, only through letters. But we do not view these as idle 'things' to be done quickly or carelessly and then forgotten. Getting communication from one settlement to another entails enormous trouble and planning. That runner you saw has devoted his life to this service; it is his sacrifice for the good of all."

Kindred marveled at the idea of falling in love without ever having met the object of that love. But Parane went on to explain that letters were a way of expressing their very being, the part of them that was the purest embodiment of what they really were.

"So much of your world is superficial, Matthew Kindred. You mass-produce letters to reach even millions in a single mailing, as you call it. Your media serve a manufactured diet of assembly line emotion, hour after hour after hour. You say, so casually, 'How are you today?' without ever really caring and, often, walking past before hearing the answer. Here, in a world that is at best a kind of purgatory, if you will, and yet one from which only death will release us—"

Parane stopped himself once again.

"What is it this time?" Kindred asked, mildly annoyed.

Parane was looking directly at the minister as he spoke.

"The truth must be shed upon you only when it is the right time."

"But why give me hints, teasing me and then stopping?"

"Because it is truth with which we have lived since the beginning of time. It is as natural as the rest of our world, however we may wish that world, that truth, were otherwise."

Kindred was about to press the matter when a warning grimace from Klatu suggested that he not do so, at least not then.

Later, after they had joined the other Dwellers at final Eat-time and were alone in the rocky cubicle that had been assigned them, Kindred expressed his irritation.

"Why is it all so mysterious? Could it be that their friendliness, their hospitality, belies their lack of trust?"

"Or is it, my friend, that the truth could be so shocking you would be quite shocked *unless* you got clues, one-by-one, and *then* the full truth?"

"Will you tell me no more now, Klatu?"

Klatu was silent for a moment, his head bowed, obviously in not inconsiderable turmoil over the matter.

"I cannot," he said, looking up. "I sense something about you. You have great sensitivity, Matthew Kindred. You *do* need to be dealt with as you have been. There is no other way."

"How can you be so sure?"

"I sense your heart—and it is sad, heavy with melancholy much of the time. You yourself have had deep tragedy before in your life. You will learn of our own soon enough. Hastening that moment would not prove a blessing."

Kindred thought of that one scene painted by Parane, demons on one side, angels on the other, and a chill started at the base of his spine and soon gripped his entire body, until extreme weariness washed it away in the midst of the sleep that claimed him.

During the time remaining at that original settlement, Kindred and Klatu would spend many hours with Parane, admiring his artistry, which flowered even under the worst circumstances.

But one day when Kindred went to see the Dweller, Parane was gone. Kindred asked where he was and was told by another Dweller, "He went off to spend time alone and die."

"Die? But from what cause?"

"He has been ill a very long period. Only writing to his loved one seemed to keep him alive. When he got her last communication, he knew he could not go on without her."

The Dweller, named Vanin, handed Kindred a patch of leather on which was written this message:

> *My dearest Parane:*
> *It is probable that I would not be alive today if it were not for your letters. The unchanging realities of our kind bear down on me with unceasing heaviness. Learning about your paintings and writing to you helped the burden of my heart for a time, but now it is worse.*

The more I grew to love the kind of individual you seem to be, the more I realized how I could not bear to be with you, talk with you directly, feel your warmth commingling with mine, the two of us as one, and enjoy the ecstasy but for awhile and then one of us having to face losing the other to that nameless abyss into which we plunge. So I think it is better that we never meet, never begin the physical joining that would make our parting all that much more unbearable.

Oh, how this has torn at me, beloved. With humankind, there is an expression: "It is better to have loved and lost than never to have loved at all." And I have heard, through stories passed down to us by those of our kind who have ventured above ground, indeed I have heard that humans usually say that to know love, to be warmed by it, to hold its sweet memory even after a loved one has died is better than the cold longing that is a vacuum where love never has been.

But, Parane, they have hope of reunion; they have hope that love truly, truly, truly never does die once it has been born so gloriously; for them it can survive the grave and continue to be felt and given for eternity.

You seem so strong. You have no illusions about the finality of death. But I am different, my love.

Even my dreams mock me, as I see in them the two of us together, blissful, forever and forever. That can never be, for reasons you well know. And so I awaken to the cruelest of realities from the most tender of fantasies.

And I know you would feel the same way. Now while we have not met, at least in the flesh, it will be bad, so bad that it will seem as though our hearts have been ripped from us. Even so it will not be quite so awful as the alternative, my love.

I go now, having no idea of my destination; I tell no one but you, for I would get nothing from them but empty talk about learning to live with my birthright.

Your letters go with me, to be read on cold nights in strange places.

Farewell,

Norisan

"He is possibly dead even as we speak," Vanin remarked. "Or he is simply wandering, as Norisan is doing, but in his case with the hope that they might meet up one day and he would perhaps convince her that a brief snatch of sublime happiness is indeed all that they or any of us have left."

Vanin started weeping. This sight in and of itself was remarkable, as Kindred thought about it, in that the Dwellers seemed not to cry very much at all, being more stoic than emotional. But here was Vanin, tears flowing as though from a broken dike no longer able to hold back a turbulent sea.

Vanin fell into Kindred's arms and cried until consciousness left him, and the minister had to put him gently down on the hard rock and get help. Ultimately Vanin was revived, but Kindred always saw, from that time on, a certain melancholy darken eyes already mirroring whatever awful burden was on the shoulders of the other members of his race.

OVER THE DAYS TO FOLLOW, KINDRED CON-
sidered frequently what Parane had said.

So much of your world is superficial....

Indeed, superficial in stark contrast to how the Dwellers lived. The truth of those words flooded his mind with vignettes that had gone unnoticed earlier: female Dwellers washing clothes in underground streams and then pounding these on flat rocks; a contingent of males going out to hunt, often deep within the earth, bringing back dead tunnel rats and other rodents as well as armfuls of bats, killed that they might be eaten; an occasional Dweller body carried on the shoulders of his comrades, moans escaping him as he hovered near death after being bitten by a poisonous insect. And always *real* light was absent; a dull, monotonous gloom, pervasive and debilitating, hung over them.

Yet they went on, no word that Kindred could catch of any committing suicide, a recourse, however sinful, that many above ground might have chosen under similar conditions, the manner of each Dweller an unfathomable mixture of melancholy and hope.

So much of your world....

Indeed so much of the world Kindred had lived in was precisely what Parane had mentioned, an obnoxious parade of vanity and superficiality and pettiness, fattened by excess, trumpeted by the media, sustained by the companies profiting thereby. If the latest fingernail polish color weren't obtained, somehow life would be emptier; if the flashiest automobile weren't parked in the driveway, the neighbors would think that hard times had come.

"It may be," observed Miath ironically, "that what is threatening us here will force us up into your world, Matthew Kindred.''

He paused and then added, ''But what will happen when that comes about?''
Kindred had no answer.

''More and more reports come to us about the effects elsewhere of pollution, atomic
or otherwise. You have heard only an occasional statement from me and others. It
is time that you see for yourself.''

Klatu joined Kindred as Miath took them first down one tunnel, then another,
on and on until Kindred was becoming impatient.

''How much longer?'' he asked.

''We must keep them isolated. We have no idea about the implications of what
they are suffering.''

...what they are suffering.

What was Miath talking about?

Kindred saw the answer a few minutes later.

Another very large cavern, reaching up several stories and more than four city
blocks in diameter. It was a separate settlement within the main one, completely
isolated.

But this group of Dwellers differed significantly from the rest. Many were quite
deformed, the very young looking much like the thalidomide babies of Kindred's world,
pathetic in their grotesqueness. Some were born without legs or arms, carried around
by those willing to help or else just left in corners, looking forlornly out at the darkness
around them. Siamese twins, joined at the temple, clumsily tried to get from one
place to another. The retarded, sitting or standing to one side, drooling, aimlessly
throwing their arms through the air or saying and doing nothing, frightened or confused by what was around them, ignorant of the truth. Some, like lepers, had open
sores on their bodies, fingers rotted away, toes gone.

And then the awful creature that came ambling toward them. Kindred was ashamed
of that word ''awful'' but found no other, however cruel it was, to describe what
he saw: a Dweller distorted grotesquely, the arms protruding out of the center of
its chest, short little protuberances, the middle fingers on each hand locked together
by a web-like piece of flesh, the legs as stick-like as a grasshopper's and shaped somewhat
similarly.

''My name is Ardenis,'' the Dweller spoke, the words discernible only with significant effort by the listeners. His mouth was a thin open slit; he spoke by sucking
in air and blowing it out again, in a manner similar to that of tracheotomy patients.

"May I show you my latest work?" Ardenis asked.

All three nodded assent.

They followed him, past other Dwellers, some looking up curiously, others enveloped by an inner world of their ultimate pain and, therefore, not aware of anything or anyone else.

Ardenis moved those strange little hands in excited fashion as he pointed out his work.

Statuary.

Each carved out of solid rock. Some were of bats poised as though for flight; some were of tiny rodents, the detail intricate down to their ears and snout and little feet. Other rock had been carved and shaped in the form of flowers, the petals delicate, the leaves perfectly formed.

And then there was the cross, with a figure hanging from it.

"My tribute," Ardenis said, his misshapen face lighting up in a smile. "I have never seen a cross, but I am told this is accurate. I have never seen Him, but this is what He is like in my mind and my heart."

Kindred went up to the cross, examining the detail: rock transformed to look like grayish wood, down to the grain, splinters scarcely large enough to be seen; a crown of thorns pressed down over the temple; the hands perfectly formed, nails through the palms; the rib cage visible through taut flesh; veins standing out on the legs, nails also through the feet.

And at the base, simple, strange words:

Lord, even though I will never stand by Your side in Your kingdom,
I give You my humble love without anger, only with joy and peace inside
my very being.

Kindred turned and looked at Ardenis, not knowing what to say. He stepped forward and took those hands in his own; then he reached out and hugged Ardenis.

"It is true, Matthew Kindred," the Dweller said as best he could. "They could have killed me right after I was born. But why? That would only be adding sin to sin. I am not as others, but then they are not as me, some of them with anger that sometimes eats up their insides, and what they spit out is pain that they have inflicted upon themselves. I have pain, yes, but it is pain beyond my control. I stand not responsible for my own suffering. I ask only that my end come quickly and, when it does, that I not linger. I have refused, over these years here, to take the life I do have and sacrifice it at the altar of self-pity."

Kindred, Klatu and Miath left a short while later, the minister looking over his shoulder. Ardenis was sitting on the ground, taking a rock already starting to look like a delicate-winged butterfly and proceeding with his primitive tools to shape the feet.

Out in the tunnel, as they walked along, Kindred tapped Miath on the shoulder and asked, "What did he mean in that inscription when he carved the words "even though I will never stand by Your side in Your kingdom"?

Miath's gaze met his own.

"Dear friend, it is the tragedy that afflicts us all."

"Miath, what *are* you talking about?"

"Tomorrow, Matthew Kindred, tomorrow you will find out when you meet with the council."

FIFTEEN

KINDRED SLEPT FITFULLY THAT NIGHT. HE SAW
in his dreams a misshapen Ardenis working away at his stone carvings, possessing
so little of anything normally necessary for happiness. Kindred felt an undercurrent
of guilt over all those moments in his life when he acted as though ungrateful to
God for a multitude of blessings, virtually all of which had been denied Ardenis and,
indeed, the other Dwellers to a greater or lesser extent.

The expression on Miath's face was chilling, because the reasons for it were so
nebulous. He had not spoken to Klatu in a similar manner. What was it that stirred
such a statement, such a look from the Dweller?

When morning came, Kindred awoke with apprehension that twisted his insides
tight, awaiting the revelation hinted at and feared for its cryptic implications.

The Council of Many was isolated, set aside in that special chamber in the
underground network of caves and tunnels.

"As I told you," reminded Miath, "it is a position of honor but also one requiring
special stamina."

"They are to remain in this fashion for the rest of their lives?" Kindred asked,
an astonished tone in his voice.

"That is correct. They have become an indispensable link with the past, and they
are looked after with all the care we can muster."

Kindred's mind was aswirl with the possibilities—each Dweller a link in a kind
of ancestral chain, his mind imbued with a whole chunk of history, one volume in

a living encyclopedia of past generations.

From the time of Adam and Eve to Noah's flood...

For a moment, the thought overwhelmed him.

...to the death, burial and resurrection of Christ.

"Are you ill, Matthew Kindred?" Klatu's voice penetrated his momentary reverie.

"No," the minister replied. "I was thinking of the implications of all this."

"As I have—the transfer of ancestral memories. Those of today reliving the lives of others from yesterday."

Kindred stopped short in the rock-walled corridor.

Miath turned to ask him if there was anything wrong.

"What an answer!" Kindred exclaimed.

"To what?" Miath asked.

"To the whole notion of reincarnation."

"What is reincarnation, my friend?"

Kindred explained to the two of them as much as he could about the New Age movement, particularly the belief in reincarnation.

"But that is wrong," Miath said. "We have detected no evidence of any of that over the centuries."

"Oh, I agree. It's all a delusion, part of the spiritual darkness of my world. But what you have here is a positive and legitimate alternative, one that in no way conflicts with the biblical standard."

"The passing of memories from one generation to another, not their spirits but instead their thoughts," Miath remarked.

"Precisely. In your case, a kind of managed, institutionalized chain of inherited recollections. Above ground it's not like that, of course, because it's entirely unpremeditated. Yet the result is similar. Just as hair color and other characteristics can be inherited, why not memories and such, lodged in the synapses of the human brain?"

"That has been part of our history from nearly the beginning," observed Miath, realizing that what was old news to the Dwellers was a discovery of mammoth proportions to Kindred.

"And yet the New Age proponents are trying to beguile millions with their version," the minister added, "one that can have originated only from Satan himself."

They had been walking again as they conversed. Now Miath stopped, bringing one finger to his lips.

"We are there now," he said.

"You were counting the steps," Kindred commented. "You didn't get distracted even for an instant."

Miath nodded, then he asked his two companions to be very quiet initially as they approached the chamber.

They all entered that mammoth cavern. It seemed darker than before. But that was hardly of concern to a race whose eyesight had adapted to an existence with so little light.

In the kingdom of the blind, a one-eyed man rules.

That quote came back to Kindred from his days in high school. But now in this huge "room," with only the faintest of shapes visible even after pupils became accustomed to the darkness, sight was secondary. Other senses tapped by the human mind, as he soon found out, would provide the "vision."

Kindred was introduced to the special ones there. To his astonishment, scores of the chosen were in the cavern, their forms more like shadows.

"Ask a question softly," suggested Miath. "Whatever you like."

Kindred broke his silence, compelled by his discovery of those ancient bodies and wondering what connection they had with the mysteries that were abounding.

"Tell me: what was it like in the days of those you have preserved and which some seem to worship?"

"You mean our ancestors?"

The response was not spoken loudly, but it might as well have been a thunderclap right next to his ear.

Our ancestors!

Kindred could hardly speak.

"Please, I...I don't understand."

Another voice came from the darkness, quite gentle, quite old, of almost unfathomable wisdom, like that of a dozen Solomons.

"It was...."

And the story began.

SIXTEEN

LUCIFER SAW THE CREATION OF PLANET EARTH. From his vantage point in heaven he watched as the planet came into being out of nothingness. And jealousy began within him.

I am God's finest, he thought. *No other can compare with me. I must have the stewardship of that world. I want it as my own.*

And so Lucifer asked God for the privilege.

And God gave it to him.

That momentarily satiated Lucifer's desires. As soon as Earth was fully formed, he could roam its surface, knowing that this was his own kingdom.

"Darien," he said to another angel, "I can scarcely wait."

Darien smiled, attracted to the magnificent Lucifer and at the same time hesitant about his display of ego. It was hardly common when he and the others were compared to the eternal majesty of almighty God, who had every reason for a similar display but never fell victim to it.

"You'll join me there, won't you?" Lucifer asked, his wings fluttering in anticipation.

Darien held back, not certain.

"Those who hesitate too long eventually lose the opportunity," Lucifer said, the warning tone in his voice not lost on Darien.

Lucifer looked down as the oceans appeared and the land masses as well, arising out of what previously had been only murky clouds of steam over the flatness of the planet.

Vegetation—the emergence of trees and bushes and flowers and much, much more. *If only I were God....*

The thought formed in his mind and lodged there, refusing his halfhearted efforts to banish it.

And then the creatures of the deep and of the land were born and lived and multiplied.

A place so beautiful that it rivaled heaven itself!

My world!

God would give him planet Earth to manage, to keep abundant in its riches, to maintain as an Eden, with no want, no pain, no death.

But I cannot do so alone, he told himself. *I must have help.*

And so Lucifer prevailed upon God again, asking Him to let any of the angels who chose to do so go with him and help in the task of maintaining the Edenic quality of life on the planet below.

And once again God agreed.

A third of the hosts of heaven went with Lucifer, those who knew him best.

Yet not the angel named Darien.

"But why not?" Lucifer inquired.

"I cannot say, because I do not know. It may seem right for you, Lucifer, but I must hold back. I must stay here."

And with that Lucifer was gone, taking with him thousands upon thousands of other angels.

Kindred was astounded by the images this Dweller was spinning with words of authority in a voice of hushed awe. He eagerly awaited more.

Life was vibrant everywhere.

Lucifer walked along a path through a garden of convergent beauty, red and yellow and orange flowers, shrubs of bright green, the air alive with the scents of jasmine and roses. Birds rested on tree branches, animals scampered in front of him. Their sounds formed a natural orchestration.

Planet Earth, he said in his mind and heart. *A world of which I am but a caretaker and then only at the pleasure of Jehovah.*

He was to prepare planet Earth for the coming of humankind.

After I have done so, and humankind has been fruitful and multiplied, I will be relegated to a subservient position, waiting on a creation of God that is infinitely inferior to me.

The more his mind wrapped itself about all this, the more enraged he became. *I could have an audience with Him and offer my concerns, but He would brush them aside with platitudinous nothings.*

Suddenly he stopped.

One of God's creations in the animal kingdom had paused in the middle of the path directly in front of him. It was dark brown, with a great deal of hair.

Lucifer stood there, looking at it, rubbing his chin as he examined the creature. *Indeed,* he told himself. *Yes, indeed!*

It was not long before he had enlisted other angels to help him gather the creatures together. Soon there were hundreds waiting with patience and trust. In this global Eden, fear was not a reality.

"We do it *now!*" Lucifer told the others. "We show God that we are His equal or better."

And it began.

"How Lucifer proposed to create new life," the Dweller said, "is unknown. That he tried is clear."

Kindred felt a chill grip him like a hand of solid ice as the story went on.

SEVENTEEN

*C*ONSCIOUSNESS CAME PONDEROUSLY, A SLIVER
of light in encompassing darkness, coupled with trickles of pain, and then nothingness
again, as though the life force were sputtering, not eager for emancipation from
an abruptly tentative oblivion.

With gathering relentlessness, the light went from sliver to blinding ray, creating
a wave of pain, thrusting the creature into its new existence....

"We have succeeded!" Lucifer shrieked.

He watched the results of his triumph come forth from its mother's womb.

"Two arms! Two legs! A mighty brain! It has my intelligence. It has me within
its very being. I have assumed a physical shape and entered its very flesh and planted
my own seed. All of us can intercourse with flesh and blood again and again and
produce more and more of them."

And so it went. Assuming physical shape, Lucifer's hordes of followers mated again
and again with the creatures of planet Earth, many of which died in the process.
Others lived to give birth to a whole generation of living beings.

It was a ghastly sight everywhere on the planet, angels engaging in perverse acts
of procreation with one particular species of hapless creatures.

The rape of Eden began slowly—not in a day or two, as day could be considered twenty-four hours, rather a much longer period of time: strange satanic
rites under a full moon; the spilling of blood for the first, the hundredth, the
thousandth time; fear swooping in and screaming its obscenities at the earthly paradise

Jehovah had brought forth out of the cosmos.

Earth became an inhospitable place of erupting mountains of molten rock and often vicious creatures of enormous size.

Life degenerated into a constant series of battles for Satan's children, against the elements and also against the ever-present flying creatures and land monsters. There was so little they could do in defense against these creatures, and so they usually ran, hoping to find shelter before they entered the giant stomachs of their attackers.

Even when safe from those predators, they had to be ready to survive poaching of their food, their weapons, their females by rival bands of others of their kind, marauders sometimes striking in the night, no warning, just their blood-chilling war cries as they swooped into sight.

And then the awful coldness started.

Lucifer stood on the top of a mountain overlooking the valley below. He was quite cold, shivering, his wings drooping from a thin coating of ice that reappeared as often as he shook it off. And he was no longer the most glorious of all angels, his countenance now repulsive and malevolent.

Beyond the mountain, spreading out to the horizon and, indeed, all over its surface, his world was ashambles. He saw the giant creatures frozen where they had fallen, their limbs jutting upward, their mouths open in a final cry of anguish before life left them.

Not a single green plant was left anywhere, not one flower alive.

The oceans, seas, lakes, rivers and streams were solid ice, destroying any of the life therein.

Lucifer looked up at the sky as flakes of snow started to fall. He shook his fist with rage.

"You have barred me and my demonkind from Your presence; You have closed the gates of heaven to us. You have left us only the physical earth and all the universes around! But not my former home."

Lucifer flung a gesture of contempt out over the barrenness not only of the earth but the vastness of the sky and the many worlds out there.

And then God spoke.

You have not created a new form of life but taken the old and corrupted it.

The words were within Lucifer, not spoken aloud, stealing into his mind from a Creator who would not be barred, no matter how hard Lucifer worked at keeping Him at a safe distance.

"You think I have failed for all time?" he spat out the words. "You think, as You have announced from Your throne, that when You start over again and make a new planet from the torn and chill fragments of the old, I will come on bended knee and be happy with whatever crumbs of mercy You throw in front of me?"

There was no answer.

Lucifer descended the mountain and walked the plain below, threading his way past the shapes frozen in their dying, their long necks like brittle icicles, their reptilian bodies hard and cold and layered with white. It was like a forest of the dead on either side of him, dumb creatures the trees of extinction.

Behind him, spreading out for as far as could be seen, were those who had chosen to serve him instead of almighty God. They flickered back and forth between a physical state and one entirely of spirit, showing off their powers to a dead and unheeding world.

Lucifer looked up again at the sky.

"We have everything but heaven itself!" he shouted. "No matter for now. We will take back heaven in time, wrenching it from the grasp of a weakened God."

The hordes of angels-now-demons chattered with excitement.

"We have all of history in which to plan for victory."

They started a chorus of chanting. And a nerve-freezing sight it was. No longer the creatures of beauty they once had been, with Lucifer the most magnificent of all, they had become loathsome beings, misshapen and cloven-hooved, still capable of projecting a pleasing demeanor but only as a disguise and only temporarily, cloaking the despicable reality.

"But for now—," Lucifer said knowingly, with a touch of fear.

Planet Earth shook with rending suddenness. The surface started to change, the ice melting, the huge, dead creatures sinking into the mud and the slime.

Not all life had been destroyed by the ice that covered planet Earth. Ironically, those beings with whom Satan and his demons had mated had been among the survivors, many of them foraging for food among cracks in the ice by digging into the soil for live worms and beetles and even ants, anything that could sustain them.

They were not of high intelligence in those days; they had no language with which to communicate with one another; they existed from sunrise to sunset, motivated only by a kind of brutish adrenaline, going from experience to experience, life to death, and knowing nothing more.

When the final destruction came, the earth seared by ferocious heat and shaken by quakes of tumultuous magnitude, they had no comprehension of what was happening. Thus many died above ground, while others scurried beneath the surface, through caves and crevices, huddling, afraid, in the darkness.

"Go after them!" Lucifer roared. "Drain their genes, their fluids from them, and then go out among the planets and stars!"

He waved his twisted, arthritic hands in a maddened sweep at the sky above and around.

"It will not end here! I want my demons everywhere, inhabiting every planet where life can be sustained. Find any similar life forms they can and inject into their alien veins that which will in time cause them to grow and develop like those we bred here on planet Earth. Linger there as their guides, their keepers; show them what they must do in order to be a threat Your domination one day. Surely You will not destroy all the planets as You have done now with Earth. Over the coming centuries I want us to be in every corner of Your creation, mocking You. In time we will do the dance of death on Your tombstone, Jehovah."

"But what about any survivors here, ones that escape our hand on planet Earth?" a demon whispered.

Lucifer turned his head and noticed a cave in the side of a mountain just before it disappeared as a molten flow.

"In time," he replied, a chilling smile crossing his cankered face. "In time...."

OTHER DWELLERS WERE READY TO DISPENSE their moments of history, and Kindred would have eagerly awaited these revelations. But in a sweeping emotional wave he was encompassed by some semblance of the awful pain Miath and Klatu must have been feeling at that precise moment. When Klatu quietly stood and left the chamber, he wasn't surprised.

Miath leaned over and whispered, "Let him be alone for awhile. That would be best for now, Matthew Kindred. He is young. He has known all this for the whole of his brief lifetime. But to be reminded of it so vividly!"

Kindred nodded. The impact upon Klatu, he guessed, was more severe than what he had experienced after Mary's death and David's paralysis, and that was a revelation in itself because over the months he had never considered anything more crippling, emotionally, than those tragedies.

For Klatu, however, it went deeper, centuries deeper, driving through to the very basis of his existence. And for Kindred it was not an easy matter, either. He had been trying to evangelize a species of animals! Creatures with no eternal spirit within them!

He remembered a science fiction story he had read years before. Some priests were studying a race of beings on another planet. They were forced to admit an unavoidable reality: that these sentient creatures had no possibility of eternality and therefore didn't actually exist because their existence would have contradicted fundamental Christian dogma. Consequently they could be only mere satanic delusion.

He shivered at the thought, realizing the absurdity and yet also seeing that the reality of the Dwellers' plight didn't change other aspects of his relationship with them. Klatu had saved his life. Others of his kind had treated him with utmost gentility.

Would he treat them in return less kindly than a dog which had perhaps alerted him to the fact that his house was on fire?

Sometime later, Kindred searched for his friend but initially was unable to find him. Then he saw Klatu, back in the chamber of the Council of Many, communing with the same Dweller as before.

"Lucifer and his demons kept our ancestors in specific caverns," the Dweller was saying, "like a herd of cattle, sacrificing first one, then another, the hard rock ground littered with their violated bodies, sucked nearly dry of vital fluids."

"And we are the tormented residue," Klatu added, "on earth, that is."

Klatu excused himself; as he approached the entrance, he saw Kindred standing there.

"You heard?"

"I did."

"Matthew Kindred, I am so ashamed. I wanted you to think of me as your equal. I wanted to be your friend. Will you forgive me? Will you—"

Klatu stopped midsentence and chuckled perversely.

"What is there to forgive? I am an animal. Does an animal *need* forgiveness for anything?"

He started sobbing then, a sight that startled Kindred because it was one of the few times he had seen Klatu do this, and never before so violently.

Kindred put his arms around him, and they walked to another, smaller chamber that was empty.

"Hearing you talk with such love about Christ," Klatu said, the words coming in a rush, "I tried to tell myself that there was hope. You see, none of us has had contact with someone like you. Whenever we have ventured above ground, our presence has made people run in fear, stalk us with guns, stab us with knives. They have treated us like animals, and, of course, Matthew Kindred, that *is* what we *are!*"

Kindred had preached hundreds of sermons to thousands of people about redemption through Christ as Savior and Lord, and he had done this because until the very moment of death any living human being had that hope. It was often difficult since many rejected Christ, preferring to live in their sin. No matter how hard he tried, those with hardened minds would continue turning their backs on Him until it was too late, and they were irretrievably headed for hell.

With Klatu it was so very different. Klatu and the other Dwellers all were willing to accept Christ as their Savior, but going through any such motions would be little more than a charade.

"Is it right of God to subject us to this anguish?" Klatu asked.

"I would ask instead: Was it right of Satan to have done so? And, of course, the answer is no. Nothing the devil ever does is right or good or just."

"But God is all-powerful. Or is He?"

"He is, Klatu. There can be little doubt about it. While we cannot understand fully how Satan could be allowed to triumph, even for a time, in the midst of a divine plan by an omnipotent Creator, that is the case. In the long run—"

"The long run?" Klatu spit out the words. "For you and other humans the long run exists. Not for *us!* Why do we even bother to honor God with our actions, if He does not reward us with His own?"

Kindred paused, uttering a silent prayer for the wisdom needed to talk to Klatu in a meaningful way.

"Is it possible, Klatu," he spoke as gently as he knew how, "that you are more disturbed by what will happen to you as you live *this* life instead? You've had all these years to absorb the truths that were repeated back there, and you still cannot. Will these truths sooner or later drive you to wild deeds, to horrible crimes because, in an eternal sense, you have nothing to lose? Is that your fear, Klatu?"

Kindred saw by the other's expression that he had hit a nerve.

"Face it: You are *not* human, and that realization continues to shake you to the very foundation of your being. Nevertheless—and think about this very clearly—human *or* animal, you are the same individual who saved my life, whose medicine cured a dying child. If this life is indeed all that you have, make it the finest life by such acts, the most productive, the most satisfying you can manage. Live with honor and dignity, Klatu. Deny Satan any sort of continuing victory. He would love to have you destroy yourself here and now. Don't you realize that, another tragedy to add to his encyclopedia of infamy?"

Kindred cleared his throat and then:

"You talk of pain, my friend. And there can be no doubt that the history of the Dwellers is filled with an overwhelming degree of pain, pain of the mind and the body."

Kindred lowered his voice to just barely a whisper.

"But it has been said that 'every broken thing is but the assurance that God is making something.' Often, through pain and other devices, He must break us in our weakness so that He can remake us in His strength."

Struggling with the words, Kindred was still being pummelled himself by the reality of what he had learned and tottered under its weight. He knew he had to project some semblance of strength, of wisdom for the sake of Klatu and, in so doing, forget about himself, waiting until later to nurse his own pain.

"You may feel that a world of suffering is on your own shoulders right now," Kindred continued, "a world of pain in your very gut. But your pain is not the only pain, nor is all that is painful centered in you and you alone. There is no such thing as a sum of suffering, according to C.S. Lewis. Your entire kind suffers, and you have but a *part* of *that*. In any event, Klatu, you are not alone, and you must not bear the suffering of all Dwellers as your own."

Klatu's expression had changed, and Kindred rejoiced at this.

"My friend—and I say that to you in the same way, whether you are human or animal—my friend, you suffer by yourself, *as* yourself, and that is wrenching, I know. Yet think of what Christ endured on the cross when He took the pain of the whole earth upon His blessed self, the filth of every sin—something *none* of us will ever have to do."

Kindred was trembling from the thought of what it must have been like for Him.

"But even more, Klatu, think of the pain that will have to be faced forever by the damned and by their deceiver, pain that you and I blessedly will never know."

Klatu held up his hand to silence Kindred.

"Should I be happy to escape the prospect of eternal torment because I will embrace only oblivion?" he asked. "Is that what you are saying? To me? To the others?"

"What I *am* saying, Klatu, is that you should not allow yourself the option chosen by those who are mired in a pit of nihilism, that is, justifying everything they do, no matter what the consequences, because—in their minds—there is neither reward nor punishment."

A number of minutes passed, the two of them sitting on two adjacent natural rock formations.

"Perhaps you are correct," Klatu finally replied. "If a king thinks he is of royal blood and finds out otherwise, that he is nothing more than a lowly commoner, he must surely wonder if suddenly he will start *acting* like one, with all the disciplines of royalty cast aside. Until I learned, early on in my life, that I was an animal, I had dreams, Matthew Kindred, such dreams!"

"And the truth is, simply, that it's up to this king," Kindred offered. "He is the one to control his own actions of today, now, this very moment, for as the Bible says, 'Sufficient unto the day are the evils thereof,' not that awful hindsight which has been thrust upon him."

Not that awful hindsight.

That truth seemed aimed as much at Kindred himself as at Klatu. Nothing could change the fact of Mary's death and what had happened to David. Time couldn't be spun backward. What was critical was how he adjusted to the circumstances—as it was for Klatu in the image he was forced to have of himself.

"But an *animal?*" Klatu said. "Your kind has animals that are cute or vicious or worthless or whatever, depending upon which species. But none has my intellect; none has my physical abilities. How could I be related to any of *them?*"

What Klatu was saying struck a raw nerve in Kindred. He had an insistent question of his own: How could he accept the reality of the Dwellers at all? How could he assume that all he had heard was correct? And for a not-so-simple reason: Nothing could be more fundamental to the Christian mythos than the conviction that sentient beings had immortal spirits and were therefore candidates for redemption, and that non-sentient beings could not have such immortality in any sense at all and were thus denied an eternal destiny.

On the other hand, Kindred knew, the Christian worldview should never be taken as an excuse for abusive behavior toward non-immortal creatures. Those in the Christian community who used the spiritless status of animals as a basis for ignoring or even encouraging the often mindless atrocities perpetrated on them in so-called scientific experiments around the world were, Kindred felt, grievously misguided.

Kindred knew he had to turn from his own shock and confusion to give Klatu yet something else that his friend desperately needed just then.

"Klatu, I look at a man named Hitler, who exterminated many millions, or Stalin, who was responsible for the slaughter of even greater numbers. I look at them and other so-called human beings like them and ask myself the same question: How could I be related to despicable devils like that?"

"And what is your answer?"

"I am related only by the blood in my veins, the flesh on my bones."

He tapped his head.

"Up here..."

And he touched his chest directly over his heart.

"...and here, there is a universe of difference. If I acted as they did—if I ordered the incineration of helpless men, women and children; if soldiers in obedience to me starved hundreds of thousands to death, beat many more senseless, shot countless numbers of others and dumped their bodies into a ditch—if *I* were responsible for *that*, then I would be no better than they were. I would be human, yes, but acting like a rabid, uncontrollable animal."

He stood before his friend.

"Klatu, you can become very much like a mad dog, snapping and tearing at everyone around you so that they run in terror from your presence. Or you can be as you have been...without change."

...*without change.*

"Oh, that it could be so, Matthew Kindred."

The prehistoric world was, by the most optimistic assessments, an inhospitable one. Survival for the so-called cavemen was tenuous, in part because of their ignorance in using the most basic tools, an ignorance that supposedly changed later as they learned to create fire and use the wheel and other devices.

Disease was a constant problem in a world without medicine of any kind, a world in which surgery and proper sanitation and much more simply did not exist, making the task of living from day to day fraught with danger, not only from within their bodies but from without, as the giant dinosaurs repeatedly sought for their own food supply among the cave people. And there were the tribes of other cave dwellers, marauders invading one another's territory.

And the elements!

In the summer, heat in oppressive waves from a blinding overhead sun, no way to cool themselves off.

In the winter, freezing cold, with a large percentage from each tribe dying of pneumonia or losing limbs because of frostbite.

A perverse, awful world, cruel and unyielding....

A world which God in His wisdom and goodness had created? And then, realizing His mistake, started over with Adam and Eve in the Garden of Eden?

Finally there was an alternative to that view, an alternative that placed the blame for the existence of this dark and ugly prehistoric era at the feet not of God but of the Prince of Darkness.

Adam and Eve were given a perfect world, without disease or death, the two of them able to walk with God, talk with Him openly and feel the objective reality of His presence. When they sinned, they were cast out into a world of pain and travail, Eden gone forever.

But as inferior as it was to what Adam and Eve once had known, it would be many times superior to the world of prehistoric times. Whom would God have been punishing? Humanity had not as yet arrived on the scene. The God of majesty and creative genius would hardly have begun planet Earth as a place of such daily dread.

It was, therefore, what Satan had made of what God had created. Not even Satan would have risked his place in heaven for the prehistoric earth.

Kindred spent time considering the implications of what Klatu and he had learned. And he realized that in the long story of the Dwellers, there was an answer to an issue that had long fascinated Christian and non-Christian alike: the theory of evolution as expounded by Charles Darwin.

The much-publicized missing link, for example. Despite intensive research, evolutionists had not found that particular species that supposedly linked humanity and the animal life from which they claimed it had evolved. And they never would be able to do so simply because there was none. Any evidence they had found of an evolving race that looked like humankind and that sprang from the animal kingdom was tied in with a singular reality—Satan's scheme to create life—which succeeded only in propagating a species with a physical appearance and an intellect that paralleled humanity's imperfectly at best. The center of humankind, its soul/spirit, could only have been bestowed by almighty God.

All the bones found by archaeologists and anthropologists belonged to Klatu's ancestors, not humanity's. When God destroyed the surface of the earth and started over again with Adam and Eve, He was literally burying the by-products of Satan's rebellion. At the same time He barred Satan from ever reclaiming heaven as his place of habitation.

NINETEEN

Shouts tore through the quiet of the underground settlement.

Kindred and Klatu hurried into the main cavern, joining dozens of Dwellers also rushing to find out what was happening.

They were approached by Miath, his face wrinkled in heavy concern.

"We have a bad situation, very bad indeed," he said. "One of our kind from another settlement went above ground with several of his friends and was attacked by some human soldiers. One of his comrades was killed; he himself managed to escape, but the rest were taken captive.

"He followed the truck into which they were herded, like so much cattle, and saw that it was heading toward a military base. Inside the base were other Dwellers, scared, shivering—there was talk of laboratory testing. He hurried from that place, and in going back underground, became confused and lost his way. He discovered us here and has asked for our help."

Kindred could scarcely believe what he had just heard. Surely there was a reasonable explanation.

"We must go up there," Miath declared, "and see for ourselves. Would you, Matthew Kindred, and you, Klatu, join me?"

Both gave assent without hesitation.

While waiting for the right route to be chosen, Kindred tried to analyze the possibility that the military were using individual Dwellers in certain kinds of experiments and wondered what had been going on in his absence from the world of humankind.

In a short while they were on their way up to the surface. It was not an easy climb at all. They fell some distance more than once, and, until near the very top, they coughed again and again, on the thin edge of oxygen starvation. And there were the bugs and slimy, crawling things they repeatedly had to brush off their clothing, their flesh. But after hours, hours that seemed far longer than others they had spent....

It was night above ground, the sky clear, stars scattered randomly over the otherwise endless black tapestry of the heavens. The air was cool, pure, the feeling of it entering their lungs exhilarating, so much so that the group of three just stood there momentarily, inhaling deeply, their eyes closed, their hearts beating faster and faster as the air's effects radiated through their bodies, nerve ends atingle with the joy of it, even the ecstasy, leaving them without words, only the sensations mattering.

Below the air was nearly always stagnant, old air only marginally refreshed by thin and vagrant whiffs of fresh oxygen seeping down through cracks in the earth's crust. It was enough to avoid suffocation but never more than that, marginal at best, making the "high" they all were now experiencing that much more memorable. Miath tuned into its sweetness to a greater extent than Klatu and Kindred, so seldom had he experienced it.

Finally, satiated, they looked at one another, a little embarrassed perhaps, a little depressed, the moment gone and already missed for what it had brought them on welcome fingers of gentle stimulation.

"It is good that we have the night," Klatu observed, his voice husky-toned.

"Yes, I was worried about the light," Miath agreed, blinking a bit self-consciously, his big eyes comfortable now—but that would not have been so under the unaccustomed glare of an overhead sun.

They walked as a unit across the still-warm sand. None of them, really, had any idea of where to go. But almost immediately the distant sound of trucks broke the silence of the desert, a silence that was especially eerie to Kindred, who had spent virtually all of his life surrounded by sound.

In supermarkets the piped-in music was a given ingredient, as in the waiting rooms of offices, at shopping malls, at car dealerships. There seemed to be something akin to a dread of silence, as though when left to the embrace of it, people would have to confront the reality of their lives, the paucity of real, deep meaning.

Yet here, in the midst of the desert, the silence was quite total. Just as the good air was so refreshing, so was the silence, a kind of natural sedative calming the nerves and quieting the spirit.

In a short while they came upon a sight so far beyond anything at least Kindred and Klatu had expected that they could not speak initially, confronted as they were by a travertine dome rising high above them, and beside it a striking blue stream of water clouded by whitish deposits of calcium carbonate.

"It is called *sipapu* by the Hopi Indians," Miath told his stunned companions. "There is a hole at the top of the dome. Legend has it, according to the tribes in this area, that an ancient race once emerged from within and sojourned for a time with the Hopi's ancestors."

Kindred turned and looked at Miath.

"Dwellers?" he asked simply.

"That seems a possibility, but then it would be a rare occurrence for my kind to spend any *prolonged* period with another race above ground."

They encountered other intriguing spots: a partially excavated Indian village that seemed to be several hundred years old, and a crater similar to the Great Crater, but much less well-known and considerably smaller.

"There are others," Miath told them.

"But was it just meteorites hitting the earth that caused them?" Kindred asked.

"It is quite probable that none of us will ever know," Miath replied matter-of-factly.

After many hours, the edges of exhaustion beginning to take over, they stopped to sleep behind a small pile of volcanic rock. Kindred's mind was filled with all the mysteries that he had been privy to during his odyssey, and despite his tiredness he slept only fitfully until the rumbling sound of some large trucks, nearby this time, awakened him and the others.

Two large ones indeed, painted army green, the storage portions only partially covered by loose canvas that flapped slightly in errant desert breezes.

Kindred, Klatu and Miath hid behind the mound of rocks, watching the trucks pass by, each having to stifle an exclamation of shock and outrage as they saw the contents of the three vehicles.

Bodies, piled so high and thick that they took up every bit of space.
Dweller bodies.

Miath had to be restrained from racing after the trucks.

"Our people!" he exclaimed with heightened alarm. "But why? Were their crimes so—"

"Down!" Kindred whispered.

Two other trucks came along. The first had a cargo similar to the others; the second was different—bodies, yes, but alive, Dwellers standing in a curious kind of trust, willing to put their faith into undeserving hands.

"We must follow them!" Miath insisted convincingly. "We must find out what is happening here."

Kindred and Klatu knew that their friend was right, that they had to put the pieces of all this together.

It was only a few minutes until the trucks reached their destination, an isolated army base. The three trucks with bodies went in one direction once inside the base; the truck with living Dwellers turned another way.

"How do we get in?" Miath said, a note of desperation in his voice. "We must do something."

What could they do? If caught breaking into the base, Kindred told them, well, the consequences would be awful indeed.

"But my people! What are they going to do with the ones who are yet alive?" Miath asked. "I have to know. You would react the same way if you were a Jew, wouldn't you, and this happened to be World War II?"

"But it's not, Miath," Kindred replied. "And this assuredly *isn't* Nazi Germany!"

"That is very true, but the deeds, as we see these now—can you ignore the similarity?"

Klatu spoke up.

"We will not know the truth until we search for it and find it."

Kindred reluctantly agreed with him. That they were actually able to make their search as easily as they did proved something else: that the typical army base was not structured to block even the intrusion of three amateurs such as they were. How much of an open-sesame it would be to dedicated, trained terrorists if that day ever came!

The three of them simply waited for an opening in a fairly isolated sector of the base, and in seconds they were inside the perimeter. But which of the buildings housed the living Dwellers?

"There," Miath said simply.

"How do you know?" Kindred asked.

"Because I feel their pain—here," Miath added, pointing to the crown of his head.

They managed to make it inside the building he indicated without being detected. At first Kindred puzzled as to why everything was so easy, particularly the lack of sophisticated detection equipment, laser-activated alarms and such. And then he realized that this must have been one of the older bases. What with budget cutbacks, there was no money to update it in any way. And besides, it was not previously an especially strategic center, rather like the almost forgotten French Legion outpost of yesterday, in an area where no one expected any trouble. Any monies would be spent at locations more crucial to the defense of the nation.

"There," Miath said, pointing toward one of the corridors.

They approached a room at the end. Hesitating for a second or two, Kindred opened the door and went inside, Klatu and Miath following him.

The room was jammed with cages, layers of these along each wall. Some held chimpanzees, with dogs and cats in others. All were oddly quiet, a kind of funereal silence dominating. Matthew Kindred sniffed the air, detecting an odor of dried blood mixed with some unknown medicine-like scent.

Klatu approached one cage that contained a tiny teacup French poodle. The dog had a contraption that looked like a battery pack strapped to it, a look of intense pain in its face.

Klatu backed away quickly.

"What's wrong?" Kindred asked.

"I heard it crying to me."

"What?"

"Some inner part of its canine brain was calling out for help, for release, and I felt that plea throbbing at my own temple."

Miath was standing in front of a particular cage, reaching his hand into it. On the other side of the bars, a chimp was also extending its own hand, nearly touching Miath's. Suddenly it drew back, or rather fell back. Its mouth opened and blood gushed out. It was then that Miath noticed a tiny little box surgically attached to its neck. Periodically a light would go on, flash for a few seconds, then turn off.

"Matthew Kindred," Miath observed, "this animal is dying. I can tell because I am sharing that death with him."

Miath appeared to be abruptly quite dizzy and then crumpled to the floor.

Klatu bent down over his friend, hugging him gently.

Kindred went over to the cage, looking in at the chimp. The animal was now shaking quite violently, banging itself against the bars of the cage but not emitting any sounds, the silence seeming peculiar, like a movie scene prior to a soundtrack being synchronized with it. Finally the chimp threw up some raspberry-colored fluid and was dead.

Miath was covered with perspiration.

"The same," he said weakly.

"The same?" Klatu asked.

"Yes, as when those of our kind die underground, except for the pain—because there are so many causes for death. But it always *ends* the same way, as though one is plunging down a deep abyss, yet there is no bottom; or at least all consciousness, all awareness, all *self* ceases before it is reached."

Kindred knew why, of course; none of the Dwellers had souls—there was nothing eternal about them. They lived one life and that was it. Over the centuries, the many centuries since the first creation, countless thousands of them would exist for a few

91

decades in each case, and that was it; no heaven or hell for this species.

Kindred shivered a bit at the thought, feeling again the disturbing finality that all of the Dwellers faced, cursed by Satan with bits and pieces of "humanity"— counterfeited glimpses of what would later be given full and legitimate expression in the creation of Adam and Eve and all of humanity to follow.

And counterfeit was unquestionably the right word. It was like having an attache case full of money, going up to a store window and seeing the most beautiful diamond ring ever fashioned by human artistry in concert with nature's processes; and though having the money to buy, being told that this money was no good, it was phony, it could not be used; and then turning away, realizing how close, how very close....

Kindred wandered over to a door leading to another room and glanced through a small, square window.

No! His mind screamed instantly at the sight. *No, they can't be doing this!*

He was suddenly very weak, his insides heaving. Klatu rushed over to Kindred. "My friend, my friend, what is it?" he asked.

"Don't let Miath look inside," Kindred said. "Please, I beg you—don't look in there yourself."

Klatu spoke very softly, very kindly.

"Embracing the truth, no matter how devastating, is for the strong, Matthew Kindred; refusing to face it is only for the weak."

Miath and Klatu took turns at the small window.

When they were through, the two of them turned aside together and went into a corner of the first room, sat down on the floor and bowed their heads, their throats emitting a loud, siren-like sound as though they were truly combined into a single entity with a single voice.

And when they had finished, Kindred could see that they were thoroughly drained of energy.

They looked up at him as one.

It was Klatu who spoke.

"They must not be allowed to endure that agony any longer, Matthew Kindred."

The minister nodded. Every bit of common sense he possessed, every rational part of his mind objected. This was government property; if caught, they all could be sentenced to long imprisonment, perhaps even death if sabotage was the verdict. And yet he also knew that the real crime was not anything they might do in the next few minutes.

The door to the second room was locked. If they were able to break the glass, perhaps one of them could reach through and try to open it from the other side.

Klatu found a hammer inside a drawer in a desk on one side of the first room.

"That'll do it," Kindred agreed, "if the glass isn't bullet-proof."

It was not.

The glass shattered into uncountable pieces on both sides of the door. Miath's arms were the longest by an inch or two. He reached in and managed to grope down to the knob on the other side.

Suddenly there were footsteps in the corridor outside, and then the door to the room they were in was flung open.

Facing them were six armed soldiers. Almost by reflex, Klatu lunged.

"No!" Kindred shouted. "It's—"

Klatu was shot in the shoulder, the force of the bullet knocking him to one side. He started to get up. Kindred rushed to his side.

"This is not the way to die," the minister whispered.

"But death is still the same. Does it matter?"

"Until death comes, we must not ever give up hope. Hope is a gift from God."

"And it is one of the most fragile, Matthew Kindred."

Klatu lost consciousness, his body falling forward.

Miath was ordered to stop just as he had found a catch on the other side of the door and was turning it.

"Stop immediately!" the command was repeated.

Miath was heedless, acting blindly, stupidly. Three of the soldiers opened fire. Miath's body was slammed against the door, which swung open, dangling him from it.

He turned his head toward a cage at his right. One of the Dwellers crawled slowly over to the cage's front bars; he could not stand because the cage was not tall enough. But even if it were, he still would have been unable to do so. A part of each leg was missing, and a gangrenous discoloration had crept up most of what remained, causing the creature's unrelenting agony.

Miath looked for a fleeting few seconds at the captured Dwellers in the other cages, arms missing on some, eyes on others, and his gaze locked in on a familiar face.

"Srepth!" Miath exclaimed, his voice hardly audible before it faded altogether, and he tumbled into the abyss of centuries.

TWENTY

Kindred was taken to a cell in the prison section of the base. He learned that a hearing was scheduled in the next few days. When Kindred was asked about an attorney for his defense, he indicated that he would rather defend himself.

Finally, as he looked out the single window in the cell, he saw across the street the laboratory into which they had broken.

Miath! Klatu! Where were they? What had happened to them?

"Rev. Kindred?" the voice interrupted his thoughts.

He turned and noticed a tall, thin, youngish man in a white smock standing in front of the cell, a uniformed guard beside him. The door was opened, and the man entered. He nodded to the guard, who then left.

"My name is Aaron Slatterly," the man introduced himself. "I'm a doctor here."

Kindred shook hands with him, and they both sat down on a cot which was directly across from the window.

"I know quite a bit about what happened, sir," Slatterly told him. "I'm on your side. What can I do?"

"Help me to stop those experiments."

"I would like to do just that, especially since I have been in charge of the ones at this base from the very beginning."

"What makes you change your mind?"

Slatterly stood and paced.

"There was always something inside me that said it was wrong. But you know how adept human beings are at rationalizing away their consciences. I convinced myself that it was for the good of humanity to see how these creatures were able to survive underground without the kinds of sophisticated medicines we have today."

He stood still and looked straight at Kindred.

"Until I found out about the *unauthorized* experiments," he said.

Kindred jumped to his feet.

"Unauthorized? By whom? For what reason?"

"We've not been able to track any of that down as yet. But the fact that these *are* being conducted is unassailable."

"How widespread?"

"Very. And there's something else."

Slatterly took a sheet of paper out of his pocket.

"One of them wrote something on this and left it in the bottom of her cage before she died."

Kindred took the sheet and read what was on it.

Klatu—farewell, my love—Taresa.

Kindred's face turned ashen.

"Are you ill, sir?" Slatterly asked, concerned. "Can I—"

Kindred waved his hand through the air and then gave the sheet back to Slatterly.

"It is a sad story," he said. "I will tell you later."

"Animals writing as that one did! These creatures are extraordinary. They don't match up with any species known before now. They play havoc with a great many scientific, biological and anthropological preconceptions."

"And some deep-seated religious ones."

"Oh, certainly! I can see it. Creatures with intelligence, moral consciousness, deductive reasoning—what a conflict with the orthodox Christian view of humanity and animals! If you admit that they have these abilities, these qualities, then you must say that they have immortal spirits. And yet there is nothing in the history of Christianity to allow that possibility since they *are* clearly animals. Animals with eternality are a seeming contradiction in terms."

Kindred was impressed.

"You have an amazing grasp of Christian truths," he said appreciatively.

"Sir, I *am* a Christian."

"Praise God!"

"Indeed."

They both sat down again.

"Being so close to them as they underwent pain started to have a severe impact upon me," Slatterly continued. "But it was a process for me that began, I must admit, sometime ago with more customary species, dogs, for example. We could stick electrodes into their brains, and still they would be wagging their tails afterward when one of us approached them. Cats could be abused terribly, and yet all anyone had to do was brush them gently for a minute or two, and they would start purring with contentment!

"When the creatures, I guess they're called Dwellers, entered the picture, that process intensified as far as I was concerned. They seemed too much like human beings and not enough like animals. Transferring some of the experimentation to them made me feel like an apostle of Mengele!"

"The Nazi concentration camp butcher?"

"Exactly. And I started reading books by theologians and others. I started to believe something quite profound about animals such as dogs and cats and, yes, the Dwellers."

"What was that?" Kindred asked.

"There is this theory that when God put Adam and Eve into the Garden of Eden, animals were there to serve them, and *they* in return were to bestow only kindness. Since you didn't have death—that came later when Adam and Eve sinned and were cast out—you couldn't have animals being killed for food. If Adam and Eve needed to eat at all—and how can we be certain that they did?—they must have partaken only of plant and vegetable life. Anything else would have involved the taking of life and the use of that lifeless animal body in each case for food.

"Those who dispute this theory point to the nature of sacrifice, the redemptive shedding of blood in both the Old and the New Testaments. My response is that this came after the fall, and not before, and that it was made necessary by humanity's sin. After all, if there were no sin, Christ's death, burial and resurrection would have been quite unnecessary.

"As proof of the animal-oriented part of this theory, I can point to the millennium prophesied in the Bible. The lion will no longer eat the lamb but will lie down with it."

Kindred recalled some reading he had done on another aspect of the subject.

"If the ideal state in Eden was what God intended for all of humanity," he interpolated, "but the intrusion of sin destroyed that and led to the gross imperfection we have presently, then we have to suppose that it isn't *natural* for animals *ever* to kill human beings. And, conversely, it isn't natural, either, for a human to take the life of any member of the animal kingdom."

"C.S. Lewis got into that, didn't he?" Slatterly offered.

"He did indeed," Kindred replied, even more impressed now. "But, of course, he went further still. He drew an analogy between wild and tame animals, and unrepentant and redeemed humanity. In Lewis's view, just as redeemed humankind becomes what God wanted from the beginning, so do tame animals become what was supposed to be their state in Eden."

Kindred leaned forward.

"And how do they achieve this 'tameness'? By experiencing the kindness of human beings. It is the vehicle of a form of redemption for animals, enabling them to shed their wild natures, just as humans shed their unrepentant selves and embrace Christ as Savior and Lord."

Slatterly interrupted then.

"Actually, sir, I must confess, *The Problem of Pain* is one of my favorite books."

"I see. So you know what I'm talking about?"

"I truly do," Slatterly replied.

"Well, then, think of this," Kindred started to say.

"May I anticipate your thought, sir?"

"Of course."

"If we continue to treat the Dwellers as animals, indeed, if we treat them actually worse than we do our pet dogs, cats, birds and other domesticated creatures, we are shoving them more and more into the arms of Satan, who will have no compunctions whatever about turning them squarely against us!"

"Right!" Kindred agreed. "On the other hand, if we turn away from the cruelty, both in the experiments on the Dwellers and in daily treatment of them quite outside the laboratory, applying the same standards of treatment—and thereby manifesting God's love—to all animals, then we can expect only God's blessing. And with that will come real peace from knowing that we have resisted that part of our own nature which Satan has been very successful in manipulating over all of recorded history!"

The two of them were silent for a number of minutes.

It was Slatterly who then spoke up.

"Sir, I have a plan," the doctor said. "Would you like to hear it?"

The minister did.

Approximately twenty by forty with a twelve-foot ceiling, the gray-toned room was crowded, two dozen spectators taking up every seat. Undoubtedly most of those present belonged to various branches of the media. Word had understandably spread with millisecond speed, or so it seemed. Some were photographers, their Nikons, Canons and Leicas ready, those with motor drives far more fortunate if anything sudden should occur. Others were reporters, equipped with portable computers or small battery-operated cassette tape recorders— but a few still refused modern technology, choosing instead old-fashioned, yellow-ruled notepads and pencils or ballpoint pens.

The room was hot, the temperature nudging eighty-five degrees. An odor of perspiration hung in the air, mixed with thin veils of smoke still remaining from nearly a dozen cigarettes and two pungent cigars before the order had been given to extinguish these just seconds earlier. Two open windows were letting in fresh air but did nothing to mitigate the heat. A blanket of it covered not only that room in that single building on the army base near Nocales, but the entire area as well. The sun was unrelenting, baking everyone and everything in a kind of vast natural oven, with only lizards and rattlesnakes and other desert life really accustomed to it.

Matthew Kindred sat at a table on the opposite side of a mahogany railing that separated the general or generals presiding over each case, as well as the accused and their attorneys, from those merely looking on, reporters or otherwise.

For Kindred there was to be no attorney; he had refused one, preferring to speak in his own defense. As he looked at the solitary individual sitting across from him, he momentarily regretted not taking advantage of the offer of counsel. This military judge projected an image of toughness and experience and did not seem the type given to compromise.

Heavy-set, with a narrow little moustache that he rubbed periodically, the only sign of what must have been impatience, he was in his mid-fifties, undoubtedly a career militarist, dedicated wholly to iron-clad rules and regulations. His deeply wrinkled face betrayed no emotion. He could have been sitting comfortably in a cool office suite, no hint that the heat was getting to him—as though it was not a human face at all, but one sculpted out of weather-worn granite. When he was not looking straight ahead, he was referring to a file of papers before him.

Kindred glanced at the stenographer ready to take down every word, a short woman in her late forties, looking as uncomfortable as all the others. His attention drifted to a non-functioning air-conditioner protruding from a window to his right. The appliance was covered with a thin layer of dust or sand or both, inescapable patches of it everywhere. Brush it away and it would return, the desert intruding. And if it were allowed to do so unchallenged—through windstorm after windstorm, and even vagrant breezes stirring up little clouds of it, not to mention the passage of feet and tires and myriad other activities—eventually it would bury whatever was in its path, as it had hidden even ancient civilizations over the many centuries of the past.

The room had little furniture in it, just the chair Kindred was sitting in, an empty one next to him, the table on which he was leaning forward and the larger table where that one officer sat, with an army guard, rifle at ease, a few feet to his right. Spectators were relegated to folding chairs hastily set up to accommodate the larger-than-usual number of those present. Added to the odor of perspiration was the smell of what could be called institutional antiseptic, similar to that found in a hospital or perhaps a city morgue. The latter thought sent a momentary chill straight down Kindred's spine.

Kindred's attention returned to the man whom he would be confronting in a matter of minutes, this crisp, efficient-looking but cold individual, a countenance perhaps even somewhat weary, the weariness of someone who had seen it all a thousand times before and merely wanted to get through the routine and go on to another matter.

But how can you be so dispassionate? Kindred thought to himself. *Have all those years of service so drained you of emotion that even the extraordinary circumstances of this particular case fail to ruffle you?*

The military changeth not, even though outside, in that sector of human society where civilians lived and worked, changes might be so devastating, so confusing and seemingly errant in one way or another that people often could scarcely make any order of their lives in a world of nihilistic triumph. Yet it was in just such a world of inconsistency that the military had to remain a kind of rock: hard, tough, unyielding, barely changed from, say, half a century ago, despite the advent of nuclear arms. So old techniques of warfare were still dominant, continuing a thread through human history from the days of Alexander the Great to Vietnam and beyond.

General Clarkson Marquand finally cleared his throat, announced the start of the proceedings and then stood, quoting the list of charges the army was making against Kindred.

As he finished, he took off his glasses, put them on the table and stared straight at the minister.

"How could you, a man of the cloth, become embroiled in all of this?" he asked, with unfeigned indignation evident in his tone.

"May I speak freely, sir?" Kindred asked.

"You may," replied General Marquand as he sat down again, as though having Kindred say anything was a waste of time; but since the rules required this, he would allow it.

Kindred stood, clearing his throat.

"You may not realize the circumstances in which I found myself over the past weeks. I have been living with the Dwellers underground, almost as one of them."

A murmur broke through the crowd. Electronic flash units went off one after the other.

"The story behind them is so extraordinary it would tax the powers of comprehension of any of us here today."

He paused then: "The Dwellers have been underground ever since the days of Adam and Eve. They are a link to the time of dinosaurs and before. But their amazing history becomes even more astonishing when you realize that they are a failed attempt by Satan himself to create human beings before God had a chance to do so. They are in fact..."

He looked without blinking at General Marquand, meeting the other's own stare.

"...a very strange combination of humankind and animalkind without, I am sorry to say, the immortal human spirit."

With that the crowd broke into a chorus of shouted questions. General Marquand managed to get order by threatening to have everyone escorted out of the room if there was another outburst.

"Rev. Kindred," the general interjected, "I find that an unacceptable and shocking statement, coming as it does from a clergyman whose Bible would completely refute such a notion.''

"But," Kindred continued, "I am not saying that the Dwellers are indeed human. They obviously have no spirits. I am talking about some of their characteristics. When I tell you just a little of what I witnessed, you will understand why it all is, I admit, amazing but certainly not preposterous by virtue of the fact that every detail is true.''

Clearing his throat again, he turned around and faced the crowd behind him.

"How many of us have had a much loved pet about which we have said, 'That dog acts almost human sometimes.' And yet it is obviously not human, though it seems more than an animal. On the other hand, when we think of Hitler, Stalin, Idi Amin, others through the course of human history, we say that their madness, their atrocities, made them little better than crazed animals, rabid beasts causing death and destruction to countless millions.''

Kindred opened a Bible that he had picked up from the table.

" 'Satan walketh about the earth as a roaring lion, seeking whom he may devour.' We are told of people giving in to passions that cause their behavior to be like brutish beasts. The animalistic metaphor is used throughout Scripture, particularly and most powerfully in the book of Revelation.''

People were starting to cough at that point, obviously bored by such "Bible talk.'' Several were whispering to one another.

Kindred ignored this as he continued. "Why did God, through His inspired writers, constantly do this? What was the precedent? Permit me to suggest that the Dwellers indeed may be the answer to all such questions.

"We cannot properly even call them creatures without demeaning their place in history. Though created by Satan, they have managed until now to thwart his domination.''

"But you lived with them. How 'human' did they seem to you?''

"At first completely so.''

"At first, you say,'' the general continued. "Did anything happen to change your outlook?''

"Yes.''

"What was it?''

Kindred spoke of the encounter with the Council of Many and the subsequent startling discovery.

"Then even this so-called friend of yours admitted that he could not consider himself human.''

"What Klatu realized long before we ever entered one another's lives was that he existed in some sort of netherworld between humanity and the animal kingdom.''

" 'Created by Satan,' " General Marquand repeated. "Isn't that a theological contradiction?''

Kindred closed his eyes for an instant as he said, "Yes, that's true. The new species, if you will, was generated by Satan. Only God can create new life. But in this case the life already existed; Satan merely warped what was already there. The animals with which Satan experimented had been created by the Lord as part of a perfect world. To a degree, the Dwellers are the handiwork of Satan as well as God.''

"Aren't we all?" General Marquand snapped sarcastically.

But Kindred seized upon that very point.

"Yes, we are. And we constantly are struggling with that duality of our natures—the flesh warring against the spirit and the spirit against the flesh.''

"Rev. Kindred," the general said, "when a dog is rabid, do we not put him to sleep?''

"Yes, we do.''

"When a human being commits terrible atrocities, do we not seek to condemn him to death?''

"Again, yes, we do. But the Dwellers have done nothing worthy of death.''

Marquand slammed his fist down upon the table.

"How can you expect us to accept that statement as valid when we have some reports from various locations that directly contradict you, Rev. Kindred? Reports that show they seem prone to the most violent outbursts imaginable. They become quite ferocious, I assure you.''

General Marquand stood, waving a thick pile of papers impatiently through the air.

"They have menaced the elderly, the crippled, the defenseless. They have sprung up from their unholy pits to begin some kind of war against humanity. If they are part divine, part demonic, then it is all too clear, sir, which side has been winning the battle for control.''

Marquand sat down, with only Kindred now standing, perspiration breaking out all over his body.

Lord, give me some words. Help me as You helped Paul at Mars Hill that day two thousand years ago....

The minister glanced at his watch.

"Is there anything further, Rev. Kindred?" General Marquand asked, drumming his fingers with studied impatience.

"Sir, I think—"

The main door into the room was opened abruptly, and two men in white smocks reeled in a cage.

Marquand stood up, as did virtually everyone else.

In the cage was one of the Dwellers.

"I did not authorize bringing one of *them* in *here!*" the general protested, his voice softening as the cage door was opened, and the creature inside was led out.

Kindred recognized him as Srepth, the Dweller seen earlier at the laboratory.

Srepth was obviously in agony. He could hardly stand, for one thing, and he seemed to be cold, shivering periodically. The fact that he was also nearly blind only made him all the more pitiable.

"General Marquand, how close a look have you ever had at one of the Dwellers?" Kindred spoke without sarcasm, more with regret.

Marquand was silent, transfixed by the sight of Srepth.

"Matthew Kindred," Srepth spoke, "am I going to die soon? I would like to die as quickly as possible. The pain in this body of mine cannot be ignored any longer."

All eyes seemed to be drawn to the metallic plate on top of his head, electrodes protruding out of it.

Kindred walked over to Srepth.

"General Marquand, Srepth here has been subjected to atrocities at the very least comparable to what the Jews experienced at the hands of Hitler's so-called medical experts."

"But the Jews were human," General Marquand protested, though noticeably without the stern conviction he had evidenced minutes before.

"But the Nazis acted as though that wasn't the case at all—as far as they were concerned, Jews were just mindless carcasses to be poked and cut and needled and drugged and God knows what else, finally to be cooked in ovens and even, sometimes, to be skinned and used as lamp shade coverings."

"But the Germans were part of a kind of cultural madness at that time, they—"

"Whatever label you attach to it," Kindred interrupted, "the fact remains that they committed atrocities. And the facts today are no different *if there is but a touch of God's handiwork in the Dwellers.*"

Kindred paused as he came up closer to Srepth, putting his hand with utmost gentleness on the latter's shoulder. Even so, Srepth winced a bit in pain.

"But let's suppose that Srepth here is *only* an animal. Are we saying that animals, though also created by almighty God, can be treated with all the contempt of which humankind is capable? When dolphins are killed by the tens of thousands in fishermen's nets, do we turn away and say that they are *just* animals, and it doesn't matter? Then why do we spend $20 million to ensure that a condor is able to be born healthy in captivity—and rejoice when that or any species is pushed back one step from the brink of extinction?

"Significant expenditures of manpower and money are authorized without a second thought to help a vagrant whale return to its ocean home. We all are appalled, recoiling in horror at graphic pictures of helpless baby white seals clubbed to death in the Arctic so vain women can parade their wealth."

Kindred did a complete turn before the audience and the general.

"And yet, now, how can we ignore all such instances, yes, ignore that small, still voice of conscience within us and suddenly sanction cruelty in the name of science, just as long as it is merely the Dwellers involved? General Marquand, as you can see, implanted into Srepth's brain are thin wires that—"

A loud shriek from Srepth interrupted Kindred.

Audible gasps came even from the hardened journalists in the room.

Srepth was pulling the plate from the top of his skull. Blood immediately spurted out. Srepth turned and held up the piece of metal.

"This was hurting me, Matthew Kindred. I had to do something."

He found his way over to the table a foot or two away and put it carefully on top.

"Good-bye, Matthew Kindred."

The cry that escaped Srepth's lips was more a sound of beauty than of pain, a strange kind of lyrical poignancy embedded in it.

The door to the room opened, and several soldiers came in. But their weapons were not cocked and ready; in fact, these had been left behind. Some had their helmets in their hands, and tears were rolling down their cheeks.

Nor were they alone in this. Many in the room were openly weeping, General Marquand probably the only one able to maintain some semblance of control over his emotions.

And it was toward Marquand whom Srepth was now stumbling, falling, lifting himself up, then reaching out his arms.

The guard to the general's right stepped over and raised a rifle, aiming it at Srepth's temple. But Marquand waved the soldier back.

Srepth stopped in front of him.

"Help my kind," he said, barely above a whisper at first, then stronger, louder, distinct for the final few seconds of his life, exhausting whatever hidden reservoir of strength he had been able to tap amidst the unrelenting anguish that ripped through his pale, thin body.

"We are not human, you know. And we have known that for some time. When I die now, there is nothing left for me, nothing beyond the grave. We have had for all these centuries a taste of humanness but not its final transcendent reward. We never will. But, please, for my kind, those yet alive, preserve that fleeting life, that fragile thread of existence. Do this, and they will serve you unselfishly until the last one passes without a trace into eternity. Give them this life, this mortality, this world for as long as you can. It...it is all they have."

Looking very proud, a slight smile on his face, he turned to Kindred and then fell dead on the floor.

Seconds passed. No one could move.

Finally Kindred sank to his knees beside the pathetic little body and picked it up and hugged it to him, sobbing.

Suddenly there was a shout. One of the few non-reporters in the room, an Hispanic woman barely twenty years old, ran up the aisle and over to Kindred before anyone realized what was happening. She drew out a knife from her dress and stabbed the minister once in the chest as he turned, briefly, to face her

She spun around on her knees and held out the blade, now coated with blood.

"He is not a man of God. He is a messenger of the devil. His 'friends' killed my entire family. He must die, too."

She started to swing the knife again at Kindred, not heeding Marquand's order to stop, probably not hearing him as he directed the guard to shoot. The rifle blast threw her to one side, against the mahogany railing, which was knocked loose from the floor by the impact.

Kindred's consciousness fled before an encompassing wave of pain throughout his entire body.

TWENTY-TWO

INITIALLY, IT SEEMED, KINDRED WAS ONCE again close to death. As it turned out, his fight for survival against the poison of a rattlesnake had been more intense, because he wasn't given "professional" help at the time. Yet having a knife rip into his chest and miss his heart by less than a quarter of an inch was hardly a negligible occurrence. It was only the third time in his life that he had blacked out, a sensation conveying the illusion of death if not the actuality of it, accompanied just before oblivion by the sharpest pain he had ever known.

He awoke briefly as he was being hurried into surgery. One of the nurses at his side pointed straight up and smiled, and he thought he could hear her whisper, "The Lord's with you." Then consciousness fled again, or rather he slipped from reality into anesthesia-induced fantasy....

"Rev. Kindred, you're going to be fine. Please, sir, relax."

How can I relax? I'm dying.

"It was touch-and-go early on, but you're going to make it. You really are. You must believe that."

Believe it? Dear God, they want me to believe that I will live. How can that be? My pain tells me otherwise.

Another voice intruded. Stronger yet softer, stern yet uplifting.

"Matthew Kindred, you will go on. You will go on and do what you never dreamed you would do. And it will be to My honor and glory. Let the phantoms of death

and despair be exorcised by a multitude of ministering angels."

He smiled then, at first forcing himself to do so, and then freely, joyously, reaching upward.

He came out of the darkness as abruptly as he had slid into it. A nurse with a cross hanging from a chain around her neck held his hand, her gentle humming of an old hymn the most welcome melody of a lifetime.

The pain didn't end with the return of consciousness. Every movement brought fresh slices of it through his body. And there was a disconcerting paralysis in his left hand at first; it gradually faded, but it gave him a scare.

His bed was next to a window overlooking the parking lot of the hospital. Several mornings after he was admitted, he glanced out to see a group of several dozen black people, ministers and others marching, placards held high, one with language that equated the treatment of the Dwellers with that of blacks over the years. Another warned of dire consequences if Kindred didn't recover fully, since the news of his defense of the Dwellers had been spread everywhere. He had become a symbol of courage, a source of hope for those fighting bigotry on a variety of fronts.

Scores of letters were sent to the hospital—from individuals in animal rights groups, environmentalists and others not belonging to any organized group who wanted to express how proud he made them feel of their own Christianity.

One letter was the biggest surprise of the bunch:

Dear Rev. Kindred:
I am wondering if you could fit some time into your schedule for me. It is regarding matters of some importance and urgency that I am making this request.
Looking forward to hearing from you.
With every good wish for your recovery.

Sincerely,

General Clarkson Marquand

Kindred immediately reached for the telephone beside his bed and dialed the number listed on the letterhead. After going through a secretary and then an assistant, he finally got the general.

"I have your note, sir," Kindred said. "Anytime would be fine. May I suggest tomorrow afternoon at 2:30?"

107

"Fine," Marquand replied without hesitation. "I'll be there...and thank you, Rev. Kindred."

As Kindred replaced the receiver, he wondered what was on General Clarkson Marquand's mind.

Marquand came in and stood quietly at first at the foot of Kindred's bed, avoiding the minister's eyes, apparently reticent to start the conversation. His cap tilted slightly to one side, the hint of a day-old growth of beard on his face, he looked and acted like someone who had had little sleep.

It was obvious to Kindred that he would have to be the one to break the ice.

O Lord, help me with the right thoughts amidst my own awkwardness. Help me to get through this man's barrier, drawn up around himself, with barbed wire at the top and a field of land mines in front, put up there over many years.

"I am sorry that you had to have what amounts to a crash course introduction to the Dwellers," Kindred said. "I, for one, wasn't aware of what was going on. When I started my sojourn underground, the chaos up here hadn't started. What happened, sir? Can you tell me anything at all?"

Several seconds passed. Marquand was noticeably uncomfortable with the demands being placed on his regimented scheme of things; what was happening now just did not compute, and he was trying with enormous difficulty to cope.

"Those reports I referred to," he finally said, "were not so much fiction, you know. These beings or creatures or however you want to describe them did indeed *seem* to be responsible for murders everywhere around the globe, down to innocent children and the elderly."

"You emphasize the word *seem*," Kindred said. "Why is that?"

Marquand cleared his throat a bit nervously before he went on.

"After meeting, I believe its name was Srepth, is that correct?"

"Yes, Srepth."

"After meeting Srepth, I conducted an examination of the facts. I had my staff working around the clock, in fact. And I pulled every string I could in Washington to get through mountains of red tape. I even had an assistant of mine board the Concorde for a quick trip to Europe, where a number of the more serious encounters took place."

"What was the result?"

"Virtually all of the so-called 'murders' were either accidental deaths or were caused by limited acts of self-defense by your Dwellers when *they* were attacked. I also have more than one report that, even when threatened, many Dwellers seemed to prefer to die rather than cause any harm to anyone."

"But why wasn't this discovered before now?"

"Why doesn't a bureaucracy perform more smoothly than it does? You would scarcely believe all that slips through the cracks, the kind of incompetence fostered by our creaky civil service system."

"Frankly, I could believe anything you might tell me along those lines, sir. I know how difficult it was within my own denomination, mediocrity encrusting what should be vibrant and effective, the cause of Christ hampered by shopworn approaches to organization and communication. I can imagine how frustrating national government and the military bureaucracy can be at times."

"Not at *times*, Rev. Kindred, but rather *all* the time. I worry grievously about how it could all mesh together and function properly if there were a national crisis, not to mention World War III. I have this private fear that we would end up bombing New York City before we ever got to Moscow."

Marquand took out a handkerchief and wiped his lips.

"Rev. Kindred," he continued, "I am here with misgivings, but I am here. That little drama earlier could have brought some display of emotion from a chunk of granite, and whatever you might have thought of me previously, please be assured that I do have deep feelings underneath what some have called this stonelike exterior."

He stopped a moment, turning his head slightly upward, and Kindred detected what he thought was a hint of extra moistness in the general's eyes.

"Surely, sir, you cannot approve of what is going on in those labs," Kindred interjected. "What you saw with that one Dweller may be repeated in other governmental as well as private sector labs elsewhere. Think of it: mass torture in the name of science or whatever. Remember, sir, that these creatures may be more human, in a sense, than animal, though not totally one or the other."

Marquand spoke slowly then, with significant effort behind each word.

"I was in the Vietnam War, you know, in charge of a platoon. I didn't view the war from behind safe Pentagon doors. I went into battle along with my men. I killed the enemy and faced the reality of their attempts to kill me. I had more than one of my men splattered all over me. Rev. Kindred, you have not faced terror and revulsion and tragedy until you have had to wipe off your own body the guts and blood of a close comrade."

"No, sir, I have not," Kindred said. "But I *have* had my wife die in my arms after pulling her from the wreckage of our car which, seconds later, burst into flame. She went on to heaven saying that she loved me, and, in that instant, I would have gladly given up my own life in order to be by her side in that journey."

Marquand wiped his left eye almost absentmindedly.

"A motion picture sometime ago gave the impression," he continued, "that the bulk of the men fighting in Nam were ghetto blacks and low-life whites, the grunts, as the film called them, the vomit of society not suitable for anything else but regurgitation on the battlefields of Nam.

"That in itself is an affront perpetrated against the poor and the underprivileged by a filmmaker whose sensibilities were supposed to make him sympathetic toward the downtrodden, but instead compelled him to monstrous deceit disguised as realism.

"It is simply not true that those were the only soldiers there. We had college kids, fine athletes and intellectuals and others, pastors' kids and farm boys and many, many more. Whatever the right or the wrong of the war, they fought with dedication, with courage, with trust—hardly the swamp scum portrayed."

Marquand's emotions were coming in a surge, and he let this happen without trying to dam them up.

"What I saw with that...that Dweller, as you call it, brought back other memories so strong that it was hard to believe that I had kept them buried so well. Indeed, it was easier to suspect that they had somehow shriveled up, turned to dust and blown away by the passage of time."

Marquand turned away at that point, hunching his shoulders as he recounted an incident so stark that he could not immediately meet the eyes of another human being.

"You don't have to go through all this," Kindred added. "I can understand that you carry with you a pain that never seems to dissipate. God knows I—"

Marquand let the words flow again, interrupting Kindred but with no intention of impoliteness. He was one of two men in that room relieving emotional anguish that had haunted them for a long, long time, and it was next to impossible to dam the river once it had begun to rage.

"This village was suspected as being the center of Viet Cong operations in a strategic delta region. We had orders to burn it to the ground. If we met with any resistance, we were to have no mercy."

Marquand gulped once or twice, then continued.

"The villagers lived only in huts, each fashioned of straw and dried mud over wood frames. Raw sewage ran into ditches on either side of the dirt road cutting through the village. The air stank. It was possible to imagine that you were in the midst of some kind of cesspool. Added to this were the odors of sweat and blood and those from the contents of pots placed over primitive fires, as well as other smells, familiar or alien.

"Setting fire to the first hut was the hardest, but the rest came easier in a sense. Yet it was never easy to see a little baby crawling away from what had been its home, its body afire, the mother trying frantically to put out the flames before it was too late—but not succeeding, holding up the lifeless, blackened form of her infant as though asking each soldier, 'Why my baby? Why my baby? See what you have done? Why, why, why?'

"And then, when no one was looking, she took out a pistol she had been hiding and shot one of the Americans in the back of the head. Then the woman herself died in a wave of machine-gun fire. Other Viet Cong came out of hiding, shooting and stabbing and throwing grenades.

"You wonder about the morality of the war, yes, but then you do understand that in some respects war tramples the morality of both sides. While occasionally necessary for the defense of liberty, there should be no illusions about its grand and glorious nobility."

Marquand was shaking.

Kindred would have reached out and embraced the man if he had been able to get out of bed. But even that moment was in the Lord's hands, he realized, because Marquand would not have been ready for that kind of human warmth from a stranger. Later, perhaps, but not then.

Marquand steadied himself a bit as he continued:

"When I returned home from the war, I found my wife in the hospital. She was dying of leukemia. I had not been told earlier, because it would have affected my judgment at the front lines. Less than a month later, I was standing at her graveside, along with our two sons. Some suggested that I get married again or that I farm the boys out to professional attendants; but I refused the latter, because that would have been like losing two parents as far as they were concerned.

"My sons grew up. Both entered the military. The oldest one died in a skirmish involving the Dwellers some weeks ago."

All this time he had kept his hat on; now he took it off and put it carefully on a nearby table.

"I wanted them dead," he said. "I wanted every last creature wiped out. And if they could experience all the pain that could be inflicted upon them before they died, I was not going to do anything to prevent that either."

"General Marquand, I—"

"Please, let me go on. I have never told anyone any of this. It has been festering inside me all this time. It has made me more than a professional military man; it has turned me into something I loathe, something without pity, obsessed with revenge that twists my feelings and wrenches me awake from nightmares that spew forth from deep within my subconscious."

Eventually, the general sank down into a chair next to Kindred's bed, his emotional reservoir bled dry.

"Do you realize that all my adult life I have put my faith in nothing but the Pentagon? That many-sided building has been the idol before which I have bowed and worshipped and from which have issued the Sinai-like commandments that have influenced virtually every minute of every day for me during the past several decades."

He had been pacing the floor, first from one end to the other, then in a circle, the sound of his footsteps forming a kind of staccato rhythm, but not obtrusive somehow, rather like the amplified beating of a human heart, only crisper.

Finally, though, he approached Kindred's bed, hesitated for a second or two, and then sat down again on the chair beside it.

"Rev. Kindred, what I am about to say probably will come as a shock to you."

Kindred said nothing but waited, studying Marquand's face. It was now more animated, a frown on his forehead, eyes wide, filling rapidly with tears.

"What does it take to become a Christian?" Marquand asked quite simply, quite directly.

"Why is it that you want to become one, sir?"

"Because I saw something in that creature's face."

"What was that?"

"Fear."

"Fear?"

"It knew it was dying. It also knew that that was the end, with the harshest possible finality. And for an instant the thought of fading away into nothingness filled it with inexpressible fear."

He looked directly at Kindred, their gazes locking together.

"And that cut through to some deep pit within me, a pit over which I had constructed a trap door that I kept padlocked. It was a laser beam vaporizing that door and revealing the contents of that pit so starkly, so vividly, that I almost passed out from what it revealed."

"What did you see?"

"Myself."

He started to turn away from Kindred, but the minister reached out and grabbed his arm gently and stopped him from doing so.

"Isn't that what you have been doing for too long now? Turning away? Avoiding the truth?"

"If I could somehow do it, I would surrender every possession I own in order to give that strange little creature even one more year of life, but life this time without the pain it was suffering. I would extend to it at least the kindness I would give to any dog.''

He hesitated briefly and then continued: ''There is so much cruelty in this world of ours: the Germans and the Japanese in World War II; the Russians under Stalin, with tens of millions of people slaughtered, perhaps as many as a hundred million; the atrocities during the Vietnam War; and every day thousands of babies die through abortion; innocent lives are taken on the battlefields that our highways have become; children are raped or used in child porn; so much, Rev. Kindred, so much indeed.

''The pollution as well: poisoned air, water, food. People smoking themselves into the grave, and all they can say is that they'll die someday anyway, without any thought about the quality of those last few months or years. What has become of this world? Why does God allow it?''

''Have you ever had an aquarium, sir?''

''Yes, a big one. One hundred gallons.''

''And you gave the fish the best environment?''

''Of course. I fed them, made sure the water was just right, gave them sufficient oxygen, all that I could. And yet one morning....''

His eyes widened.

''One morning,'' Marquand continued, ''when I went over to the aquarium, which I kept in my study at home, I saw one fish brutally attacking another. In fact, the one fish had already torn apart the other and was in the process of eating it.''

''See my point, sir?''

''Yes. I gave them the best environment I could. What they made of it and how they treated each other was up to them.''

He saw Kindred's Bible on the table beside the bed.

''Show me what this salvation you preach is all about. Would you show me that, please?''

Over the next few minutes Kindred read to the general from the New Testament, taking him through John 3:16 and other verses. Totally out of character, but not caring for that short while about image or protocol or any of the baggage from his military career, Marquand got down on his knees and spoke softly, not to Kindred, but to God Himself.

A little later there was a knock at the door.

''Come in,'' Marquand said, standing quickly.

One of his assistants entered the room.

''Sorry to disturb you, sir, but you have a dinner engagement with Senator Bridges.''

Marquand straightened his uniform, putting on his hat.

"Newkirk, I want this man released as soon as he is well enough to leave."

"Drop all the charges, sir?"

"Every last one of them."

"Yes, sir!"

Marquand turned, winked at Kindred and then walked out, his bearing once again strictly military.

As the door was closing, Kindred heard the general add: "Newkirk, tell Bridges I want him to get to my place a little early, if he can. We're going to be talking to the president of the United States this evening."

Kindred HAD PLENTY OF TIME TO READ.
Apart from the Bible, he devoured newspapers and magazines, eager to find out whatever he could about current events pertaining to the Dwellers. He picked up a noteworthy thread among all the written material and television news: Uproar over the experiments was increasing. Demonstrations were being held all over the world, even in countries with no record on human rights, let alone animal rights.

Celebrities were becoming involved. The host of a popular television game show held a press conference during which he demanded that the Dwellers be accorded the same protection as any endangered species.

But it was a tough issue for many religious groups. After all, the Dwellers were undeniably a direct link with Satan. Some clergymen argued that the Dwellers could be a devilish fifth column, and were already rising against human beings.

Nevertheless, others reasoned, God had created the original creatures. And wasn't every birth a miracle in itself, the way God had endowed each species, human or otherwise, with the ability to perpetuate itself? Could the current generation of Dwellers be held accountable for events over which their long-ago ancestors had no control?

What prevailed was a public consensus that the experiments must be stopped.

And stopped they were.

Marquand called to tell Kindred in advance of announcing it to the media.

"The president will make everything official at three this afternoon," Marquand said, his tone strangely subdued.

"Clark, are you OK?" Kindred asked.

Marquand changed the subject.

"Apparently you'll be released soon. I'm very glad, Matthew."

"Clark, you *do* sound—"

"Forgive me, Matthew, but I have to make preparations for the presidential press conference. We'll talk later."

Promptly at three o'clock, the president of the United States announced that all Dweller experimentation had ended two hours earlier and would be permanently forbidden.

TWENTY-FOUR

PRIOR TO THE PRESIDENT'S PRESS CONFERENCE, it seemed that any atrocity could be committed against the Dwellers. Like most Jews during World War II, except those in Warsaw, who fought to the last living Jew, they were to offer notably little resistance, those instances of self-defense notwithstanding, resigned to the suffocatingly superior forces of their tormentors. The similarity was quite unnerving when it included the notion among Jews as well as Dwellers that they would never be anything but a doomed, melancholy race, destined for eventual oblivion; to fight back ran the risk of making matters worse than was the case already. Surely the witnessed inhumanity was a poisoned well that would soon run dry.

For the Jews, their racial delusion proved suicidal. For the Dwellers, perhaps it meant they were *not* the supremely intelligent animals they had appeared to be otherwise, their behavior akin to dumb cattle led to the slaughter. That was why those who did strike back seemed to stand out so blatantly.

Now, surely, with no more Dwellers put on laboratory tables and injected with germ cultures or cut apart so that their organs could be studied or the various other medical and scientific "procedures," any encounters with Dweller survivors would be peaceful. Therefore, it was reasoned, a new era between humankind and Dwellers could begin, however falteringly so.

But that was where everyone who speculated about the matter was proven quite wrong. During that summer of 1993....

At first the incidents were considered unrelated. Some fish washed up on the shores of Lake Michigan; garbage on the Atlantic City beach; fecal material at Malibu.

But then it kept happening elsewhere, not only in the United States but at Brighton, England; Cherbourg, France; Cairo, Egypt; Perth, Australia.

One of two incidents that brought everything to a head occurred midday at Cape May, New Jersey.

The air had a curious taint to it. The little girl wrinkled up her nose, hesitating to go into the water because that seemed to be where the stench was originating.

"Mommy, Mommy, it smells like a hospital here!" she exclaimed.

The mother had noticed the same thing and was about to call her daughter in to the shore. But suddenly the child started screaming in pain.

Her mother's instinctive thought was that a shark had attacked. But that was absurd because the child was in only a foot or so of water, very, very close to the shore.

She ran into the surf, grabbed the six year old and pulled her back. It was then that she noticed the hypodermic needle jammed into the left foot.

"Mommy, please, it hurts. Take it away. Please, take it away!"

There were other such incidents along that particular beach within an hour or so of one another. Children, young adults, the elderly all reported not only hypodermic needles but also vials of blood washed up on shore.

All contaminated. Some with the AIDS virus. And finally....

Two thousand miles away at a Houston hospital with a special infectious diseases clinic....

Gone!

"The whole lab full of them!" exclaimed the intern.

"But where?" the resident director asked. "Who and where?"

The phone rang.

"Yes," the director said, after he grabbed the receiver. "Are you sure?"

Finally he put the receiver back, the color gone from his face.

"Follow me," he said.

They went outside toward the rear of the hospital's property line. Standing there,

118

looking extremely nervous, was a female nurse, pointing a few feet ahead. Flung into a drainage ditch were test tubes, small bottles and round, flat containers that had held virulent disease cultures.

Intern and director looked at one another, their throats constricted with shock and an awful feeling of helplessness.

Houston and Cape May. Not garbage. Not ballpark-type refuse.

The most deadly diseases thus far discovered had been under intense study, especially the AIDS virus and its new offshoots, which were probably more contagious than the parent cells. They were broken out of safe storage and dumped into the ocean in the one instance and a drainage ditch in the other. In a matter of weeks it was proven that these were not isolated happenings.

More of the truth stood up and shouted its unwelcome presence when a wave of deformed babies swept the world.

TWENTY-FIVE

I<small>T MUST HAVE BEEN PAST MIDNIGHT. NORMALLY</small>
the hotel would not pass calls through after eleven. Many of the guests were elderly, having come to Nocales for the hot mineral springs a mile or so from the town proper. For that unwritten rule to be broken meant an emergency.

Kindred fumbled for the phone receiver, knocking it on the floor. Leaning over the edge of the bed, he managed to find it through thick layers of sleep that hung on stubbornly.

General Marquand.

After apologizing for the hour, he asked, "Matthew, can you meet with me?"

Marquand's voice betrayed his anxiety.

"If I can be of any help, certainly," Kindred replied, hiding the irritation he felt.

"A car will pick you up at eight tomorrow morning and take you to the airport, unless that creates a problem for you."

"No, that's fine."

"Thank you."

Kindred replaced the receiver on its cradle and fell back on the bed.

Two forty-five.

He tried to fall asleep again but failed, guessing why Marquand had called. All the reports on TV and in the newspapers gave clues, of course, carefully orchestrated so as not to cause panic. Despite the president's announcement, the Dwellers had presumably decided to go beyond occasional instances of self-defense and instead strike back in a more systematic manner, avoiding the mistake of an *en masse* strategy that would have been destined to fail.

Why?

The question nagged at Kindred. World opinion had clearly shifted in favor of them. After achieving what surely was essential, without unduly endangering themselves, why did they respond now as they did? It made not the slightest sense.

Animals....

They were, in fact, animals. What was rational behavior to humans might have been, in certain circumstances, beyond the grasp of the Dwellers. Some animals had a tendency to lash out when any circumstance seemed threatening, although in calm and familiar situations they were amazingly sensitive and loving. It was also quite possible that the Dwellers were unaware of the president's directive.

But tipping him off about what may have been behind Marquand's out-of-the-blue telephone call was the encounter he had had earlier that day.

He had decided to stay in the Nocales area after recovering from his wounds. It was relatively isolated, like a retreat in some respects, ideal for those wanting to enjoy the springs without large crowds to face. He needed time to get himself back together. After all, he had been through more than most humans would ever experience if they lived to be Methuselah's age. And all this had come on the heels of the exceedingly traumatic period that drove him to flight in the first place.

...that drove him to flight.

He had repeated those words to himself often, knowing that they were an admission of his weakness in dealing with Mary's death and David's crippling injuries. But perhaps even more devastating was the realization that they were a mirror showing his lack of spiritual depth and stability. Yes, he believed in Christ as Savior and Lord. But the question was how much personal trust in God he had had over the years, preaching about salvation, the inerrancy of Scripture and so much else with faith, trust and devotion only implicit in all of it.

At the core he knew he had been preaching from the cushioned cocoon of good health, flourishing pastorates and the growing public recognition of his abilities as a pastor, even on a national scale. When the bad times descended, like swooping hawks snatching away all that he had come to rely on, when he no longer had the accustomed crutches that had insinuated themselves into his life, everything truly went to pieces.

David....

As he went walking that afternoon, breathing in that now-familiar air, his mind went back to the moment when Miath, Klatu and he had emerged from underground and drunk in its exhilarating sweetness. And he remembered the tragic aftermath.

"Srepth!" Miath had exclaimed, his voice hardly audible before it faded altogether *and he tumbled into the abyss of centuries.*

That was the last he would ever hear from his friend or see of him.

What have they done with your body? he said to himself. *Have they thrown it on a pile of others and then poured acid over the heap? Or have they doused you all with gasoline and set everything afire?*

And Klatu....

Are you dead as well, your wound fatal? Have they buried you in some unmarked place?

He caught himself doing again something of which he had been embarrassed and ashamed earlier: thinking more about Miath and Klatu and other Dwellers than of his own son.

He had not tried to contact David since coming above ground.

What hypocrisy! I bemoan the fate of a misbegotten species of animal while ignoring the welfare of my own flesh and blood.

Kindred decided to return to the hotel and call the boy. It was then that he noticed the automobile at the side of the road. It had been there earlier but didn't make an impression the first time. The fact that it remained aroused his curiosity.

He saw that the right front door was open. And then he heard the sounds.

The cries of a baby.

He approached with caution. Lying across the front seat was a woman, blood covering her body, her face a mask of frozen pain. On the floor was possibly the smallest live baby he had ever seen—with no arms or legs!

Kindred wrapped the fragile little body in a blanket after he had determined that the woman was indeed dead. Her child was barely alive. He started to hum an old hymn to it, and the fear that had brought forth those cries quickly dissipated. The baby settled back quietly, trustingly in his arms.

The little body was so light that he had no difficulty carrying the baby back to Nocales. The town's doctor happened to be in his office and took the child from him.

After examining it briefly, he took it into a side room and then came back to talk to Kindred.

"Sweet little child," the doctor commented. "Another victim, I'm afraid."

"Victim?" Kindred asked, playing dumb.

"Of those...those so-called Dwellers."

"Can you be sure?"

"Not a hundred percent, naturally. But we see very few deformed children in these parts. We live a healthy life-style out here. This has happened only since they've gone on the rampage. Some of us call it a war."

"Are you serious, sir?"

"Yea, World War IIIa, one columnist quipped."

The doctor paused, then added, "You were near the springs."

Kindred nodded.

"Could that be the source? So many around here use it. I wonder if they poisoned—"

His eyes widened.

And so did Kindred's, the same thought occurring to them both.

The springs!

The doctor was on the phone immediately.

After staying a bit, Kindred went back to his hotel room, thankful that General Marquand had arranged for a governmental stipend, at least for a few more months.

No arms or legs.

And the point of origin may have been the hot mineral springs, possibly now poisoned beyond reclamation.

The sight of that truly helpless infant stayed with Kindred throughout the night in his dreams and when he was awake tossing in bed. He had repeated mental snapshots of the blood-spattered dress on the woman in the car with no one else around. And had reported it all to the local police.

Dweller sabotage had probably been responsible, some chemical or virus or whatever in the water the mother had consumed. Undoubtedly there might have been clues, signals that something was wrong. Other women might have taken the easy way out and had an abortion. But not this mother—and she had died because of it, sacrificing herself rather than her child.

Kindred thought to himself about how he would have liked to have known such a woman....

Deciding that he couldn't go back to sleep after all, what with the dreams and then Marquand's call, he got dressed and went outside.

Nocales was actually too small to be called a town—"village" was more like it. It seemed almost stereotypically Western, like a movie set.

What an unlikely spot for it all to begin, he told himself, the irony clear.

He walked the mile or so to the hot springs. The steam-shrouded waters seemed very much as always. Had the Dwellers managed to poison such a source of natural refreshment and benefit? Had that mother soaked in the water through the pores of her skin and doomed her baby as well as herself? How many elderly men and women would die in great pain now after coming to the springs in well-nigh a worshipful manner?

Where is it all going to end, Lord? What will this world become?

At precisely 8:00 A.M., the black sedan pulled up in front of the hotel. Kindred was waiting in the hotel lobby. As soon as he saw it, he walked outside. A quite tall and thin Secret Service agent held the back door open for him and then slammed it shut after he had climbed inside.

"Rev. Kindred, General Marquand wanted you to have this before the meeting," the man said, handing him a manila file folder with a thick pile of papers inside. "He was hoping you could somehow read through it during the ride to the airport and on the plane."

"Fine," Kindred said, taking the folder from him. "I'll start immediately."

"Thank you, sir."

Stamped on the front were the words: *TOP SECRET.*

What he saw was a mixture of reports and summaries. Much had been covered to a greater or lesser degree in the media. But a great deal more had not been, and the whole context certainly deserved the top secret designation.

The worldwide health problem as a result of the water and other contamination was considerably more serious than the public seemed to realize. And it wasn't just the current problems, either. The documents were terrifying:

The incidence of birth defect has risen higher in a month than anyone would have thought possible. Downs Syndrome, leukemia, elephant man syndrome—these are the tip of the iceberg. New forms altogether are starting to show up, especially as offshoots of the AIDS virus.

As devastating as all this is, the impact upon future generations holds the potential for causing massive social disruption, indeed, even widespread collapse.

Genes are being altered. This produces immediate results, as we have seen. But what of the next cycle of babies? And the one after that? And we must also consider the effects upon plant and animal life....

Kindred felt the muscles in his throat become hard, barely able to function, as he read the next few paragraphs:

Already we see the various harbingers. Two- or three-headed cats, once the rarest of biological accidents, now are much more common; dogs are being born with

124

the tendency not toward rabies (which is itself contracted) but toward the typical symptom of that disease: madness. Apparently the chemical composition of their brains is being altered before birth. Ultimately this produces whole litters which act as though they are rabid yet do not have the disease itself. As far as we know, this condition is not subject to a cure.

In short, what is being projected, and not out of any alarmists' tendencies but from an objective, pragmatic analysis of the facts, is a world only a few years hence that has become, to put it mildly, destabilized.

He swallowed as best he could, his whole body trembling.

And Satan shall run...

That snatch of a verse about the end times surfaced in his mind.

...seeking whom he may devour.

"Sir, we're at the airport. Can I help you with your bags?"

The Secret Service agent's voice interrupted his solemn introspection.

"No, I can—"

Kindred dropped the folder. The agent helped him gather the pieces together.

"I'm familiar, sir, with the contents. I don't blame you for being nervous."

In half an hour Kindred was on the plane, heading toward Washington, D.C. He had several more hours to spend going through the contents of the folder. Each page seemed to bring another revelation, another nightmarish detail as a piece in a puzzle so terrifying that he almost resolved a dozen times not to read any further.

Somehow we could get along if all we had to deal with was the animal population. For there the numbers would be great, but in comparison to the insect population....

The genetic impact upon insects! From the smallest fleas and ants to beetles, flies and....

Once again our speculation is based upon what we see happening already—reports of bees the size of small birds; spiders once capable of inflicting only mildly irritating bites, such as common strains of the tarantula, now with poison so strong that any human or animal attacked dies in a matter of seconds!

And we cannot ignore what might happen to plant and vegetable life, for example, poisonous pollen carried from flower to flower, creating roses whose odor is quite deadly; and then there are the sources of so much of what we eat: corn, wheat, apples, lettuce, grapes, much more.

By concentrating on our water supplies, the Dwellers have found the Achilles' heel that exists for even the most technologically advanced countries. For Third World countries the same results would occur but at a highly accelerated pace since maintenance of uncontaminated water supplies as well as adequate waste disposal is often questionable. In such countries very little would be needed to cause epidemics so devastating as to make the Black Plague look innocuous.

As he sank back into the seat, having to put down the folder yet again, his mind drifted back to that time with the Council of Many, to the revelations about Satan's plans for planet Earth, how he would never stop trying to turn what was left of Eden into a gigantic hell-hole. In the end Satan would join with the other fallen angels in the lake of fire as his final place of judgment and eternal punishment, but *until then....*

There had been chills up and down his spine before, but in that moment his whole body felt like a block of ice.

After arriving at Dulles International Airport, Kindred was escorted by another Secret Service agent to another black automobile and then on to the Pentagon. His pulse started to quicken as he entered the building.

A short while later he was in a conference room alone, waiting for Marquand to arrive. A screen had already been set up, as well as a film projector on the long conference table.

Marquand entered a couple of minutes later and shook Kindred's hand.

"Clark, I'm sure you called me to talk about the lingering Dweller problems," Kindred said. "But I can't believe it's all as bad as I've been told."

"Believe it It's worse.'

"But how *could* that be? The president ordered a permanent elimination of the laboratory use of their kind. And other governments followed suit. I can assure you that that would satisfy the Dwellers, for it was the only *real* problem they had with us, apart from the underground nuclear testing. They aren't so vengeful as the news reports would have everyone to believe. Hysteria sells better than calm reasoning and fact."

"Agreed. However, have you thought of *why* they were venturing above ground in such numbers and so visibly, as opposed to the stealthfulness that had characterized them for centuries?"

Marquand was correct; he had not considered that at all. The Council of Many had gained their knowledge from forays above ground, but only under the most cautious of circumstances, and never in any significant numbers. And as far as he knew, none of the other Dwellers had ever spent so much as ten seconds "upstairs."

"Matthew, there has been a great deal of discussion in recent years about nuclear wastes and..."

Kindred immediately anticipated the rest of it.

"...its being stored underground in increasing amounts, driving the Dwellers upward.

126

That's why I heard talk among them about whole settlements disappearing!"

"Bull's-eye."

"But they never understood why. It was an alarming mystery to them."

"They do now."

Marquand hesitated, then added, "There is more, Matthew. I must tell you that there were some in our government so entranced by the potential of using Dwellers as guinea pigs in everything ranging from simulated space flights to germ warfare tests that they decided to flush out greater numbers of them and add to the available pool."

Kindred tried to avoid the thought that surfaced then, the truth it conveyed so disturbing that his mind froze for a moment.

"Are you suggesting, Clark," Kindred managed to say, "are you really suggesting that the disposal of nuclear wastes was stepped up and deliberately shifted to areas of suspected Dweller habitation?"

"It is not a suggestion, my friend; it is damnable fact. The containers were, shall we say, less than accidentally put together with faulty seals."

"But the potential damage to people, Clark, to all of us!"

"Since when have the political types been known to possess any discernible degree of foresight?"

"But what is the political advantage?"

"It's a short-cut. It's a chance for certain senators with certain medical or scientific projects in their states to point to stunning successes much earlier than originally anticipated. They receive kickbacks as well as votes."

"And claim at least some of the credit?"

"Right on the nose, Matthew. And it was being done in strictly covert fashion. Recall the accusations during the late 1980s about a shadow government taking courses of action of which even the president was unaware?"

Kindred nodded, the memory all too vivid.

"The chaps responsible, right as we speak, make those other guys look like kindergarten amateurs."

He reached over to a button on the wall and turned off the lights, after which he switched on the projector, using its remote control unit himself.

"And this is the price we are paying for what they have done."

The first scene was in a small village in China.

"Even the communists are cooperating with this one," he added.

Dead. Everyone was dead.

"At first no one had any firm idea why they all died. It could have been from the water, they thought. You can rule out air pollution in such a rural environment.

But then there was the story given by an elderly woman shortly before she coughed her life away.''

"What did she say?'' Kindred asked.

"Listen for yourself.''

Marquand freeze-framed a shot of the "main street'' of the village, bodies everywhere, some piled on top of one another; then he took out a cassette tape recorder from a small, narrow drawer underneath where he was sitting and turned it on.

First the Chinese woman spoke and then an interpreter, the tape alternating between the two:

"They came up from beneath the earth, first a hand, then an arm, then another hand and arm, and they popped up everywhere. But they didn't come after us. They just took some old cans and opened these and spilled the contents onto the ground. And then they went back under the earth.

"Many of us started coughing, and we were throwing up, and I spit out blood again and again. And my friends were falling, screaming, blood everywhere. I grew faint, dizzy, and....''

Several seconds passed before Marquand stopped the recorder and took the projector off freeze-framing.

The scene changed.

A hospital in Calcutta, India. Patients were dead in virtually every ward, along with the doctors, nurses and interns. Lying in the corridors. Half in, half out of their beds. An operating room was filled with unspeakable carnage.

Kindred stood up.

"Please, stop the film!'' he said. "I've seen enough.''

"No, Matthew, you really haven't. I'm doing this to show you the scope and the bestiality of what the Dwellers are perpetrating.''

Kindred reluctantly sat down again.

Other scenes spun past his eyes, across a broad global swath.

"Obviously some of what you have been shown has filtered out to the news media. Something as devastating as this on a worldwide scale can hardly be kept a secret. Even so, we try to dam the tide, so to speak, whenever possible, hoping at least some of it will not be broadcast in banner headlines or trumpeted on the evening news. We haven't been very successful, but we comfort ourselves with the knowledge that the public doesn't know absolutely *everything*.''

He turned and looked directly at Kindred.

"Trying to avoid global panic is the worst part. When people feel threatened, feel trapped, they resort to the most animalistic behavior themselves. They act as much like animals as the Dwellers are doing. Can you imagine, if that final spark is ever lit, what kind of jungle we all would be plunged into, Matthew? If that ever happens, the Dwellers win, for we would then be totally at *their* level!"

Marquand calmed down enough to run off the rest of the film. Finally the "show" was over, and he turned on the lights.

"I do apologize, my friend. But I could not take any chance that perhaps you might have thought the danger was somehow being sensationalized by the media. This time they have tended to modestly *downplay* it, as much as possible."

Kindred could not speak at all, monstrous images crowding his mind.

Marquand allowed him some time to calm down.

"We need your help. Purely and simply, that's it."

"But how?" Kindred asked weakly. "What can I do?"

"Matthew, it is *extremely* awkward for me to have to tell you what I must, but, you see, your friend is behind all of this."

"My friend?"

"Yes—Klatu."

TWENTY-SIX

IT TOOK SOME TIME FOR WHAT MARQUAND said to be accepted by the rational portion of Kindred's brain.

Klatu alive!

He had assumed that Klatu had died from his wounds at the laboratory melee. Nothing more had been mentioned about his friend.

And Klatu was leading the Dwellers to strike back!

Marquand's voice broke into his thoughts.

"Are you all right, Matthew?"

Kindred looked up, still stunned, at Marquand, who had placed a hand on his shoulder, extreme concern on the man's face.

"Yes...," Kindred replied uncertainly. "I...I wonder how you can be so sure?"

"That, Matthew, is the next part of this show."

More film! More scenes—carnage around the world. But this time the camera spotted something different: a name written on a wall or a sidewalk, scrawled in blood.

Klatu...

Sometimes by itself. Often with other words added to it.

Our savior...Our messiah...Freeing us from the human yoke...Liberator... We worship you.

Tears streamed down Kindred's cheeks.

"Did you know that the Bible actually talks about more than one antichrist?" he asked.

"No, I hadn't realized that."

"Call them tinhorn antichrists until the real one appears."

"And it starts now with the Dwellers?"

130

Kindred couldn't talk just then, nodding instead as a reply.

Marquand had to sit down, his left cheek twitching noticeably.

"Am I to be a commander in the last battle of humankind?" he mused, his voice uncharacteristically shaky.

Neither of them spoke for several minutes, each lost in a maze of thoughts.

The end of the film, sputtering off sockets in the projector, brought both out of their thoughts.

"You want me to help?" Kindred observed.

"I know of no one more likely to be able to accomplish what must be done."

"You mean catch Klatu to stand trial for execution, don't you? And there is another possibility as well, one that would save a lot of trouble in the long run."

Marquand's gaze met Kindred's.

"It has to be faced, you know."

"You do mean the chance, more than a slight one, in fact, that *I* could become my friend's executioner. Isn't that the possibility everyone is hoping for? It saves the time, the money of a trial, which would be awkward at best since Klatu simply isn't human. How many times has an *animal* been put on trial? And yet Klatu is human *enough* that you run the risk of bringing up controversies brewed by those opposed to capital punishment, along with the animal rights groups. And what with the pollution foisted upon the Dwellers in *their* world, you're going to have the environmentalists, the conservationists, and who knows who else! *That* is a recipe for a stew that you would prefer not to have to eat."

"I would be less than honest, Matthew, if I denied any of that."

"But you can hardly ask a minister bound by Scripture and all that it dictates to kill in cold blood!"

"That is the point, Matthew. Would it be in cold blood? Or—"

"—self-defense?" Kindred finished the sentence for him. "We are told by God not to murder anyone. But the commandment given to Moses does not preclude defending oneself. If Klatu were to attack me, and I had to kill him, that would resolve everything quite neatly and conveniently, wouldn't it?"

Marquand's manner changed as he stood and started pacing.

"Matthew, I wonder how much of what you say now is influenced by feelings for Klatu that are obscuring just what he has become?"

He reached down into the drawer under the table and pulled out a folder filled with photographs.

"I was hoping I wouldn't have to show you this."

Kindred took it from him and started leafing through the shots.

"Time is short, Matthew, for two compelling reasons. You are looking at one of them."

Roads collapsed!

Shots in and around New York City, London, Paris, Rome, elsewhere. Vehicles smashed into one another. Bodies lying half in, half out of the wreckage.

"They are taking advantage of their existing tunnel system and digging others, causing the ground to collapse under the weight of constant traffic on major thoroughfares all over the world," Kindred surmised. "By poisoning the water, by contaminating the food supplies, by turning nature's order inside-out and by bringing transportation largely to a halt—cutting off possible escape routes—they cause civilization to become unhinged. We've lied to people, called most of these events just natural disasters, however terrible, however devastating."

"And that is when they attack *en masse*, Matthew. They may already have tested the feasibility of that eventuality."

Kindred had come to the last dozen or so photographs. He saw shots of Dwellers surrounding an isolated village in the Swiss Alps.

"Those were taken by an amateur photographer who managed to escape with his camera and film intact," Marquand pointed out.

The evidence was irrefutable. The Dwellers had changed, truly; the satanic part of their nature was now dominant. But how could he be sure that Klatu was their leader?

The final shot provided the answer.

Klatu was standing over a woman who had fallen out of a wheelchair and was lying beside it, looking frantically up at him as he raised a very large knife.

"He's their leader, Matthew, *and* a participant. Look at the expression on his face."

It was more than anger. More than even the taste of revenge initially so sweet. The face was contorted, the eyes wide.

There were other shots, and then Marquand showed additional scenes on video involving Klatu—usually in acts of violence.

"It's catch-as-catch-can, I'm afraid," Marquand pointed out. "Naturally none of us can *predict* when he will appear. I can tell you that videocams have become standard equipment at military and related installations all over the world."

Kindred felt a chill, deeper than any before in his lifetime.

KINDRED KNEW HE WOULD HAVE TO DECIDE overnight whether to aid in the capture of Klatu or remove himself from that task. He was torn. He asked for just a bit more time. That was when the general reached into a drawer set in the side of the conference table and pulled out what appeared to be a mangled pile of paper scraps, some waterlogged, others with burnt edges, some merely dirty.

"Take these with you," he said.

"What are they?"

"You'll have to decide that one for yourself."

Kindred had had no idea how long he would be required to stay and had brought along with him a change of clothes. Marquand put him up at one of the hotels frequented by members of the foreign service.

After checking in and getting dinner, he went back to his room, laid the bits and pieces of paper out carefully on the floor, and sat down Indian-style to study them.

I remember only a little...waking up on that table, with another beside me and on it a body they had cut apart, most of the insides removed.

That expression on his face!

Mouth frozen open, eyes wide.

They had strapped him down and operated without anesthesia!

Kindred couldn't make out the rest of that particular "page." Others were almost totally undecipherable.

...didn't die...so close...on the edges of...what matters anymore?

The next scrap of paper riveted his attention for one obvious reason.

...I miss...where...now?...need to know...need to...Matthew...I....

His hand trembled as he turned over another sheet, then others, trying to find ones that were more intact.

I don't want to do these things. When he was nearby, and I could talk to him, it was easier...but...now...Satan beckons with words of hate..find myself listening to what...wants me...to...hear.

Kindred put the sheets down and stood. He walked over to the closet and slipped on a heavy coat; then he left the room and got an elevator to the lobby.

Outside there was a stiff breeze, a cold one, but as he walked, he hardly noticed.

...a body they had cut apart, the insides removed.

Klatu must have been taken from the laboratory at the army base after they were separated and used in one of the experiments, before a halt had been called to those invidious undertakings.

To return to consciousness and see one of your fellow beings already dismembered! And to know that you were probably next!

Had they gotten to his brain? As with Tar—

Kindred fell to his knees in the middle of the sidewalk, and undoubtedly the passersby thought he was on drugs. But there was nothing he could do, no strength left in his legs, no thought in his mind except to stop and cry and pray that he didn't lose his sanity on that cold avenue in the nation's capital.

When he was nearby, and I could talk to him, it was easier.

"Dear God," he said out loud. "What is next, Lord?"

Eventually he managed to stand and walk for many more blocks until he became quite lost. As near as he could tell, he was in a section of the city where women openly made their living by selling themselves for the pleasure of others. One of them approached him, put her arm around him and asked if she could do anything for him that night. He brushed on past her and saw others, but none came up to him.

All seemed pathetic, with makeup so garish that a mannequin in a department store window appeared to be more human than they.

A derelict jumped out in front of him, pleading for some money. Kindred gave him a couple of dollars. Then he heard some commotion down an alleyway.

Two men were beating a Dweller to death.

Kindred ran up to them, hit one man in the jaw, and judging by the snapping sound, broke it as well. The man ran then, screaming in pain, followed by the other man.

Kindred bent down behind the Dweller.

The creature coughed up a mouthful of blood and fell back against Kindred's own body.

"They hate...us...so much," the Dweller said weakly.

134

"But you continue your attacks," he replied, though not harshly.

The Dweller looked at him, as though not hearing this.

"You!" he said, his voice momentarily quite strong.

"You know me?"

"We all know you, Matthew Kindred. You are the one who will help us. You will save us from this suicide."

"How can you say that? I am one man."

"You are Klatu's friend. You can take the dagger—"

More blood dribbled over the edge of his lower lip.

"None of us can do this. He has mesmerized all Dwellers. He—"

The eyes closed, the breathing barely visible.

"By fighting for our survival Klatu will guarantee our...destruction. We do not hate him. But his...yoke must be taken from...our shoulders."

And then he was dead.

Kindred put the broken body back on the ground and covered it with refuse.

He stood beside it for a moment, his head bowed.

"It has to end, Lord," he prayed. "There is just too much suffering. Show me what to do."

He somehow steered himself back to the hotel, made his way to his room and read more of the sheets of damaged paper.

I have not God nor man. I have only my own kind. We must go on until death claims the last one, no graves set aside for us nor tombstones in memorial. Perhaps we will revitalize the ground, fields of green springing up from our decay. Could it be that dandelions will be part of the legacy of our defeat? At least then God will send rain to satisfy the thirst of what has been given back out of our mortality. That is something...isn't it?

He phoned Marquand the next morning and recalled during their conversation how awful it once had been to put a dog to sleep that he loved very much.

TWENTY-EIGHT

"Years ago, Bangladesh became a symbol for the Third World," the helicopter pilot was saying. *"Then it was Ethiopia, especially because the government just wouldn't feed its own people, since many of them were deemed to be on the wrong political side. There are places in the world now that have more starving people; there are places where disease is in fact even more of a nightmare. Just a few years ago, in the prosperous 1980s, who would have thought that it would be Rhode Island one day?"*

The helicopter was flying over an area virtually sealed off, with food and medicine airlifted to it. Rhode Island was for all practical purposes surrounded by water so badly polluted that the stench seemed to reach up to them. With this calamity out in the open, nothing could be hidden from the American public any longer.

"It was really insidious," the pilot continued, *"I mean, how the Dwellers planned it all. The water was polluted in stages, with chemicals that were virtually undetectable in smaller quantities, which were gradually increased. By the time everyone was aware of what was going on, well, it was too late. So many people were poisoned, so many diseases were spread, that Rhode Island had to be quarantined for the good of the nation."*

What Kindred saw below seemed more like a scene from the Dark Ages of plague and despair. Men, women and children behaving like lepers, running furtively from place to place.

"Everything possible is being done to help," the pilot added. *"But their minds are gone, in most cases. And they are very easy prey."*

Even as they looked, those words became fulfilled prophecy. Several Dwellers....

At that point he awoke the next morning, sweat covering him. He felt more alone than he could have imagined possible. He was being asked to betray a friend, a friend not human, but one who had saved his life.

Do I try to take his life after he gave me my own? Kindred had asked of the darkness earlier that night.

Ultimately, he realized that the choice might have to be that of putting aside any question of loyalty and placing himself instead totally in the hands of God, coming before Him with the burden of decision and asking for the rest that Scripture promised.

And then there was David....

He thought often of his son, of course, thought of the cold metal of the wheelchair, thought of the accident that had crippled David, the funeral and the eventual running away, and all the rest. He thought especially of the guilt—the smothering, stultifying guilt that blocked any communication between them, feeding on itself, the absence generating more guilt and prolonging it.

By then David must have built up within himself a very tall and broad fence, a fence not of guilt but resentment, resentment that just at a point in his life when having a father was critical, he was missing both a father and a mother. He had grandparents to whom he could turn, and they were kind and loving, but it wasn't the same, not the same at all.

Kindred knew where to call his son, but David had no idea how to contact his father.

He reached for the telephone next to his bed but stopped in mid-air.

Please, Lord, help me!

He knew the number by heart and started dialing; then he looked at the clock beside the phone.

Nine-thirty.

For David it was two hours earlier.

He finished dialing and waited for the ring.

Once...twice...a third time.

Mary's mother answered.

"This is Matt," Kindred said.

"Yes," she replied, her voice devoid of warmth.

"Can I speak with my son?"

"After all this time, Matt?"

"God knows I regret it all."

"Matt?"

"Yes?"

"We've been praying that you would call."

"What?"

"We've been asking the Lord for this very moment."

137

Kindred's eyes filled with tears.

"Has he been healthy?"

"Yes—but very lonely. He needs you."

"But he must hate me now."

"Only if you were never to return, only if you abandoned him altogether."

"Has he left for school yet?"

"No, Matt, he's right here beside me."

David! So close. Ready to—

"Dad!"

The words wouldn't come at first. *Months later. An eternity of experiences. And now....*

"Are you there? Dad, please say something."

"David, please, please forgive me!"

"I forgave you the day you left. I told Grandmother that...."

Kindred just sat and listened to his son's voice, enjoying the sound of it, the reality of it, the joy of its familiar inflections. David often had asked to be taken to his mother's grave. He had prayed, begging God to send an angel to watch over his father.

"I didn't want anything to happen to you, Dad. I love you so very much."

That was a year ago.

"But if I had just been more careful, had paid more attention, had—"

"No, no," David interrupted, "it's not that way. It was Mom's time to go. God called her home. She's happy, Dad. She just wants us to be happy, too. She's walking with Jesus. Don't you look forward to doing that someday? *I* do! I want to see Him at last, as Mom does. I want to shake hands with the angels, too."

Kindred used to preach about angels. David would respond enthusiastically to what the Bible had to say regarding them. He read some good Christian books about angels. And he would doodle with some paint brushes, creating scenes on canvas that showed majestic beings with wings and faces so white, so pure.

"Dad, come home. I need to see you again."

That choice again—stark, compelling. To catch a plane and return to his son's side. Or to go on the mission that Marquand had laid out before him, descending into the tunneled world of the Dwellers, commencing a mission of execution.

"David," he said, "I have to go somewhere first."

"Dad! Dad! You've been away long enough. Please, please, come home."

"I will, but—"

Click.

David had hung up.

And in that sad little moment, the tears flowing more freely than ever, he realized that Klatu wasn't the only one he had been asked to betray.

THE PLAN WAS FOR KINDRED TO RE-ENTER THE Dwellers' tunnel system and try to regain their trust, assuming, in his case, that that trust had been squandered. There remained the possibility that he had escaped becoming an object of revenge and was still thought of as a friend rather than one of the enemy.

It was decided that the best place to start was where it all indeed had begun for Kindred, back near Nocales, New Mexico.

At a distance from the original cave entrance, Marquand expressed the beginnings of second thoughts.

"You will be completely at their mercy, you know," he said. "One man against a horde of them."

"But we all suspect that they are doing this only because of Klatu," Kindred replied. "He has become the rallying symbol. If he is changed, if he is—"

He was about to say "removed," but the word wouldn't come out.

"There isn't any other way, is there?" he said, picking up on Marquand's own mood.

"I have prayed that there was."

He stopped, seemed surprised at himself, then continued. "Prayer has had such an impact on my life these days, Matthew. Even when God doesn't give the answer *I* want, I know that there will be *His* answer regardless."

They talked for a few minutes longer, and then Kindred waved good-bye.

"Matthew, there's something else," Marquand said.

"Yes?"

Marquand hesitated, smiling wanly, then: "Never mind. It's not important just now."

"Are you sure?"

"It can wait for your return."

139

Kindred could not have conceived what would happen between that moment and the next time Marquand and he would again meet face-to-face.

The original settlement was in shambles. Dead Dweller bodies were everywhere. The odor from decomposition was almost overwhelming. Parane's artwork had been largely defaced. Kindred stood there, a host of memories flowing over him.

Parane spent most of his free time painting. Initially his canvases were the walls of his cavern. But he also was then allowed to paint the corridors and other places throughout the region occupied by this particular group of Dwellers.

Kindred was impressed by the gentleness of most of the images—scenes of Dweller family life: a number of portraits of little ones not more than a few years old; male and female Dwellers holding one another tenderly; elderly Dwellers. It was artwork of sensitivity.

How things had changed since then.

A group of octopi performing what seemed to be an underwater ballet, indeed dancing through the water with a natural grace comparable in its own way to any movements of the Bolshoi.

And whatever happened to Nessie?

Nessie turned slowly over on her back, causing Kindred to follow this movement until he ended up on her stomach. The creature's head, tiny in relation to her body but large by any other yardstick, poked up through the water, and she let out a low sound that was a combination of pig's grunt and cat's purr.

A few months ago or a hundred years? He had lost all sense of time. He wouldn't have been surprised to find that none of it had happened and that he would suddenly awaken in a psychiatric ward, confined there due to a severe breakdown, heightened by the pressure inflicted by the notion that Christians just didn't have breakdowns.

But, no, it all was real, and he was back, on a mission that he would probably relive in his mind a thousand times in successive years and regret as often.

He knew he had to get out of that settlement. It was dead. It had been destroyed after ten million years of existence. Evolutionists were correct in their measurement while being intrinsically incorrect in everything else: A hundred thousand centuries had passed since the Dwellers first went underground.

A figure darted across the tunnel to his right.

Then he heard the sound of sobbing. He entered the tunnel and followed it until he saw the familiar figure huddling to one side, the tears flowing in spasmodic little jerks.

...and then the awful creature that came ambling toward them; Kindred was ashamed of that word "awful," but found no other, however cruel it was, to describe what he saw, a Dweller distorted grotesquely.

Ardenis!

Kindred bent down beside him.

"I am hurting all over," Ardenis said, his voice trembling pitifully.

"Let me take you above ground. Let me get help."

"No! They will use me in a lab. They will poke and pry and tear at my awful flesh."

"They have stopped all of that—as a gesture of good faith. But it didn't work, Ardenis. Klatu caused—"

Ardenis started laughing, so hard that he weakened himself even more.

"How easily you...," he whispered.

He reached up to Kindred with that webbed hand of his and closed it around the minister's shirt.

"Klatu has only tried to...to save us. But in doing so, he unleashed that satanic part of our nature. It must have been part of the deceiver's master plan; how do you say, yes, our button was finally pushed. And we all fell into its entrapments."

"What are you trying to say?"

Kindred would never find out, for Ardenis fell back against the hard rock wall of the tunnel and lapsed into semi-consciousness.

Kindred sat there for a number of minutes, holding Ardenis's nearly limp hand in his own.

Abide with me, fast falls the evening tide....

Ardenis began singing those words from the hymn that Kindred had taught many of the Dwellers.

The darkness deepens....

Tears came to Kindred's eyes as Ardenis turned and looked up at him.

"There is darkness, Matthew Kindred," he said. "And it is much more than what exists here in this dank world of ours."

When other helpers fail, and comforts flee....

"Matthew?"

It was the first time any Dweller had called him simply by his first name.

"Yes, Ardenis?"

Hold Thou Thy cross before my closing eyes; shine through the gloom....

"Matthew, my friend, the darkness is a wave rising up before me. I want to see the cross of the Savior before it is too late."

Kindred could not speak.

Ardenis's expression changed. There was no fear this time but rather concern, not for himself but for his human friend.

"It matters not, Matthew. We were born from the dust. The dust reclaims us. It was not your doing. Please, Matthew...."

His eyes started to close. But as they did, Ardenis uttered in a faint whisper a few final words.

"Dear human friend, this animal loves you with mind and body though I cannot offer my soul as well. Please take my love as a pitiful gift this fleeting second before I head into the abyss...."

And he was gone, putting his frail grasshopper-like arms around Kindred's midriff and embracing him, as though hugging a rock before a giant wave wrenched him out to sea.

Kindred had to pry the arms apart and, in the process, broke off one of the spindly fingers. He nearly passed out from the shock, but he hadn't known how fragile Ardenis's hands had really been.

Kindred cried out, every nerve in his body shuddering. Finally, he looked for the cavern where Ardenis had created his carvings.

Many were quite deformed, the very young looking much like the thalidomide babies of Kindred's world, pathetic in their grotesqueness. Some were born without legs or arms, carried around by those willing to help or else just left in corners, looking forlornly out at the darkness around them. Siamese twins, joined at the temple, clumsily trying to get from one place to another. The retarded, sitting or standing to one side, drooling, aimlessly throwing their arms through the air or saying and doing nothing, frightened or confused by what was around them, ignorant of the truth. Those like lepers, with open sores on their bodies, fingers rotted away, toes gone.

Still there!

They were still there. All were alive, though just barely in a number of instances. And food! Food had been placed in the cavern in such quantity that they probably could go on for many more weeks.

On the one hand, the Dwellers were dealing disease, pain and death above ground. But there in their own world they were capable of the most profound compassion.

The Dwellers noticed him. Quite a number became genuinely excited, as those having any awareness at all of what was going on around them told others. Dozens of them came hobbling, crawling, even rolling toward him when they lacked arms and legs.

"Where is Ardenis?" asked a Dweller, whose head was attached directly to the upper part of his torso, no neck visible.

"Ardenis is dead," Kindred said forthrightly.

"Ardenis is dead...Ardenis is dead...Ardenis is dead...Ardenis is dead...."

The cry vibrated through the multitude, some shrieking the words, some moaning them, some uttering them in a kind of singsong.

"Please, Matthew Kindred, let us have him," said another Dweller.

"But he...he...."

"Yes, he will decay and stink if we do not do something. Where do you suppose we have put our dead through the centuries?"

The Dweller who spoke was perhaps the most normal-looking he had seen in that cavern. His only disability was that he had a single leg and that leg was in the middle of his lower torso. When he moved, he did so with a hop.

"Please bring Ardenis back, and I will show you where we will put him."

Kindred did what this Dweller wanted, and without any difficulty, since Ardenis had lost a great deal of weight and was not much of a burden to carry.

Kindred followed him, and virtually all of the Dwellers in the cavern fell in line behind the minister.

A number of minutes passed before they reached their destination.

Kindred smelled sulphurous odors that he had never before noticed. These became more and more intense as they came closer.

"Here, Matthew Kindred, is where our dead go."

He stood before a three-foot-wide hole in the ground with steam coming up through it.

"That leads deep within the bowels of the earth to the molten epicenter, we believe."

Kindred hesitated, not quite sure of what to do.

"Commend him back to the ashes from whence he came," the Dweller who had led him there said sorrowfully.

Kindred dropped Ardenis over the edge, and the thick whitish steam claimed him.

Kindred stepped aside as one by one the other Dwellers came to the hole and spoke briefly, or just stood and bowed their heads, and then returned to the main cavern.

Perhaps an hour later, Kindred sat and talked with the Dweller who had led him to that spot.

"What is your name?" he asked.

"Yucarek."

"What happened here? I saw so much that could only have come from violence."

"And violence is what caused it, Matthew Kindred. Many of us had no desire to follow Klatu. Sin is not fought successfully with more sin. We may be only animals in one sense, and when the Bible talks about sin it does so in the context of commission by your kind. But there is no other label, forgive me, for describing what Klatu and the others wanted to bring about.''

"And so?"

"Dweller turned against Dweller. Left behind are the bodies of those who refused to bow to Klatu's will.''

"What changed Klatu?"

"Knowledge.''

"Of what?"

"Lies.''

"What lies?"

Yucarek looked at him curiously.

"You really have no idea, do you?"

"I guess I don't.''

A flicker of irritation crossed Yucarek's face.

"And you shall not find it out from me.''

"But I need to know. To what lies are you referring?"

Yucarek's manner softened as quickly as it had hardened.

"You would then be a man with no world to claim as his own, no race to call his people.''

"I don't under—''

Yucarek gently put a finger on Kindred's lips.

"It is not knowledge you could face just now, Matthew Kindred.''

Kindred left them a short while later. He was given reports of where Klatu might have been heading, and he embarked on the next segment of a journey whose destination was a mystery not yet dispelled.

KINDRED MANAGED TO FIND, UNDAMAGED, one of the diving contraptions made out of plants. Using it, he was able to navigate the underwater tunnel network as before, but this time he was going alone.

And a wondrous journey it was. Periodically the tunnels would widen substantially, and the three of them would surface again and meet other colonies of Dwellers. Mile after mile, as portions of each tunnel linked in with other tunnels, Kindred had growing appreciation for what Miath had said about becoming lost. Furthermore, the minister could find no hitch in his "equipment." The plant mass functioned better than any scuba-diving gear he had ever used.

Klatu and Miath had swum it with him. Both had become accustomed to it over the years, but Kindred was aghast at the wonder of what they were doing. And now Miath was dead, and it would be better for everyone if Klatu....

He emerged into a somehow familiar chamber, exceptionally large, the ceiling quite high. The rocks were nearly pure white at that point, as though they had been polished. They emitted a kind of glow, although there was no light that could penetrate through both rock and the sea water itself as far beneath the surface as the chamber happened to be.

Nessie!

This was where he had frolicked with the fabled creature, the spot to which she returned periodically.

The prehistoric amphibious reptile was resting momentarily on the edge of an outcropping of rock. Nessie spotted them well-nigh as soon as they entered the cavern and roared so loudly that the walls vibrated to the sound.

He wanted desperately to see her again. That sounded strange, perhaps, but the

145

experience of meeting Nessie was a highlight of the travels on which Klatu, Miath and he had embarked. To relive it....

Nothing.

She was gone, as so much else was gone. He started to reattach the plant when suddenly he thought he heard a roar, not of triumph, but of despair and pain.

Directly in front of him the water started moving, and then abruptly Nessie's head appeared. She looked quite different from the last time. Her skin was pale, covered with sores, and one eye had been eaten away.

He shook his head.

The tragic vision had fled from his mind; he just prayed it wasn't prophetic. He supposed she would continue roaming the seas until the increasing pollution mired her in its noxious net, dooming the remaining representative of a species that had survived for millions of years.

He encountered other Dweller settlements, some deserted, others quite active, the latter receiving him gladly.

"Matthew Kindred," said Arnac, the leader of one of the settlements, "you seem surprised that we take you in without hostility."

He had to admit that was the case.

"We know that you are not like the rest of your kind. We know that you would do nothing to hurt us. Why wouldn't we welcome you with the greatest respect and affection? You are an important symbol to every Dweller."

"A symbol?"

"Yes."

"But of what? I am—"

"Human? That is true. You are what we wish we were. You are of the best that humankind has become, not those who hunt us down, who shoot us."

"But what are you doing in return, Arnac?"

"Fighting back."

"Only the Lord has the right to seek vengeance."

"So we are just to let them destroy us?"

"I didn't mean that."

"But then what is it that you are trying to say, Matthew Kindred?"

"Do you know just how bad it is up there?"

"We get reports."

"What do the reports say, Arnac?"

"That victory is coming closer."

"Victory on the backs of deformed babies? Is that the kind of victory you desire?" Arnac fell silent.

"I am told you all have a cavern in which you keep those suffering from the effects of underground nuclear testing. I want to see your own. Please take me there, Arnac."

Arnac, still not speaking, stood and motioned for Kindred to follow him.

They walked down a tunnel to a rather small cavern.

What Kindred saw was not what he expected.

There were, as before, the twisted bodies of radiation-doomed Dweller young. Since this community was not as large as the others, the number of deformed was noticeably smaller than at the original settlement.

But then there were additional members not ordinarily present: human babies being coddled by Dwellers, held and sung to and swayed back and forth, being fed with utmost care and concern!

"Dear God!" Kindred said, not profanely.

He walked among them, found a baby sitting by itself and picked it up gently. A girl.

The nose was nothing more than two openings in the face, with little or no bridge. The eyes were so close together that they nearly touched. The mouth had been formed at a forty-five-degree angle. As a result of all this, the baby couldn't see or breathe or eat properly.

Kindred felt a tug at his leg.

He looked down and saw a male Dweller child, probably less than seven years of age.

"Give me," he said simply.

Kindred hesitated and then handed the infant to him. With utmost tenderness, the child took the baby to one side and started to feed it some liquid nourishment through a hollowed-out reed.

Finally Kindred returned to the tunnel. Arnac was waiting for him. His original intention was to point to the misshapen Dwellers and use them, in a sense, as visual props to illustrate what was going on with human young. But obviously Arnac and the others knew all about it. At least that was his initial assumption.

"Now do you see yet another reason why this has to stop?" Kindred said. "How can the deformation of an entire generation of the innocent be justified as part of any plan for revenge?"

Arnac looked at him with a total lack of comprehension.

"Arnac, perhaps you didn't—"

"No, no, I understood perfectly, Matthew Kindred. But I fail to understand why human babies used in experiments have anything to do with our actions?"

...human babies used in experiments.

"Is that what you've been told?"

"No. It's obvious."

"In what way?"

"Our battle for survival, brave and noble, could hardly have caused what you are suggesting it has caused."

Kindred was stunned, but as the seconds passed, his amazement turned into something resembling a television picture of astounding clarity. He understood, vividly, what was happening.

There was a self-righteousness about the Dwellers, the manner of many who belonged to suffering groups of one sort or another, a kind of delusionary mantle which they wrapped about themselves and which often cloaked the most heinous acts. The Iranians were certainly guilty of it in the 1980s, looking on themselves as freed at last from the Shah's repressive yoke and valiantly battling the forces of Satan both in the Western world and within Islam itself.

It was also true in other countries: Angola, Nicaragua, Uganda after Idi Amin. In nearly all instances, the successors to despotism showed tendencies more brutal than those of their predecessors. It was not that their grounds for rebellion and overthrow were illegitimate, but that the means they used proved despicable, and once in power they seemed to multiply atrocities to an alarming degree.

And so Klatu was able to become a messianic symbol. Unlike the apostles and disciples of Jesus Christ, whose mission was truly divine, Klatu's followers became blinded to the bankrupt morality of how they were trying to accomplish what was certainly necessary: short-circuiting the possible extinction of their kind.

Our battle for survival, brave and noble, could hardly have caused what you are suggesting it has caused....

They could not admit the unspeakable tragedies that were being caused above ground under the guise of liberation from the spectre of annihilation. This would conflict with the righteousness of their cause. So they blocked it out, undoubtedly under the careful maneuvering of Klatu himself.

Another light went on in Kindred's mind!

If Klatu realized the truth and sought to divert the minds of his followers from it, how long before the images of masses of innocent babies and the others who were dying backfired into a torrent of acid rain-like guilt that would destroy him also? Kindred knew Klatu all too well, and he shuddered at what Klatu might be capable of doing when caught between revenge and remorse, each tearing him in diametrically opposite emotional directions.

"Matthew Kindred!"

Arnac's voice penetrated his momentary thoughts.

"You need to rest," Arnac said sympathetically. "Perhaps by Awake-time you will have decided to join our crusade."

The expression on Arnac's face didn't tell him whether the Dweller was jesting or quite serious.

In the middle of what passed for night in the world of the Dwellers, Kindred was awakened by a Dweller dwarf from the cavern he had visited earlier. This by-product of radiation-spawned genetic damage was rather normal in every regard except his size.

"Matthew Kindred! Matthew Kindred!" the little voice pleaded.

Kindred had been asleep in a little cubicle not far from the main cavern where the other Dwellers made their beds.

He jumped a bit when he saw the little one.

"I am Usuf. Please, I must talk with you."

Kindred came awake surprisingly fast, considering how exhausted he was.

"Of course," he replied. "I will listen."

"We cannot survive here. I know that. Not being involved in their crusade, I have been able to stand apart from it. I am strange in my physical being, but my mind is quite clear. I cannot say that I am smarter than my fellows, but I see the poor chance for success they have. It is not freedom for any of us if the fabric of civilization is pulled down around everyone, Dweller and human alike."

"The law of the jungle," said Kindred, "is a poor substitute for the rule of the civilized world, whatever the shortcomings of the latter."

"Well-put, Matthew Kindred. Here is what I suggest."

Kindred liked Usuf. He seemed rather similar to others the minister had met during the course of his various pastorates, people who compensated in mental prowess for what they lacked in the physical realm.

What Usuf had in mind was for those in the cavern to escape above ground.

"It will not be easy," he admitted, "and some may be lost along the way. But to attempt this is our only hope. We do not have the proper medicines or anything of that sort. We have coped for many, many centuries with the natural plagues of life in this world of ours, but what has been forced upon us in recent days is beyond the reach of our primitiveness."

Both Kindred and Usuf were sitting on the ground Indian-style at that point. Usuf looked up at the ceiling of the cubicle.

"That is our sky," he said, centuries of sadness in his voice. "Sometimes it is quite a bit higher, soaring above our heads; sometimes it is so low that we have to crawl on our bellies."

He shivered a bit, hugging himself tightly.

"You have preached about hell, have you not?"

"I have."

"Could the age-old descriptions of hell have been given to God's prophets by a Creator who had our world in mind as a hint of hell, something that was easy for humankind to grasp, a finite symbol for a place, a punishment that is infinite? Am I so far from the truth, Matthew Kindred?"

Kindred recalled that hole into which Ardenis had been thrown, with its whitish steam and sulphurous odors. And the darkness of their world, the seeming unchanging atmosphere and nature of it.

"It matters not," Usuf interrupted the minister's thoughts. "It is nevertheless a hell from which we must extricate ourselves, even as the real one entraps forever."

The plan was a simple one. Wait another Day period until the next Sleep-time, and then, while the other Dwellers were asleep, they would leave through a route that Usuf had had in mind for a long time.

"As soon as I heard that you had re-entered down here, I—"

"You heard?"

"You do know how word travels in our world?"

"Yes, but the quickness just took me by surprise."

Usuf got to his feet and said good-bye, waddling back to the cavern. Kindred leaned against the hard rock wall of the alcove, one thought sending tendrils of dread through his body.

Klatu must also have heard!

ARNAC WAS EAGER TO SHOW KINDRED SOME OF the plans being hatched by his kind.

"I am a divisional commander," he said. "Klatu has conferred on me quite a lot of responsibility."

How easily they trust me, Kindred thought silently. *It doesn't occur to them even for an instant that I am here to thwart their cause.*

"We have compromised the purity of their drinking water, as you know," Arnac continued. "We have tampered with their germ storage. And we are undermining the integrity of their roads, their bridges. Eventually we will move on to food supplies."

"And after that?" Kindred asked with much trepidation.

"Contamination of their fossil fuels."

The world's oil supplies!

His mind drifted back to the embargo of the 1970s, just two decades ago, and yet it seemed like ancient history, not something that would ever be repeated. No particular lessons had been learned, no consuming pursuit of alternate means of power initiated, no impact whatever made upon any basic philosophy of conservation, leaving civilization vulnerable once again.

"All of it is underground, of course," Arnac continued. "The oil fields represent a wonderful opportunity to bring their civilization to a crawl, if not a shuddering halt altogether."

"At most they would have just the supplies set aside for emergencies to keep them going, at least for awhile, and what may already be in refineries," Kindred observed.

"And nearly all of the emergency supplies are, need I say it, in *underground* reservoirs!"

"You have easy access to all these vulnerable resources, that is, underground supplies of water and fuel and the foundations of transportation thoroughfares. But the germs—all of those were kept—"

"In buildings placed deep within the earth's surface, because, it was reasoned, there existed less of a chance for *accidental* exposure. Once they went into the ground, they entered *our* domain."

"But what about the increasing attacks above ground?"

"Most weren't attacks, Matthew Kindred."

"But I've seen the reports through the media."

"How trustworthy have you *ever* considered the secular media to be, my minister friend?"

Arnac had a point, of course; whatever made a good story, that was the goal, with accuracy and objectivity often the casualties. He shuddered at how vicious the media were in attacking ministries in the late 1980s, eagerly exposing major as well as minor difficulties, like animals stalking their prey in the journalistic jungle.

"But if not attacks by Dwellers, what were those confrontations?"

"Slaughter by hysterical humans."

"*What?*"

"Some of my kind had suggested that peace gestures were in order, that we could negotiate a settlement. They got very little chance to make any offers; they were murdered, Matthew Kindred. As you can imagine, that didn't exactly fan the fires of pacifistic intent among my kind. You might say that it made us more determined than ever to conquer rather than compromise."

Kindred's mind raced. *Was that the revelation Marquand had started to tell me about? And was it the knowledge to which Yucarek had referred?*

"A Dweller named Yucarek told me that there was information I would find so hard to accept that I might be tempted to reject my own people," Kindred recalled out loud. "Is there more still that I do not know, Arnac?"

An inscrutable look crossed Arnac's face.

"It is possible that you may ultimately accept no one, my friend. All of us have deceit at the very core of our beings."

The biblical theology of that statement did not escape Kindred.

The remainder of Awake-time was spent listening to Arnac and other Dwellers telling not only of plans for stepped-up activity, but also of what they would do after winning control of the surface.

"We will administer more benevolently than any of the humans have shown themselves capable of doing," observed Warnuk, a rather large Dweller with a slightly self-conscious bravado about him. "We will ask probing questions of great depth and insight before we shoot them down."

There was laughter from Arnac and others gathered nearby in the settlement's main cavern. When they saw that Kindred failed to grasp any humor in what had been said, they acted a little embarrassed.

"Forgive us," Arnac said, shifting his feet. "You seem so much more like us than like other humans. Please forgive our lack of sensitivity."

"My question is, Do you give up on peace?" Kindred asked of them all. "Do you say because of the way the initial attempts turned out that you should abandon *any* hope for peace?"

"Hope is always present," Warnuk interjected. "We hope to win this war we have been waging. We can take the initiative now virtually whenever we want. As for peace, how often have human beings waged war in order to secure that very peace? You had peace when the British ruled the United States, but you chose war in order to throw off their yoke. You *could* have decided to remain British subjects.

"You fought two world wars to keep from falling under German, Italian and Japanese domination. At one point you became the only country in history to attack another with atomic weapons; the rationale? An act of war designed to hasten peace, but an act for which generation after generation has continued to pay the price in pain and suffering of one sort or another. You fought in Korea and Vietnam, all supposedly in defense of liberty. War is part and parcel of human decision-making, whether the fighting is confined to a single country or a dozen.

"In the Bible, war was repeatedly waged in Old Testament times. At Masada, Jews held out for as long as possible before taking their own lives rather than submit to the Romans. In fact, Jesus was rejected as the Messiah because His promise was that of a future liberation, not the present one for which they had been hoping."

"So you are determined to follow Barabbas rather than Christ?" Kindred asked at that point.

"The one fomenting revolution who was freed instead of Jesus?" Warnuk asked. "Yes."

"Have we any other choice?"

There was more discussion. Kindred had no doubt about the sincerity of the Dwellers around him. And that made them all the more frightening, in fact; those insincerely committed to a cause tend to drift away from it in time, but the zealots remain, pursuing that cause even to the point of their own deaths if necessary.

He studied the ones seated around him at that moment as they were cooking their food over a fire in their midst: burly Warnuk; smaller, thin Arnac; and the others, none as big as Warnuk but many as tough-looking. Others seemed so frail in appearance that it was impossible to conceive of them as warriors at all. All indeed were true guerrillas, avoiding confrontation with superior forces and instead clandestinely hitting their targets, then retreating to their underground havens, shapes in the night leaving disease and starvation in their wake.

How different the mood! Kindred observed to himself. *I sit here as an apparent friend among those who are actually enemies. How long ago was it that they had been peaceful, wanting to join with human beings and share the future, denying victory to the demonic within them, ready in time perhaps to exorcise themselves altogether?*

Finally, as the time grew late, they went separate ways. Kindred headed back to the cubicle where he had slept the night before, his mind filled with a kaleidoscope of thoughts.

Take away the water, the food, the medicine, the routes of transport and the fuel to run the motors of industrialized societies—and indeed civilization will be plunged into perhaps fatal turmoil, without a single shot being fired by the perpetrators. All the nuclear weapons, the tanks, the submarines, the computers and the vast hordes of soldiers with their rifles and grenades are like kiddie toys in comparison....

The realization struck him like a physical blow. Nuclear bombs could poison much of the world of the Dwellers, as had been the case already, and nuclear wastes could cause enormous damage. But then an all-out attack along those lines carried attendant risks: the possibility of generating earthquakes and tidal waves, the further poisoning of worldwide water supplies—not to mention other by-products with long-range implications so devastating that such action could only be deemed wholly untenable.

But there was one other factor the Dwellers had failed to take into consideration—and Kindred was brought face-to-face with it only a short while before he was to join Usuf and the others.

He had started to doze off when he heard the screams. He jumped somewhat groggily to his feet, and a Dweller he had never met before ran right into him.

"Sir, sir," the male said, "it is awful, just awful."

"What is?"

"My name is Bucran. I come from the next settlement east of here. I come to see Commander Arnac. To tell him about the water. The water has turned bad on us. My loved ones are dying. So are others."

Kindred helped Bucran to find Arnac. Warnuk and others joined him. The story Bucran told them was indeed horrendous.

"It all happened within the course of a few days. The sickness started, then premature births, the babies dead from the womb or dying. During one three-hour period, a quarter of those in the settlement were gone.

"Their pain," Bucran told them, "their pain was so awful. With some it was as though the blood backed up in their veins and came through their skin pores. They couldn't keep food in their stomachs. Their screams tore through the night."

Arnac was truly stunned.

The water has turned bad on us....

After hearing the rest of Bucran's tale, Arnac instructed that he be given food and drink and allowed to rest.

"But my family?"

"I know. I know. But you do them no good whatever if you collapse and become as sick as they are," Arnac soothingly told him.

After Bucran was gone, and Kindred and Arnac were alone, the minister confronted him.

"Arnac?"

"Yes, Matthew Kindred?"

"Don't you see what is happening? We all drink the same water. We breathe the same air. We probably catch the same diseases. You aren't safe just because you stay here!"

Arnac's reaction showed that while his kind were smart, they were not, however, capable of deductive reasoning to the same extent as human beings. They understood that the havoc they were creating could undermine human civilization, but they had failed to realize that theirs also could go down the tubes, and for the same reasons.

"When a cat wants to climb a tree," Kindred remarked, "it knows it can do so with great agility. What it does not realize is that it may not be able to get down unaided."

"What is your point, Matthew Kindred?"

Kindred curiously felt a degree of pity for Arnac. Nothing he had said was getting through. Arnac was thinking and acting according to the full extent of his intelligence, but there was that final leap, that missing link, between what was Dweller in origin and what was human. Almighty God had created humankind in *His* image, with various intellectual and other gifts and abilities; Satan had attempted to create the Dwellers in his own image, but Satan had only a fraction of the abilities of God. All that he could ever pass on to the Dwellers was as limited as he was.

The historical parallels were striking. Satan, unwilling to admit the reality of his ultimate defeat, would continue to fight against God until he was thrown into the lake of fire, along with those who followed him, human and demon alike, as the final judgment from God. The Dwellers apparently would go on as well, blind to the consequences of their actions: that they would die of the same poisons, diseases and starvation they sought to heap upon humankind. With the Dwellers outnumbered, they would become extinct while hundreds of millions of human beings would survive. It would be an initially nightmarish world, but a world that, given time, they could reconstruct, not quickly, not pleasantly, but a world rising phoenix-like from the ashes of what once was. The Dwellers would have disappeared, extinct at last, the vanquished rather than the victors as they had hoped.

Kindred verbalized all this as best he could, as simply as he knew how. Arnac seemed pale suddenly, far more so than usual for his kind. He had to sit down on a nearby rock, his hands shaking.

"I see...."

That was the extent of what he said at first.

Warnuk, walking nearby, came over to see what was wrong.

"You look awful," he said. "Are you becoming ill, Commander Arnac?"

Arnac looked up at the other Dweller.

"You have been crying!" Warnuk said in astonishment.

"I have, my friend, my brother," Arnac replied. "I have been shedding tears for the mad folly with which we have deluded ourselves."

Warnuk and Arnac had been close friends for a long time; they were of a similar disposition, ready to carry the battle to the very centers of human civilization, ready to wrest the control of planet Earth from humankind.

Seeing Arnac in such a state had a profound impact upon Warnuk. No longer the self-confident soldier, he sat down beside his friend.

"Please tell me...."

Arnac did precisely that, as best he could. He concluded:

"We are cats in a tree, Warnuk, so proud of ourselves, looking at the world around us with triumph because we have made the ascent. Yet, though we cannot remain in that tree forever and survive, we have nevertheless conspired to kill the very ones who can save us!"

Warnuk was silent initially, his big head with its golden mane bowed in shock as well as deep thought.

Finally he stood and paced as he spoke.

"For many months now I have relished the role of secret warrior, making my forays into the enemy camps under the cloak of night and dealing crippling blows to the underpinnings of their civilized way of life. I have dreamt during Sleep-time of going above ground during a day of final victory and walking proudly under the sun, with my head held high and human beings at my feet."

His voice broke for a moment, and he had to clear his throat.

"That will never happen. We have only the following choice: Live this life of hell beneath the surface of this planet called Earth, or lay down our arms and submit ourselves up there to the mercy of humanity."

"No! No!" a voice rose in opposition.

Bucran came forward, having overheard much of what was said.

"My family is dying back there!" he shouted. "That would never have been the case if human beings had treated us with other than contempt, if they had not forced us to such desperate actions."

Arnac, who had been silent, walked up to Bucran.

"My friend, it is not possible to base every breath we take on the 'ifs' of life. If you were to ask me, I would have to say that humankind is as weary of all this as we are, were we to hold to the truth instead of noble delusions that are like emotional quicksand, drawing us down into its suffocating embrace. For us of all beings there is, need I remind you, no comfort whatever in the grave. We have this life and this life only. So we must make of it the very best we can, for this is the goal worthy of our pursuit."

Bucran obviously wanted to object, wanted to drown out Arnac's righteous statement with some compelling words of his own. But he could not.

He bowed his head and fell into Arnac's arms, sobbing.

"I am so tired of not feeling the warmth of the sun, so tired of arthritis in my bones because of the dampness, so tired of eating insects and rodents, so tired of... being what I am, what all of us are."

Arnac hugged his fellow Dweller with utmost gentleness.

"We are of our father the devil, Lucifer, Satan, whatever we might call him," Arnac spoke softly. "But that does not mean that we have to be his *obedient* children. He gave us the life of bastards, but we don't have to live the life of criminals."

Bucran looked up at last, his cheeks wet, his eyes red.

"He has had too much victory already, hasn't he?"

Bucran turned around and faced the hundred or so of the Dwellers who had been gathering to one side, observing the little scene that had ensued.

157

"We stop all this now," he told them. "We turn this moment into a defeat for all that is unholy, that is unforgiving, that is vengeful within us. We cast out Satan and allow all that is divine within us to take over, to blossom into a measure of what the Lord wanted in the first place, creatures obedient to *Him* while yet alive, the eager, loving friends of humankind, comforting those in pain, bringing joy to the needy, guarding the helpless and going into the darkness at the end with gratitude for what was."

Arnac turned and pointed to one of the tunnels adjoining the cavern.

Usuf was standing there—holding an especially deformed human baby.

"He's dying," that barely audible voice said. "What can I do? Please tell me what I can do?"

Convincing one settlement of dwellers
to forego the battle was a victory, of course, but there were hundreds of such settlements underground all over the world.

"We need to be able to point to some gesture, some act on the other side," Arnac was saying, "that indicates a willingness to end all this. I will start the process, preparing them for something, but it cannot be merely words after all that has happened in the past."

"Let me go back above ground," Kindred replied. "I think I can get the right person to listen."

Arnac paused, then: "I will join you. Let us take Usuf and the others. If they see that both sides are indeed suffering, then they should do all that is necessary to bring peace."

Everyone pitched in to help. Makeshift stretchers were assembled out of pieces of wood and vines strong enough to hold the bodies that were to be carried.

But then the task was actually to get them to the surface. Reaching the areas of Dweller habitation from above was awkward, at best, but with crippled youth, Dwellers as well as human, it would take enormous patience and resourcefulness to get back up there.

In fact, it became obvious that perhaps the task might prove to be impossible, at least without injury or death. Many of the youngsters were simply too weak to stand up under a great deal of strain.

Kindred came up with an alternative.

"You and the others," he told Arnac and Warnuk, "are able to go above ground because you are in top shape for the climb."

159

"But it would be exhausting despite that," Warnuk admitted.

"Exactly. Carrying bodies at the same time, many of which—"

"What is your solution?" Arnac interrupted, a trifle impatiently.

"Getting help from others of my kind."

"Letting *them* down here?" Arnac spoke in disbelief.

He and Warnuk looked at one another. There was a time when the very idea would have been unthinkable. But that time had been swept away on a sea of violence and resultant suffering.

"Letting them down here?" Arnac repeated, as though saying the words again would make the implications more palatable.

"Isn't this the time for trust to start again?" Kindred asked simply.

"You are correct, Matthew Kindred," Arnac agreed, after pausing briefly. "I suggest you take one of the smaller young, a baby perhaps. We can rig up a sling in which he would fit, and yet your hands would be free. And I want one of my kind to go with you to help, if necessary."

"And I volunteer."

It was Warnuk who spoke, the consummate warrior, surprising Kindred.

Kindred hesitated.

"Is that not acceptable?" Arnac questioned.

"Oh, yes, yes, it is."

"But what is the difficulty that I see so transparently on your face?"

"We should take two of the young."

A light seemed to go on in Arnac's eyes.

"One human, one Dweller?"

"Indeed. To show that both sides are truly suffering."

"Agreed!" Warnuk said, and to symbolize how he felt, he took a long, knife-like stone weapon out of his waist harness and threw it to one side.

They shook hands, all of them, and prepared for what was to come.

First Kindred had to know their location.

"We are near Cincinnati, a few hundred feet away from a...a...," Arnac said with uncharacteristic hesitancy.

"A prison, Arnac?" Kindred asked.

"No."

"A zoo."

"Not at all."

"A toxic waste dump?"

"Nothing like that, Matthew Kindred."

"Then what are you trying to say?"

"A convent."

"A convent?"

"Yes. I know you are a minister and...and...."

Kindred started laughing, louder and harder than he had done in a very long time. Finally, when he was able to control himself, he looked up at Arnac, Warnuk and several other Dwellers standing near him, concerned. And he realized something, then, something quite poignant.

The Dwellers didn't know how to laugh!

They had no comprehension of why Kindred reacted as he did.

Even after trying to explain it to them, he could see that they just weren't fully aware except in a distant sort of way.

"My friend," Arnac said to him, putting a hand on his shoulder, "it may be that we have had no reason to laugh all these many centuries."

During the next Awake-time they were ready to go—Kindred with a human infant in a sling hanging from the back of his neck, and Warnuk likewise outfitted but with a Dweller infant instead.

Just before starting the climb, they were given a farewell by the gathered Dwellers. Each of the several hundred remaining carried a lit torch. Holding these straight above their heads, they swayed gently back and forth a number of times, singing a song that had a lilting quality to it, rather like an Hawaiian melody that Kindred had heard on Maui years before.

"It is a farewell, but we all hope not a permanent one," Arnac told them. "Perhaps, Matthew Kindred, when this is all over, and there is peace between our two worlds, you can teach us to laugh."

Ten minutes later the climb had begun.

Getting to the surface was a bit like climbing a mountain, but from the inside. And this time the babies added a burden in every sense of the word, particularly when a rock face offered only the smallest opening, barely enough for Kindred and Warnuk to navigate by pressing their backs against one side and pushing themselves up with their feet against the opposing wall. With a baby hanging down their backs, this would have been impossible.

So when they encountered that sort of problem, Kindred would climb up alone as far as possible. Then both babies were tied to a rope made out of dried vine and pulled up ever so gently, followed by Warnuk. They would rest for a short while and then climb a bit more, stop, transfer the babies and go on. It was slow and tedious, but it worked.

But it wasn't always so cramped. Occasionally they emerged into a subsidiary tunnel and cavern system with wide routes heading toward the surface. It was then that they would rest for at least a little while, each holding his young charge.

"It's so hypocritical, Warnuk," Kindred mused out loud.

"What is, Matthew Kindred?"

"Babies such as these in my world are frequently used as justification for abortion."

"I, too, have heard about that practice. I can say that it is unknown among the Dwellers."

"Why is that, Warnuk?"

"If any race has *reason* for aborting its young, we certainly have. The world they enter is not what any of us cherish. We tolerate it but we loathe it at the same time."

"Why don't you practice abortion?"

"How can we hope to escape the control of Satan if we give in to him in such an important matter as this one?"

The baby Warnuk was holding was quite possibly one of the most pitiful Kindred had ever seen. A male, this little Dweller's head had grown to twice its normal size at the upper skull area, but the lower part with his eyes, nose and mouth was considerably closer to normal size. There was no hair on the top; due to the extended nature of the bone structure, the veins were pressed very close to the outer skin. And that was true of the veins in much of the rest of his body, close to the surface and vividly apparent, making him almost a living textbook diagram.

And so pale!

The average albino was deeply tanned in comparison to this baby. His skin, quite apart from the visibility of the veins, had a totally transparent look, giving the impression that close examination would enable a view of various inner organs.

And those eyes: the pupils nearly white, much like those of a cataract sufferer. They would have to be careful if they emerged above ground in daylight hours, because after even a brief lifetime with minimal illumination, blindness from sudden exposure to sunlight was a distinct possibility.

The baby in Kindred's arms was male also, his head quite normal but all of his fingers on each hand formed as one, "melted" together and looking like a single thick finger. The toes were the same way. There was no way to tell whether or not his eyes were normal, because he had been born with no movable lids, just an unbroken patch of skin from below his eyebrows down to his cheek on each side of his face.

"They'll have to cut open the skin and somehow work with the motor reactions of his cheek muscles," Kindred speculated.

"And what of his insides?" Warnuk added. "How normal are they, I wonder? What is he missing? What organs are joined together abnormally?"

He shuddered from the thought.

"You have caused us anguish," Warnuk said, "and we have done likewise to you. And a thousand times ten thousand will suffer well into future generations because of our mutual transgressions against the innocent."

"Warnuk, that isn't even as many as are murdered each year in abortion clinics in the United States alone."

"How sad...," he said, his voice trailing off into silence.

Finally they approached the surface. "Fresh air," Kindred said. "Smell it?"

Warnuk inhaled deeply.

"We are close now."

"Very," Kindred agreed.

They were able to push through the surface dirt after carefully wrapping the babies with a gauze-like fiber from a particular underground plant, allowing them to breathe but preventing any dirt from getting into their mouths and noses.

The sky!

It was night.

"I've never been above ground, you know," Warnuk admitted wistfully. "I've trained those who have, but I myself have spent the many years of my life down below, with its stale air and its dampness and all the rest. And now this!"

Amazement and appreciation turned his voice into a whisper.

Ahead Kindred noticed a building.

"The convent?" Warnuk asked, noticing it as well.

"I think so."

The wall around it was a good twelve feet high. In the back where they were, Kindred could see only a single door breaking its stuccoed surface.

A minute or so later that door was opened, and a nun came out. At a time of drought she was following a municipal directive by watering a modest little garden at night.

Kindred and Warnuk approached a short while later.

She looked up at them, her eyes widening, and screamed, not so much from seeing Kindred with his dirt-covered face and torn clothes, though he probably gave the appearance of an escaped convict, but from the sight of Warnuk, tall, broad, alien-looking, and the malformed infants they were holding. She dropped the hose she had been using and ran back inside, slamming the door shut behind her.

Kindred and Warnuk sat down on the ground and waited. Less than fifteen minutes later, flashlight beams pierced the night's darkness. Followed by more screams, the babble of voices.

"We must be quite a shock to them," Kindred observed. "One thing's for sure—they're not going to shoot us."

"The brides of Jesus carry no shotguns."

Kindred looked at Warnuk, startled that this Dweller would know such a thing.

"This is not the first time nuns have spotted my kind, particularly those at isolated convents out among the mountains in various places."

"What did they do?"

"Scream."

"And after that?"

"As they are doing now."

Kindred turned his attention back to that small door. It was opened again. A head popped out, then back in again, then out. Finally the nun came gingerly outside, followed by several others.

They stood at a distance for a number of minutes. Then, single file, they approached Kindred and Warnuk.

"Hello, sisters, my name is Matthew Kindred," he said as he stood. "I am a Baptist minister. This is my friend Warnuk."

The Dweller stood as well.

All of the nuns took several steps back virtually in unison. One was scratching her chin as she eyed Warnuk. Then she walked up to Kindred and, in semi-conspiratorial fashion, asked him the most obvious of questions.

"*Who*—no, shall I say, *what*—is he?" she blurted out.

The other nuns scolded her for being so forward. Her cheeks reddened with embarrassment.

"Forgive me, please. I—"

Warnuk walked over to her. The expression on her face was one of utter fear.

"We need your help," he said and held out the baby in his arms.

The nun's face softened instantly.

"What is wrong with the poor child?" she asked.

"He was born as you see him," Warnuk told her. "There are many more as bad as he is or worse."

Her apprehension had turned completely to sympathy.

"But where? You must take us to them."

Warnuk pointed downward.

"Where?" the nun asked, her forehead in a deep frown.

"In my world."

Warnuk could have handled it differently, but he was being mischievous.

"There?" the nun said, looking at the ground beneath her feet.

Warnuk nodded, smiling.

"Oh...."

The apprehension was back on her face. And the other nuns had started to back away. It was then that Kindred intervened.

"Sisters, Warnuk is, well, having a little fun at your expense. He's not a demon from the netherworld. You see, he's a Dweller."

It was obvious that they had no idea what a Dweller was, so complete was their isolation, even from the chaos elsewhere in the world.

Kindred took a few minutes and gave them a primer course on current events.

"We have a chance to bring everyone together," he concluded. "And we need your help."

One of the nuns had approached Warnuk and gently took the baby he was holding.

The nun with whom they had been speaking accepted the other baby from Kindred.

"So innocent," she whispered.

She looked at Kindred and Warnuk and smiled.

"Please come inside," she said. "We lead a humble life here but we cannot turn you away after so hard a journey."

As Kindred and Warnuk fell in line behind the nuns, Kindred noticed that a single tear was tumbling down his friend's left cheek.

THIRTY-THREE

"COULD THE POPE HELP US WITH GOD?"
Warnuk asked the next morning at a modest breakfast in the convent's dining hall.

He offered that question loud enough so that most of the several dozen nuns present could hear him, though that was probably not his intent. Warnuk was simply used to speaking in what could only be called a robust fashion.

Mother Veronica, who had introduced herself the night before, looked up from a bowl of farina and tried to smile.

"And what would he be saying if indeed he were to do that?" she asked in reply.

As yet neither Mother Veronica nor the others were aware of the central predicament faced by all Dwellers.

"About salvation," Warnuk said.

"You are concerned about yours?" she inquired.

"Yes, very concerned. We are denied it."

"And why is that, pray tell?"

"Because we have no souls, none of us."

Mother Veronica choked even on the farina. Sister Martha, the nun first encountered by Kindred and Warnuk, patted her gently on the back.

Then Mother Veronica leaned over to Kindred, who was sitting to her left.

"What theology have you been telling this poor man?" she whispered.

"He only looks somewhat like a man, I'm afraid."

Her expression was one of utter disbelief. She turned away as though glad she was a Catholic and not a Baptist and thus not confused about such matters.

"Your name is Warnuk, am I correct?" Mother Veronica asked.

Warnuk, directly across the table from her, nodded.

166

"Warnuk, why in this world are you so convinced that you have no soul? All men and women have had souls breathed into them by God Himself. You are surely no different."

"But I am."

"But how?"

"I am not human, you see."

The hall became quieter than ever.

Mother Veronica glanced at Kindred and then back to Warnuk.

"God created you in His image, and since you are not an animal, you have to be human, Warnuk."

Her manner was that of a teacher trying to be patient with a slightly slow student.

"But, Mother Veronica," Warnuk said, "I am an animal—and God did not create me."

As a unit, all of the nuns stood, saying nothing, their astonishment expressed by this single action. Each one turned toward Mother Veronica, who was still sitting but who had tipped over her farina at those last words from Warnuk.

"Rev. Kindred, would you step into my office, please? And...and Warnuk?"

They followed her at the same brisk pace she was walking. Her office was some distance away from the dining hall.

Once inside, she slammed the door behind her, obviously outraged.

"What exactly is going on?" she asked, her eyes wide with emotion. "And, please, no more games!"

After the three of them were sitting down, Kindred repeated as much of the story of the Dwellers as he could piece together, with Warnuk filling in most of the gaps.

Mother Veronica interrupted impatiently.

"They are, in part, why Satan fell from grace?"

"Coupled with everything else that he intended."

"But they obviously have great intelligence, if Warnuk is any indication."

"The most intelligent..."

He looked at Warnuk, who simply nodded.

"...animals ever born."

"For millions of years right under the surface of the earth?"

Kindred nodded.

Mother Veronica proved amazingly astute in the various questions and insights she offered. Kindred developed considerable respect for her.

After nearly an hour, she leaned forward on her desk, a thoughtful expression on her face, and asked, "Let me pose to you a question that you may not have considered. Is what Warnuk represents right now a triumph for God or Satan?"

167

Kindred hesitated only a bit.

"For God indeed."

"Let me add this: When someone accepts Christ as Savior and Lord, is that not also a divine triumph rather than a satanic one?"

"That is true, Mother Veronica."

"Do you ever give in to the devil in your daily life?"

"More than I would like to admit to you or the Lord."

"And does God reject you as a result?"

"Not at all," Kindred replied. "His love for us is eternal."

Mother Veronica smiled in appreciation.

"I quite agree," she said. "I quite agree."

Her own manner showed her growing respect for this Protestant clergyman.

"Can murderers go to heaven?" she continued. "Rapists? Ruthless dictators?"

"They can as His redeemed ones, if they seek the Lord's forgiveness."

"If there is mercy for the most despicable criminals when they fall before Him and confess their sins and accept Christ into their lives, can you imagine our blessed Lord turning His back on these helpless ones who had nothing to do with how and by whom they were created?"

She cleared her throat, then added: "So then what we have here is only the *assumption* that the Dwellers are denied heaven."

"But the Bible seems to say—"

"Rev. Kindred, in the Old Testament the Bible *seems* to say that we also end up as dust, just like the animals, as you surely know from Solomon's heart-wrenching lament."

"But that is a verse taken out of context, of course, which is easy to ascertain when viewed against the rest of Scripture."

"*That* is my point. Now, I ask you, my brother in Christ, couldn't the same be said for those very few verses that *seem* to suggest that animals do not have eternal life? Can we surmise that one set is out of context and the other not so? Most critical of all, do we in our foolish and ignorant presuppositions ensure that our doubts become a self-fulfilling prophecy for the Dwellers by discouraging them any longer from seeking Christ?"

Abruptly Mother Veronica fell against the high-back chair in which she was seated, closing her eyes, muttering a prayer under her breath.

A minute or so later, when she opened her eyes, Kindred and Warnuk could see extra moistness in them.

"I used to be a missionary in Africa," she told them, her voice quite mellow. "At first I didn't want to go. I wanted to minister to the civilized world, not brute savages. Somehow the latter seemed very much beneath me. Of course, later when I learned that the pope had specifically requested that I be sent, I had no alternative."

She glanced at Warnuk.

"God would have none of my human frailties, my protestations based purely upon inflated self-esteem. I heard Him reminding me, within the depths of my soul, not to think of myself more highly than I ought. That there was no difference between myself and the Africans in God's sight. They needed a Savior just as I did."

Mother Veronica smiled a bit.

"You know what they called me in later days?"

They both shook their heads.

"The Mother Teresa of Africa. I ate with the natives. I cleansed their wounds. I wiped up their vomit. I held them as they died. And prior to being transferred here, I actually thought of refusing to leave Africa. I couldn't understand why the Lord would take me from that mission field. But now I know why."

She looked at both Kindred and Warnuk.

"I cannot bestow a soul. No mortal has that power. I personally do not even accept the doctrine that my church holds regarding excommunication. So I cannot put Warnuk into heaven nor can I deny him heaven. Only almighty God has that responsibility; only He can make that decision—not any group of mere mortals."

She paused for only a second or two.

"But I can help to make *this* life less horrendous. What I am saying is that I am at your disposal, as your obedient servant."

The first request Kindred made of Mother Veronica was to use the convent's only telephone, which was on the desk in her office. She handed it over to him without hesitation. Marquand had provided a special number that went directly to his office at the Pentagon.

Less than half a minute passed before Marquand answered.

"This is Kindred. I haven't located Klatu as yet but—"

He heard Mother Veronica say something, and he excused himself.

"Klatu?" she asked.

"Yes."

"Is this how you spell that name?"

She handed him a Polaroid snapshot of a wall. On it were scrawled five letters: *KLATU.*

He nodded excitedly.

"Sir," he said back into the receiver, "we may have stumbled onto something right here."

He explained where they were and what Mother Veronica had shown him.

"I will have a contingent of men there by noon, if not sooner," Marquand remarked. "And I should be able to join them not long thereafter."

"Thank you, sir. I pray that we are nearing the end."

"That is my prayer also, Matthew."

Kindred replaced the receiver.

"I must prepare the nuns," Mother Veronica said. "We aren't accustomed to this sort of excitement."

"The name Klatu—where did you find it?"

"In the basement. On the wall next to an old tunnel."

"A tunnel?"

"Yes. We have no idea where it leads. My fellow sisters and I aren't a very adventurous lot, I suppose. We never bothered to explore it."

"Did you ever try to discover the significance of 'Klatu'?"

"May I borrow an expression from the Baptists?"

"Surely."

"I suspect it was a case of just waiting on the Lord, Rev. Kindred. What He wanted us to know, He would reveal in His own good time."

Waiting outside the office was Sister Martha. Mother Veronica asked her to take Kindred and Warnuk to the basement to show them the tunnel. In the meantime, she would call the other nuns together in the dining hall to let them know what was going on.

On the way to the basement, Kindred gave Sister Martha a capsulized version of the circumstances.

"In just a short while, the Lord has led you through more adventures than a dozen people in a dozen lifetimes," she said, appreciating what Kindred had told her.

"And some of it can never be repeated," he said, thinking of Klatu and so many, many others.

The tunnel....

There, on the wall to the right, was Klatu's name, scrawled on the concrete blocks with something like a crayon.

"How long ago?" he asked.

"You mean the name?"

"You've known about the tunnel for a long time. How recent is the name?"

"Just a week ago, Rev. Kindred."

Just a week ago!

That might mean that Klatu had been gone for a week, and the search for him would be as arduous as ever.

"Mother Veronica forgot to mention these," Sister Martha said.

She took a leather pouch out of her habit.

The pills!

He looked inside—only a few left. *Could this mean that Klatu was ill? Could it be that he—*

"What are they, Rev. Kindred?"

"The most remarkable pills known to humankind."

"They heal, don't they?"

"How would you know that?"

"I was told that I had cancer," she said. "But no longer."

He wanted to ask her why in the world she would take anything of such an unknown origin.

She sensed his thoughts.

"When you have great pain, and you pray to God for healing, and He directs you to such a strange little bag, you realize that He may have placed the answer right before you."

"If the pills could be duplicated and distributed effectively, that would end virtually all disease, I am convinced, from cancer and AIDS on down to the common cold."

"We can help. Mother Veronica's father is a renowned doctor. He works at one of our leading Catholic hospitals."

"But why would he leave them here?" Kindred mused out loud.

"I do not know him as you apparently do, but let me suggest that, if someone who is ill leaves behind the very thing that could cure him, he may not want to live any longer."

"But we don't know that Klatu has become sick."

"We do not know that he hasn't."

"May I keep these for a bit?" Kindred asked.

"You may," she said, an angelic smile on her face.

Warnuk and he looked more closely at the outer part of the tunnel.

"What was this complex originally?" Kindred inquired.

"A Civil War army outpost," Sister Martha told him.

"And this must have been an escape route."

"That is what we suspect."

Kindred turned to Warnuk.

"I can almost guarantee we will find that Klatu happened upon it accidentally as he followed the natural underground tunnel system."

"Rev. Kindred?" Sister Martha said. "I've just recalled something."

"Yes?"

"About a week ago, the other sisters and I had the impression that we were somehow being watched. Normally that is not anything special when you try to live as close to God as you can, without all manner of worldly distractions; after all, God is there watching you constantly. But this...this was different somehow."

Her mouth dropped open.

"What is it, Sister Martha?" Kindred asked, concerned.

"We had a group of terminally ill sisters from other orders here. They didn't stay more than a few days. It was a special fellowship arranged by the archbishop of our diocese."

Kindred's hand went to the pouch of pills in his pocket.

"And that was why Klatu left these behind!"

"To help," she added. "And we had no idea about any of it."

Tears started to form in Sister Martha's eyes.

"I discovered the pills in time to help myself but not the others. They had already left."

Kindred reached out and cupped his hands around her cheeks.

"There are only a few left. You would have been in the position of choosing which ones would live and which to leave condemned to death."

He smiled sympathetically.

"And, dear sister in Christ, once the pills were gone, there would have been nothing left to study. Now, when the pills are mass-produced, millions will be helped."

"You are so kind," she said. "So many ministers look on us almost as Satan's deceived ones. They preach sermons against our church."

They were about to hug one another when suddenly the lights went out, plunging the basement into darkness.

ABOVE THEM THEY COULD HEAR CONFUSION.
"Everything must be off," Sister Martha told them, "the lights, the kitchen equipment, everything."

"I'll head on up first," Kindred said. "Here, take my—"

Warnuk's shout interrupted him.

"In the tunnel!"

Kindred looked and saw movement inside, a shape partially outlined by flames, presumably from a hand-held torch.

And then it was gone.

"Go up with Sister Martha," Warnuk declared. "I'll investigate."

Kindred did just that but reluctantly. He would have preferred going with the Dweller on the hope that they had perhaps spotted Klatu lurking inside the old tunnel.

As soon as they reached the first floor, one of the nuns saw them and ran over to them.

"Outside," she said, barely able to speak. "We are surrounded by...by...."

She took them outside where they saw Mother Veronica running toward the convent's entrance in the wall that surrounded it.

"Mother Veronica!" Kindred shouted. "What is it?"

"See for yourself," she shouted back, though not unkindly.

He reached the entrance almost as soon as she did. Several nuns stepped aside and let them look through the tiny windows in the double doors.

Dwellers.

Scores of them.

"All seem very much like your friend Warnuk," Mother Veronica remarked.

"We need help," said a nervous nun standing nearby. "I must call the authorities."

"The phone is out also," Mother Veronica told her. "The lights, the appliances, all dead. We have absolutely no power."

The nun was becoming hysterical.

"They're demons. They came up from hell itself. Satan created them. They...they...."

Sister Martha tried to reason with her but finally had to shake her fellow sister, and not gently.

The nun fell silent, with no apparent anger, only an expression of embarrassment on her face.

Kindred saw that the Dwellers were slowly growing in number, new ones coming up from holes in the ground, emerging more than likely from the tunnel system that Warnuk and he had used to get to the convent the night before.

And something else!

Females started to join the males, each carrying an infant, many of these deformed as were the babies Warnuk and he had brought along with them.

"Holy Mother of God!" Mother Veronica exclaimed prayerfully, looking at Kindred out of the corner of her eye as she did. "They aren't here to hurt us, are they?"

"I doubt it," Kindred answered. "They want help."

"And we shall give it to them," she said firmly. "We shall surely do that."

She opened the double doors wide and walked outside, looking regal and even angelic at the same time.

That Mother Veronica was in her element was apparent as the Dwellers gathered around her. Gone was any impression of estrangement. If their origin, if their very condition as not-quite-human creatures mattered to her, she succeeded in hiding any such concerns. They needed care and love, which she was dedicated to giving to them.

Kindred could never accept some precepts of Catholic theology, but unlike many Protestants he had known over the years, he wasn't going to be the least bit surprised when one day he entered heaven and found untold numbers of Catholics there, with perhaps a few self-satisfied Protestants missing.

Mother Veronica clearly showed the love of Christ as she moved among the Dwellers, smiling, talking, hugging. Just before taking them into the convent itself, she bowed before them, raising her hands to the heavens and asking God to take away their pain and their sorrow and to give them health and joy. The Dwellers followed her through the double doors a bit like children marching to the tune cf a beneficent Pied Piper.

The other nuns took a bit longer to get used to the unusual group of more than a hundred pale creatures with thick, bulging foreheads and considerable body hair in the case of the males, their clothes made of leather and sinewy plants.

In a short while, the grounds of the convent were filled with voices, Dwellers beguiling wide-eyed nuns with stories from the past million years or so.

"They swim through an underwater series of tunnels all over the world," Sister Martha said excitedly, as Kindred walked by, "using only plants that turn water into oxygen."

"Yes, yes, they've even been feeding the Loch Ness monster, really they have!" exclaimed another nun.

Mother Veronica was especially captivated—as were dozens of nuns gathered with her—by what one Dweller was telling them about their own Council of Many.

"You talked to someone who has been a link in a chain of inherited memories that include being at the birth of our holy Lord," she repeated, "and on through to His death, burial and resurrection?"

The Dweller male named Tarue nodded, obviously pleased that Mother Veronica and the others were so interested.

"Yes," he told them. "One of our ancestors saw the stone at His tomb being rolled aside by an angel and then passed that sight on to another, and many more, through the centuries to follow."

He reached out and took Mother Veronica's hand in his own, then dropped it suddenly, tears coming to his eyes.

"You are very much like an image in a dream I have from time to time."

"What sort of dream, Tarue?" she asked.

"I dream that, after a long night's sleep, I awaken in heaven, allowed to go there after all, and the first face I see is so kind, so caring, so sweet and beautiful that I rejoice at the Lord's mercy. That dream, I know, will never be reality, but having seen your countenance, I also realize that part of it at least has come true for me."

Mother Veronica, seated in front of Tarue as were most of the nuns in that group, reached forward and hugged him. Suddenly he pulled away, shivering, rubbing himself as though to get back a little warmth.

"What is it?" Mother Veronica asked him.

"I feel so strange."

More than a minute passed, and then Tarue looked at her with the most sublimely tender expression Kindred had ever seen.

"I felt a wave of sorrow, and then it was swept away on wings of joy."

"Please tell me, Tarue," she implored. "Do not hold anything back."

"I saw an angel standing by your side, Mother Veronica. The angel seemed to be saying that you would soon be walking a street of pure gold—at your side a multitude of those whose lives you had touched on planet Earth; ahead the Savior, His words so simple, so wonderful: 'Welcome, good and faithful servant....' "

Mother Veronica stood and excused herself.

"I wanted to please her," Tarue said, watching her go. "I didn't mean to make her sad."

"I don't know what it is," Kindred answered. "I'll go to her now. Will you join me?"

They approached Mother Veronica's office. The door was ajar. She was kneeling with a Bible in her hands, looking up at a stained-glass window which depicted the ascension of Christ, multicolored light shining onto her face.

Tarue walked over to her and put his hand on her shoulder.

She turned and smiled at him.

"I'm not sad," she said. "You have made me very happy, Tarue."

"I have?"

"Oh, yes. I *have* been thinking about death lately. I have been wondering why someone as unworthy as myself would ever be so greatly blessed as to stand in Christ's presence one day."

"You unworthy? I feel your goodness in my very being."

Mother Veronica stood with some difficulty.

"I hadn't told the others, you know. You relieved me of that responsibility in such a beautiful way."

"You are—"

"Yes, I am dying. And you have eased the journey, Tarue, more than you'll ever know."

"But the pills," Kindred said, "you took none?"

"Sister Martha is impulsive. But I am not! Some things cannot be cured so simply, I'm afraid!"

She wiped her eyes, straightened her habit and walked toward the door.

"We should rejoin them now, don't you think?"

They went back with her to the courtyard where everyone was gathered. Its normal atmosphere was a rather stately calm, ivy growing up the stuccoed walls, little sound except for an occasional bird, the air carrying scents from the flowers grown and tended to by the nuns.

And now with so many gathered inside its confines!

Humans and Dwellers together, young and old, with no hint of animosity or uneasiness.

Mother Veronica started to speak, but her words were drowned out by the sounds of military helicopters.

WㅤITHIN LESS THAN HALF AN HOUR, THE HELI-
copters had been joined by an array of tanks, jeeps and trucks carrying dozens of
uniformed soldiers. Anticipating more than token resistance, the men entered the
courtard of the convent. They saw thirty-eight nuns, a minister in his late thirties
and seventy-nine Dweller adults together with fifteen deformed human and Dweller
babies.

"What the—?" a sergeant said, his mouth dropping open.

Before anyone could answer, Marquand entered and, without breaking stride, walked
up to Kindred and shook his hand.

"Amazing!" he exclaimed, looking around. "Tell me, though, Matthew, why did
we need a mini-army to come in here? It looks as though you have everything quite
well in hand."

Mother Veronica approached Marquand.

"May I suggest, General, that a battle-ready stance may be inappropriate for your
men at this time?" she said more in good humor than consternation.

Marquand turned and saw dozens of soldiers with rifles poised and ready and the
turrets of two tanks aimed at the middle portion of the convent wall.

He shouted a command to them, and they relaxed.

It didn't take long for the soldiers to mix with nuns and Dwellers alike. What
started out as a potential confrontation became an event no one could have predicted.

The nuns prepared a tasty meal for everyone, creating a picnic-like atmosphere
with humans and Dwellers laughing together.

"Delicious!" General Marquand exclaimed. "All of it prepared and cooked here,
I suppose."

"Yes, everything from the cream of asparagus soup to the Saint Huebert fish stew," Mother Veronica said.

"And the dessert, the very best I have tasted in a long time," Marquand added.

"Yes, that's Saint Placid's pumpkin chiffon pie."

Even Marquand had managed to relax, taking off his helmet well before the meal, and the soldiers, catching this signal, did likewise.

"I am quite full," he remarked contentedly.

"But the meal is not over," Mother Veronica said.

"What?" Marquand replied. "We've just finished dessert."

"But there is a special custom of ours. It involves an after-meal course as a treat for visitors."

Just then several nuns brought in loaves of bread baked in the convent's kitchen and juices made by the nuns from the fruits of an orchard on convent property directly beyond the wall.

After enjoying this additional food, Marquand stretched a bit, sighed contentedly and turned toward Tarue.

"What caused your fellow Dwellers to come here in peace?" Marquand asked.

"We got a message from the last settlement that Matthew Kindred visited."

"Already?" Kindred questioned.

"We have ways," Tarue said wisely. "If we can pass along the memories of a million years, surely doing so with the words of a few days ago is not an impossible task."

"The memories of a million years?" Marquand asked uncomprehendingly.

"Ah, yes," Tarue continued, "forgive me. You see, we have a group called the Council of Many...."

And Tarue proceeded to tell Marquand about this wondrous aspect of Dweller life underground. Marquand was nearly speechless.

"I...I...," he stuttered, then, embarrassed about losing his composure, he gathered himself and said, "What a wonderful academic tool for students of all ages."

"Indeed, General," Tarue agreed.

"And these, sir," Kindred said, showing him the pills.

"The ones you once mentioned to me?"

"Yes. There are only a few left, though."

"I hope that we can uncover the exact formula. It would go a long way toward curing so many of the diseases afflicting us over the years."

Marquand hesitated, then added, "The possibilities regarding Alzheimer's disease, for example. My mother and my father both had it."

He cut himself off, unaccustomed to skittering on the edges of an emotional display in front of so many strangers.

After an hour or so, it was time for the Dwellers and their offspring to be taken to treatment centers where they could be cared for properly and questioned, and some plan worked out for their future circumstances. Marquand had ordered two buses in for transportation—one reason for the wait—as well as several ambulances to take the crippled young.

Outside the convent wall, the nuns saw the soldiers and the Dwellers off, waving to them, real expressions of love on their habit-shrouded faces.

"Tarue," Mother Veronica said, "would you wait just a moment? There is something in my office that I forgot to give you earlier."

Tarue smiled and said that he would be happy to wait.

She went back past the double doors.

"General Marquand," Kindred started to say, "what do you think about—"

Mother Veronica's scream tore through the air.

Everyone turned in that direction. Kindred, Tarue and Marquand, a pistol in hand, hurried inside the courtyard.

Mother Veronica was standing there, the front part of her habit pierced by a long wooden spear with a stone tip, the white portion red with blood. She looked at them and collapsed.

Directly ahead of them, standing in front of a door leading to the convent's basement, was Warnuk!

"Warnuk!" Kindred shouted in shocked disbelief. "Why? In God's name, why?"

Warnuk's body tottered and fell as Klatu shoved it to one side.

"He was only a shield, you fool!" Klatu shouted, as he turned to run back inside.

Marquand took aim and managed to hit Klatu in the shoulder with the first shot; the second missed altogether.

Marquand turned and started to shout to his men, but Kindred stopped him.

"I'll do it," he said. "Wasn't that my mission?"

"Take this," Marquand insisted, handing him the pistol.

"I'm not—"

"Self-defense, Matthew. If you have to use it, that will be self-defense."

Kindred nodded with a sigh of reluctance.

He went over to Mother Veronica. Tarue was already there.

"She wants someone to read her the last rites," Tarue said frantically, "but there is no priest here. Can a nun do that, Matthew Kindred?"

Kindred didn't know, but Marquand motioned to one of the nuns now gathered inside the double doors.

179

Mother Veronica smiled weakly at him, their eyes meeting, as she whispered, "Whatever happens, my Baptist brother in Christ, it'll be all right. With our Savior by our side, who can prevail against us?"

Kindred then approached Warnuk's body. The eyes were closed, the limbs still, but he wasn't quite dead, his lips moving though nearly imperceptibly.

Kindred bent down beside him.

"Warnuk, my dear friend, I—"

A profound shivering motion radiated through Warnuk's large body, the skin assuming, momentarily, a very slight bluish tinge.

"The abyss, Matthew Kindred, the abyss...."

And then he was gone.

THIRTY-SIX

THE MANMADE TUNNEL HAD BEEN DUG UNDER a dozen feet of earth, the ceiling and sides timber-reinforced. There was a smell of age as he entered, damp wood precarious in its strength after more than a century.

Rats scurried across his path. Worms dangled from the dirt ceiling. Kindred noticed an old rusty shovel to one side. He almost tripped on the barrel of a musket that looked more like a relic from the War of Independence than from the Civil War.

The darkness was so complete that the flashlight didn't reach very far. He slipped a couple of times on the wet ground. After the first fall he simply got to his feet and went on. But the second was different: he fell and kept on falling.

Another tunnel, this one probably made by nature, and leading straight down!

He screamed at the swiftness of the descent. Mud splashed across his face. He felt something slimy fall onto his neck, only to be shaken off as he continued falling.

Is this what it's like on the way to hell? The thought flashed across his mind, a chill gripping him.

On and on he fell, the contents of his stomach coming up into his mouth. There was nothing that he could detect to grab onto, nothing to brake himself.

Until he hit a hard stone floor.

Every bone protested, along with his muscles and all his nerves.

He blacked out.

Consciousness returned in bits and pieces, a bit of light here, some sensation there, an oil-like odor penetrating his nostrils. Finally he opened his eyes and examined his surroundings through a gradually dissipating haze inside his brain.

The huge cavern had a wide ledge that extended completely around its circumference. The latter was filled with faint shapes barely perceived in the encompassing darkness; most were motionless, perhaps dead, while others were in unspeakable pain, moaning, their bodies moving weakly.

"Dear God!" Matthew Kindred spoke audibly, though with trembling voice, not just in his mind and spirit. The words, not capable of containment, forced their way very nearly of their own volition across his tongue into the air around, a score of witnesses unheeding, wrapped as they were in their embalming torment.

Kindred fell to his knees, throwing his head back, salty tears issuing up over his eyelids and down his cheeks, and some dribbling into his mouth.

They cried unto the Lord in their trouble, and He saved them out of their distresses. He brought them out of darkness and the shadow of death, and brake their bands asunder....

The Lord also will be a refuge for the oppressed...and they that know Thy name will put their trust in Thee: for Thou, Lord, hast not forsaken them that seek Thee....

He looked up, recalling from memory words so familiar that they once had lost their impact, and yet now, there in his mind and spirit, a vibrant gift from God exactly when needed.

Yea, though I walk through the valley of the shadow of death, I shall not fear the evil around me....

As that last word was spoken, the walls seemed to shake with a certain fury, savage, hellish.

"How do you know, Matthew Kindred, that it isn't too late for spiritual profundity of that sort?" the familiar voice boomed against rock and stone, the words echoing as ghostly, fading images of themselves, carrying a hint of physical pain no doubt from the bullet wound. "Perhaps that time is long past; perhaps that path will never be trod again by me or any of my kind."

Klatu!

Kindred spun around.

Klatu was standing a few feet away, holding a long spear in his left hand and a burning torch in the right, a changed Klatu, his hair matted, smears of blood and dirt on his face. He stooped a bit, not tall and straight as he had been only months earlier. There was nothing proud or majestic about this Klatu, his eyes rimmed with the redness of nights without sleep, filled with the regurgitated visions of what the awful, awful days had brought him.

"You look amazed, Matthew Kindred," Klatu said, though not harshly, a strange softness underlining his words.

" 'Amazed' hardly describes what I feel now. Revulsion is much closer. What madness—"

"Madness is the word, you know. What unbearable burdens does it take to drive a species to the brink of insanity and then over the edge *en masse*, lemmings heading for their own destruction?

"The answer is simple: It takes suffocating wave after wave of outrage and frustration, day after day of seeing their kind slaughtered and at first not fighting back, at first sitting there before those serving as executioners—no, murderers—enduring the carnage like *obedient, trusting dogs!* Surely these humans knew what was right, what was wrong—surely my people, the victims, had done something so awful that the punishment of death was the only recourse they deserved."

Klatu was nearly choking on the words.

"Madness starts not quite then, Matthew Kindred, not even during the period when trust, however misplaced, however naive, continues to rule the minds and hearts of the lowly, an innocent time when they can still accept virtually anything at the hands of those—"

He dropped the spear, probably without noticing that he had done so, the words coming in an unstoppable surge.

"Madness does rear up and take over and forces out anything else at that awful moment when trust withers away at the gradual realization that they had done nothing to deserve what had befallen them. They did not ask to be born of Satan, fathered by demonic conceit. They did not ask for the torment of two natures, one a quasi-humanity, the other somehow animal though not fully so— nor the agony of knowing about redemption, *comprehending* it, yes, even quivering with eagerness for it, and yet being told that it was never to be theirs.

"But once that madness, born of all this, takes hold, it consumes like an emotional malignancy, forcing aside all normal, all good, all kind and decent thoughts and motivations. Finally *nothing* less than total malevolence rules in waves of hatred as the thousands of my kind are cut down like so many stalks of wheat. Yet that is not the correct analogy, because they are neither human nor animal, and so they are the chaff instead of the wheat, but cut down just the same."

"But all this, Klatu, all this *torment* that you have inflicted upon innocent bodies?" Kindred asked, waving his left hand at the dimly seen figures.

Klatu's expression changed to one of disbelief.

"You think they are your kind, Matthew Kindred? You think we kidnapped human beings and brought them here to get some satisfaction out of their pain?"

"It does seem that—"

Suddenly Klatu started walking just below the ledge, lighting small torches placed around it.

He turned around and faced Kindred.

"Go, clergyman. Look at one of the bodies. See for yourself why you are so very, very wrong!"

As Klatu stepped aside, Kindred approached the ledge cautiously, looking more closely at the bodies.

"Klatu! Klatu!" he exclaimed, not wanting to comprehend what was surely the greatest madness of all.

"Yes, Matthew Kindred, yes...."

Kindred had difficulty believing what he was seeing.

Dozens of bodies, not human as he originally assumed, but Dwellers' bodies...no! no!...the Council of Many!

Some were not as yet dead, but delirious, rambling on aloud about those memories they had been raised to perpetuate as the sole purpose of their existence, memories passed on from generation to generation so that there were living links with the past.

"The dinosaurs...dying...their bodies shaking the earth as they fall, their mightiness so abruptly...vanquished."

"The flood...sweeping all before it...except the ark...people banging on its doors...begging to be let in."

"Christ...the Son of the living God...divinity incarnate...His blood flowing out as a Roman spear pierces His side...Mary is weeping for her beloved Son...."

"Surely the plague will soon end...fields of the dead...the stench...more dying...."

"Bodies floating in the midst of rice paddies...."

On and on it went, the voices filled with pain, pain that grew, inexorably consuming memories so carefully collected and preserved over the centuries, yet so ethereal, transitory, like the images flickering through a movie projector until the film runs its course, leaving only the white, blinding light flickering, flickering, flickering.

"But why *this*, Klatu?" Kindred shouted, incredulous.

"You think any of *us* are responsible? You think I have become so debased that I would inflict such wounds on my own kind? What you see here is what is left after *your* people get through with them."

Kindred saw what must have been tears rolling down Klatu's smudged cheeks.

"They are flesh and blood fragments of more than one council. Most have been brought here from many, many miles away. I carried them myself, Matthew Kindred,

I and a comrade, before he died, coughing his life away from some unknown sickness. I didn't want them to die alone. I wanted them here, and I intended to bring the nuns down to see—"

"Even if it is as you say," Kindred interrupted, "what about that group of terminally ill nuns at the convent? When you saw them, you left behind the pills, and yet a week later, how does that explain your attempt to kill Mother Veronica with a spear?"

Klatu jumped down from the ledge.

"I saw how friendly she was with the enemy...just like the rest, a traitor."

It was clear, though, that there was little conviction in his tone of voice or the expression on his face. He looked instead like someone who had acted rashly and now regretted it deeply.

"Klatu, did they experiment with your body before you managed to escape?" Kindred asked suddenly.

Klatu froze just a few feet away from him.

"My body?" he repeated. "As with Taresa?"

"Yes, did they—"

Kindred cut himself off. "You *know* about her?" he asked, stunned.

"I do. What do you think was the final, inescapable piece in this puzzle with which I was faced? I found her in one of the labs."

Klatu let out a giant roar of rage then.

"She was still alive, Taresa and our child! She had given birth, and the baby had been taken from her, and both of them, my wife and my son, were cut up and poisoned and...and they both died in my arms, and they...."

He started choking on his emotions and had to stop briefly.

"I know what pain they endured, Matthew Kindred, for I went through the same ordeal. They stuck wires into me also, and they sent electricity through my cells."

Something happened to Klatu then. He abruptly seemed more like a child, caught in a series of acts well-nigh beyond his comprehension but embarked upon in any event, and now the price had to be paid.

"After I escaped, I found some tunnels and wandered through them for the longest time. I nearly died then. The pain squeezed my *mind!*

"I was found, though, and I recovered, at least physically; yet it was not the same. I wanted revenge. God knows that consumed my very being!"

A plaintive tone entered his voice.

"But, Matthew Kindred, I did try so hard to get beyond what they had done, to fight the desires overwhelming me, to be what you and others like you wanted, and in that I was no different from my fellow creatures. Until I found Taresa and

185

my son. In the end I and the rest of my kind could only lash out as the brute beasts we are.''

He tilted his head slightly.

"Even now God continues to speak nothing to us," he said. "Our yoke remains. He has not taken it upon Himself.''

"But, Klatu, how can any of us probe the mind of God and claim to know, without equivocation, what He has in store? Can you be so certain that God is who you imply Him to be? So uncaring, so brutal that He would set you aside on some kind of eternal garbage heap, to lie there, rotting, until your body had disappeared, with nothing else left?''

Kindred walked directly up to Klatu then.

"Give me the torch," he said.

"Please, Matthew Kindred, I will take it and burn this worthless flesh," Klatu said, bringing the flames close to his body.

"No, my friend," Kindred said, "no, you will not. We are brothers in a way, bound together by the saving of one another's life. I cannot let my brother destroy himself.''

"But your brother, Matthew Kindred—if I could *ever* be called that—your brother has the blood of countless innocent ones on his hands.''

Klatu dropped the torch, and it rolled to one side. He held out his hands.

"Look at these and imagine the horrible things they have done.''

Kindred took those hands in his own, though Klatu tried to pull away.

"I see other hands as well, dear friend," he said with utmost tenderness. "I see the hands of Saul.''

Klatu looked at him with an uncomprehending expression.

"Please, let me tell you about Saul," Kindred said.

And he repeated words from Acts that had been long ago memorized.

" 'And falling on his knees, Stephen cried out with a loud voice, "Lord, do not hold this sin against them!" And he died....Saul was in hearty agreement with putting him to death. Thereafter, Saul began ravaging the church even more severely, executing many, entering house after house; and dragging off men and women, he would put them in prison.' ''

Kindred looked straight into Klatu's eyes.

"And then he had an experience that changed his life, Klatu, that made him into an apostle, the most influential of all the apostles of that time. Later, he died quite violently, it is said, for he was beheaded. But he gave his life to Christ.''

"Yes, Matthew Kindred, I know, God knows I do, but for him there was life eternal, not oblivion.''

"But which is more worthy, your life in rebellion, your life as a series of acts of infamy—or a life that in the living of it says to God, 'If this is all there is for me, let me be at peace with Thee. Though humankind looks at me in disgust, though they torment me, though they do all manner of evil against me, I shall no longer do the same in return. They may choose to act like beasts themselves, insensitive to the pain of others, but I shall not duplicate the evil that consumes them. I shall honor Thee with my very being, and leave the rest, O God, in Thy loving hands.' "

Klatu started sobbing then.

Kindred reached out and embraced him, ignoring the dirt and sweat and blood, embraced him with tenderness that must have come directly from the Lord, for it was a tenderness that ignored the violence of what had been, ignored the loathsome sin, placed all of that under the cleansing flow of Calvary.

"How can I ever accept what you are—," Klatu started to say.

And then a voice interrupted them.

One of the council members.

Kindred and Klatu rushed to his side.

"The abyss!" he was crying. "I see beyond the abyss. It is gone!"

Kindred and Klatu glanced at one another, excitement starting within them.

"I see...."

And knowledge surged through like an atonement from heaven as the council members spoke.

In that era wickedness had spread everywhere. It had invaded the places of worship. The home. Even the seats of government. Scandals were a regular occurrence.

They laughed at the good. And embraced the profane.

God was cast from their thoughts. Babies were sacrificed. Sex became a commodity on streets of desire.

Satan had another ignoble opportunity. He had failed during the pre-Adamic period in his original intention to create life. He would try again, this time through demonic sexual intercourse with the human females of those days.

And so he sent legion after legion of his fallen angels into the homes of immoral women, into homes where God was not honored.

None could withstand the awful creatures, monstrosities of cloven feet and sharp teeth and foul odors, their red eyes burning with the intensity of flame-drenched hell itself.

In nine months and less, the children started to appear, normal-seeming and yet, as they grew, not that at all. A unique bone structure was one of the differences. Other irregularities became apparent only later, and more would have been instilled within them if not for warnings heeded by their mothers.

"Your fathers return," cried the women. "Your fathers return soon, to take you away. We feel them nearby."

The unwilling mothers had grown to love their strange offspring, never deserting the maternal need to protect even those born of rape.

"We cannot leave them to the horrible creatures who violated us," the women said in gatherings. "It is not their fault that demons gave them physical life."

So the mothers decided to hide.

"A great storm is coming," they said, pointing to the sky. "The judgment of God upon us all. If we do not flee the devil, that judgment will fall upon us as well."

And so they ran for caves, for crevasses leading deep within the earth. Some turned and looked up at the sky for the very last time.

"See!" they cried. "It has begun."

The fathers of their children were hovering above, ready to descend. But they could not. The storm was fierce, thunder and lightning and great sheets of water without end.

And in the midst of it, an ark began to float as the waters rose....

"Matthew Kindred!"

"Yes, Klatu, I hear, praise Jesus, I hear!"

"We are not animals. Our mothers were human. We are...."

Their joy grew with each second.

Some water seeped in below, some rushed in torrentially. Many of the mothers did drown, their babies with them.

But many more survived.

And in the centuries to follow, they were fruitful and multiplied, thousands of them, hundreds of thousands, deep within the earth.

Progeny after progeny, taught many things but none more important than the central reality of their lives:

To cast off the yoke of the demonic within them and to embrace almighty God with every bit of love of which they were capable, until one day He would reach down into their world, and He would lead them above again.

But in time that vision grew dim, very dim indeed....

The first few Dwellers with whom Kindred and Klatu were communing grew very weak and could not continue.

But others took their place.

Centuries more passed. The original fervor of their commitment dissipated, as did the memories of their origin.

And so Satan got them in time to believe a lie so awful, so twisted and evil, that he would stand back and roar with exultation.

"God has not won after all," Lucifer the Fallen would tell a triumphant gathering of his unholy followers. "These children of mine in time will never know that they cling to a lie that I foisted upon them from the start. This lie was repeated so often down through the annals of history as an ancestral truth that it became an idea they never thought to question, a lie I have hung as imprisoning chains around their very spirits, spirits they will carry with them into the hell that will be my home and theirs."

The ecstasy they shared was blasphemous at its core....

THIRTY-SEVEN

KINDRED AND KLATU COULD SCARCELY SPEAK, staggered by the profound truths they had heard—but their spirits were soaring at the same time!

"Matthew Kindred, God hasn't deserted us!" Klatu exclaimed. "He's here, by our side, and we will walk with Him along the golden streets of heaven. We—"

Then his eyes opened wide, and in seconds his head fell forward, his shoulders slumped.

"What is it, Klatu?" Kindred asked, deeply concerned at the about-face in his behavior.

"But thousands of my kind *have* died in ignorance. They died thinking that God indeed had no place for them. They will be in hell while others rejoice through eternity. How can I bear the burden of knowing that they have only torment?"

Kindred hesitated, silently praying for the kind of wisdom desperately needed in that moment.

"No, Klatu, no, I don't think God turns His back on any who seek Him."

"The Buddhists then are in heaven? The Muslims who worship a vengeful god? The cults who claim Him even as they twist His truths?"

Kindred closed his eyes and held up the palms of his hands.

"Lord," he said aloud, "precious Jesus, give me the words my beloved friend must have."

When he opened his eyes, tears were streaming down his cheeks.

"The Buddhists worship a counterfeit set before them by Satan himself. The Muslims bow before a god whose only purpose is the shedding of the blood of the innocent, and in their ravings they fail to see that they stand before the devil instead and gladly receive the knife that he hands them so that they can plunge it into the hearts of their enemies. The cults spring mostly from blind or possessed puppets instilled with the demonic powers of hordes of fallen angels eager to deceive if it were possible the very elect.

"Klatu, Klatu, the difference between those blasphemous perpetrators of unholy deeds and your kind is that many, many Dwellers indeed have offered up their praises despite the cloud of hopelessness wound so tightly around them by their original father—despite even what seemed the indisputable reality of many millennia."

Klatu raised his head.

"Taresa!" he fairly shouted. "My beautiful Taresa!"

Instinctively he half-reached his hand out at his side, then blushed as he caught himself.

"It is as though I can feel her already next to me, her hand in my own."

"Ardenis, too!" Kindred said, as the miracle of realization brought back memory after memory.

Kindred went up to the cross, examined the detail, rock transformed to look like grayish wood, down to the grain, splinters scarcely large enough to be seen; a crown of thorns pressed down over the temple; the hands perfectly formed, nails through the palms; the rib cage visible through taut flesh; veins standing out on the legs, nails also through the feet. And at the base, simple, strange words:

> *Lord, even though I will never stand by Your side in Your kingdom, I give You my humble love without anger, only with joy and peace inside my very being.*

"And Parane, dear Klatu, Parane and his beloved!" Kindred said with great joy. "They offered up worship even when believing that God would not hear them."

"No longer separated," Klatu savored the words.

"Now nothing, not all the deceptions of Satan, not all the demon hordes at his command can ever touch them again."

All of the council members in that place would die over the next several hours.

But even in the midst of their pain, the ebbing of their life force, they were content because, one by one, Kindred was able to lead them to a full acceptance of Jesus Christ as the Savior and Lord after whom their kind had hungered for centuries.

At the end Kindred and Klatu each held a Dweller in his arms, wiping off fluids that sputtered periodically from between their lips, crying with them, laughing, holding hands that would suddenly become weak as life drained away.

"No more pain, Matthew Kindred," one of them said.

He reached up and brushed away some tears from the minister's own cheek.

"Rejoice, my brother in the flesh and—dear blessed, blessed truth—in the spirit."

The hand fell, but the eyes remained open for a few seconds longer.

"Oh my!" the dying one said, his face lit up with a sublime smile. "How beautifully they sing, how soft their wings against my...."

And so it went until both were gone.

Kindred and Klatu sat quietly, not immediately able to let go of the now-lifeless forms in their arms.

"Why was there no joy earlier?" Klatu asked, after Kindred and he had finally laid those last council members gently on the rock floor. "Why has the joy suddenly burst out, like a moth from a cocoon, liberated into something so beautiful?"

Kindred's mind went back to the atmosphere of despair that he had sensed among the Dwellers from the very beginning.

"Delusion again," he replied after prayerfully considering the matter for a few minutes. "Satan *knew* that redemption was possible after all, but he kept the Dwellers prisoners to their ignorance. It was only as they actually died, as they actually experienced the reality of that redemption, that joy flooded them."

"Yet Dwellers were redeemed, not just now, but centuries ago as well. Even so, I have never heard of what we have seen here. Surely everything would have changed for us if it had been otherwise, if my kind could have witnessed just one incident like any of these today!"

"Could it be, Klatu, that there were moments similar to these, but your ancestors, still under blindness, ignored the truth anyway?"

"But I—," Klatu started to say.

"The Jews in the Old Testament were witnesses to God's power again and again and again. After they were freed from Egyptian domination and led safely through the Red Sea onto dry land, saved by the miraculous intervention of almighty God, they turned to false gods and graven images rather than to Him.

"Think of that, Klatu. God stepped down into the fabric of finite time and space and parted those waters, holding them back long enough for every Israelite to get across, and then He lifted His hand and destroyed the pursuing Egyptians by letting the waters overwhelm them, drowning the entire army of soldiers!"

Klatu was silent, contemplating his friend's astounding words.

"Could it be that there really were such moments, as you imply," he finally said, "when my kind had the veil lifted briefly, and then, succumbing to Satan's delusion, they let it drop once again?"

"That might be the answer, Klatu; it might indeed," Kindred agreed. "But something else is more important."

"What is that, Matthew Kindred?"

"Not what is past, not settling every unanswered question, but rather the *reality* of what we have seen, what we have experienced here, today! God has chosen not just to lift the veil but to rip it asunder. That should be the cause of joy abundant, not nagging questions, my brother."

"And *brothers* we are, Matthew Kindred; brothers we have *always* been!"

Some time passed as they savored what had transpired, as they soaked in the sheer beauty of that time, that place. Then finally....

"Can we not bury them somehow?" Klatu asked, standing before the wise ones.

"Yes, let's gather some rocks and—"

Klatu suddenly held up his hand, cocking his head slightly.

"Matthew Kindred, listen!"

"I don't—"

And then he heard it, too.

A rumbling sound.

"An earthquake. That's the first sign, like thunder before a storm. You learn about such things when you have lived underground for millions of years. We must leave immediately."

As they started to run, the ground shook.

A falling rock hit Kindred on the forehead. He fell, nausea engulfing him. Realizing with a stark and compelling clarity that the cavern was beginning to collapse around him, and yet his own strength was suddenly gone, he felt arms lifting him, dragging him. And then the darkness came fully.

THIRTY-EIGHT

He COULD NEVER REMEMBER, IN TIMES SINCE then, where they picked him up. There were vague images of trees and a river. But even these were as though viewed through the thickest fog, surreal in how they appeared to him in moments of retrospection.

It was, they told him, quite a distance from the convent. He had apparently been dragged far from that cavern where he confronted Klatu for the last time, through long stretches of underground tunnels; and he had then emerged above ground, where he wandered dazedly....

Matthew Kindred ultimately came back to life, having existed for a time in some sort of limbo between awareness and oblivion. His identity, his past, his memories were kaleidoscopic fragments which he would grab ahold of, only to have each torn from him.

That stage in his rehabilitation passed, to be replaced by the residue of all that previously had battered him emotionally...before he was aware of anyone named Klatu, long before his time with the Dwellers, Nessie and dancing octopi, and a beckoning crystal pyramid on the ocean bottom. Indeed his mind returned to that last day with his family—the car hitting the tailgate on the highway, flipping over three times, landing in a ditch beside the road; the smell of gasoline as they were pinned within the crumpled metal; his wife's still, bruised, bloody body, then standing by her grave weeks after the funeral, his son in a wheelchair, looking up at him with eyes accusing him beyond redemption. The months of flight, the cowardice this personified, along with its implicit self-pity, his sin nature triumphant and gloating, swooping upon him, vulture-like, picking the bones of whatever was left of him.

He dimly recalled a sermon, a piece of confetti in the wind, and at first without

194

context, at first with only the vaguest of hints as to its purpose. But gradually, as it came more and more in focus, he recalled it as a sermon about a believer becoming so filled up with the things of the world, so dominated by self, that the Lord had to begin an emptying process, draining everything so that the void could be refilled in a way honoring to Him. The fact that he had once delivered it only served to underline his hypocrisy.

One gloomy morning, rain beating against the window in his room, he slowly got out of bed and walked to the mirror in the adjoining bathroom. They had said that weeks had passed. It could have been years. As he looked, it seemed that he had aged that much, or more. His hair! Completely white! Dark circles underlined bloodshot eyes. The forehead had lines that looked like miniaturized furrows in a farmer's field.

He sank to his knees then, realizing that the way he looked matched what he had become inside. It mirrored the corruption of those tenets upon which he had built his ministry, tenets preached with zeal, yes, to others, but from which he had fled when it was no longer sufficient to indulge them as easy-to-dispense platitudes.

Yet there was a difference in the way he viewed everything this time. Back in that cavern a miracle had happened, perhaps a series of miracles. If there could be an answer for the long nightmare of the Dwellers, then surely, with God's help, he could pull himself out of his own pit of despair.

He realized that he hadn't been out of his room since he was rushed to wherever they had taken him. But he would stand at the window across from his bed, which he did more times each day than he could actually count or remember, and see mountains in the distance, snow at the top of each ridge, and at their base a city with skyscrapers. On the grounds directly below, there was a surfeit of trees, together with a large pond and an Oriental-style bridge over it, people walking the numerous pathways. Through the open window, carried on gentle stirrings of air, was the aroma of flowers, sweet and natural, nothing else to detract from it except the absolute purity of the air itself, laced with a hint of coolness that felt invigorating to lungs that only recently had filled with the smoke of burning flesh.

...to wherever they had taken him.

It may not have been far from the convent; it may, in fact, have been hundreds of miles, if not thousands. He just didn't know. They were more interested in saving his life and getting him back on the road to stability than providing directions on a roadmap.

They....

One day, there at the window, he thought he saw Marquand, but he wasn't certain. It was a military officer getting into a black sedan, then driving off.

They....

The nuns with whom he had sensed some real rapport, because of their kindness. The fruit of the Holy Spirit had been displayed through the way they acted without hope of reward, merely out of a desire to serve their risen Lord through serving one of His disciples. He saw none of them, and he looked each day with utmost care, hoping that Sister Martha might pay a visit or...

...Mother Veronica.

...standing there, the front part of her habit pierced by a long wooden spear with a stone tip, the white collar red with blood.

Would there be some kind of miracle for her as there had been for him?

"REV. KINDRED," THE VOICE SAID, "YOU HAVE a visitor."

Kindred was sitting in one of the two overstuffed chairs in his room, reading his Bible. He looked up at the smiling young intern.

"A friend stopped by to say hello."

The intern stepped aside, and Kindred saw the familiar figure of Marquand.

"Hello, Matthew," Marquand said. "I understand you are feeling quite a bit better."

The intern excused himself.

Kindred sighed with notable weariness as he stood and shook hands with Marquand.

"I don't feel worse," he replied. "I guess that means I *am* feeling better."

Marquand wore a light yellow sports jacket, patterned shirt and yellow slacks—a marked change from earlier occasions when he seemed to find it necessary always to look "military."

"I almost didn't recognize you," Kindred joked.

"I am the same man in or out of uniform, make no mistake about that, soldier, er, I mean—"

They enjoyed a good laugh then. Both sat, stretching out comfortably.

"I was thinking how much alike our lives have been, Matthew."

"Alike?" Kindred said, surprised. "I don't see that at—"

And then he remembered the pain Marquand had endured through the loss of his wife to leukemia.

"Oh, yes. Losing our loved ones. Fighting battles against various enemies. But you didn't break down."

Marquand's expression turned serious as he looked straight at the minister.

"How do you *know* that, Matthew?"

Kindred realized that his assumption was nothing more than that, based upon the impression of strength that Marquand continually projected.

"My fellow officers never knew, that is, except one, a chap I'd known since my grade school days. I got through it during what the others thought to be just a vacation."

"You were able to recover in just a few weeks?"

"That was the problem and, if you will, my salvation."

"How do you mean? Recovery can hardly be forced, with a time limit set on it."

"I might have agreed with you if it were not for my own circumstance. Knowing that my career would be severely damaged or destroyed if I didn't get myself together in four weeks admittedly added to the pressures and tended to make everything worse. But the fact was that I had no choice. I would either collapse or I would pull myself up from the emotional gutter and get on with my life. There was no gray area, no intermediate one, no compromise whatever."

"You said, when you came in," Kindred remarked, "that you understood I was feeling quite a bit better. That's true...today. But tomorrow might be different."

He tapped his forehead.

"There is yet an awful lot of mischief going on in here."

"Well, we're going to do something about it."

"We?"

"I've arranged to take some time off. I'll be staying here with you, to help."

"You?"

"You heard correctly, soldier," Marquand said, smiling.

Less than a year before (or was it longer than that?), he had had someone else by his side, holding him, an anchor truly, until he survived the poison of a rattlesnake. Now it was a different kind of poison in his system, and once again he would not be alone.

Having Marquand with him, talking out everything not with strangers alone but with a friend as well, proved to be the link he needed, especially when another kind of guilt he had been harboring rose to the surface.

How could ministers have breakdowns? Surely that meant unconfessed sin in their lives. How could they succumb to a variety of temptations, sexual or otherwise? Wasn't the breakdown in each case an indication of something rancid and unholy, a foothold of Satan's that had to be exorcised before they could get on with life?

He had to deal with that notion head-on. It proved to be the source of underlying guilt that had eluded his awareness, like cancer undetected and, therefore, running wild inside him.

But finally it came out in a verbal torrent as Marquand and he sat in front of a pond inhabited by a multicolored population of large *koi.*

"Every minister who has any rapport with his parishioners is confronted daily with a dozen, a score, maybe more, of individuals reaching out to *him* for advice, for help, for solace, for some drop of wisdom from his personal well of spiritual strength. If he cares, he really gives himself to them without holding back. He—"

"—does it for so long," said Marquand, completing the thought, "so unselfishly, that when he must go to that well for help in his own life, it is nearly bone-dry."

"How did you know?" Kindred asked, stunned.

"A military officer, especially a general, has a similar situation. The men under him have been *trained* to turn to him for their orders. If he exudes a reasonably sympathetic manner, rather than that of a harsh dictator, he becomes a father-figure—forgive me, Matthew, even something of a God-figure to a degree—and they turn to him in off-the-cuff moments as a fount of wisdom."

Marquand stood and walked to the very edge of the pond, looking down at the *koi,* which averaged two to three feet in length.

"Three times a day, Matthew, an intern comes here and feeds them. It is quite a sight. They all jump out of the water virtually at once in a frenzied grab for food. I wonder, in their creaturely dumbness, if they somehow look on that intern in a way similar to how people look to you and to me.

"The trouble is that you and I can keep going on for a certain period of time only. When our inner well is dry and we are of no help to anyone, including ourselves, we collapse, Matthew. It's as simple, as inexorable, as that."

He sat down again and faced Kindred.

"The key is whether we allow the water level to rise again, or whether we further deplete everything within us until we merely go off, screaming, into the night and never find our way back?"

He rested his arms on Kindred's shoulders.

"My friend, David's waiting for you back there."

"Here, now?" Kindred said, alarmed, panicky.

"Not literally, Matthew, not back there. But he's waiting somewhere, though."

"He rejected me."

"That is not altogether what happened."

"But, Clark, he—"

"Your son hung up on you, yes, I know."

"But I don't remember telling you what happened."

Marquand brushed that aside.

"I suspect David felt you were offering just another round of excuses for not returning home immediately."

"But why would he think that? I was the one who made the call, Clark."

"If you haven't been able always to react as an adult, Matthew, how can you expect a teenager to do so?"

Marquand's tone was gentle, and Kindred took no offense.

"I wonder if I will *ever* forgive myself for not being the father he needed. I should have shouldered his burdens rather than adding to them."

Marquand swallowed once, twice, and then asked, "Tell me the truth when I ask you a question now?"

Kindred nodded.

"Aren't you worried, with all this other stuff a kind of smokescreen, aren't you worried, really, that somehow you can get forgiveness from everyone, even David in time, but that God has turned a cold shoulder to you?"

Kindred sat there, quietly, his friend's words assaulting him full-force.

"All those Sunday sermons about Christ's death purchasing redemption," Marquand went on, "His blood washing away sins, and yet every bit of it has remained up here..."

He tapped his head.

"...but it hasn't gotten through to here."

He pointed to his chest.

"You, the one so forthright in your articles and your radio broadcasts condemning those country club Christians who go through dead ritual Sunday after Sunday while nothing sinks in, who merely mouth words of faith—just noises from their vocal cords. And yet, Matthew, in this one crucial area, you are as spiritually recalcitrant as they are."

...that God has turned a cold shoulder to you.

As Kindred thought back over the recent past, he realized that Marquand had hit a bull's-eye. He started crying then, without shame, the tears necessary.

"Yes, I think that's it, dear God. I *know* it is."

Both men lapsed into silence for the next few minutes.

"Clark, there's something I've not told you as yet," Kindred ventured.

"What is it?"

"It's about the Dwellers."

'Well, go ahead."

"They are not animals, Clark. The Dwellers were born of human females. Their mothers were women."

200

"You're over the edge on that one, Matthew. You—"

He saw the expression on his friend's face.

"You aren't talking fantasy or delusion here, are you?"

Kindred shook his head.

"But what about their fathers?"

Kindred told him what he had learned back in the cavern.

"But their mothers refused to give in, you're saying? They refused to dedicate their children to the devil?"

"That's right."

Marquand fell back against the bench, his head turned toward the sky.

"I've just come from one of our bases on the East Coast, Matthew. I've been forced to deal with another case of ritual child abuse."

"Another case?"

"There have been dozens of these at army bases around the country. Parents giving up their sons and daughters to the whims of satanists who have been infiltrating the military."

He looked at Kindred then.

"We condemn the Dwellers, and yet their mothers resisted the devil—while in our own nation we have a growing conspiracy involving entire families who sell their very souls to that...that monster."

Marquand shook with anger.

"One of the ringleaders is a lieutenant colonel who has had high security clearance for a number of years."

"Satan keeps repeating himself, doesn't he?"

"Oh, yes. Thousands of years ago. And now again today at places that are the heart of this country's security."

Marquand fell into silence then.

A couple of minutes passed.

"There's something else, Clark," Kindred probed. "I know you too well. You've not told me everything."

"Yes, Matthew, there is. But I would be guilty of a terrible federal crime if I told you just yet. Let me say only this: The good news is that the Dwellers are not condemned to oblivion. The bad news is the nightmare that such a revelation hastens along for the rest of us as we try to face the crimes committed against them."

Another lull. Then....

"There's something at the other end of this property that I think you should see," Marquand said as he glanced at his watch.

After wiping his eyes briefly, Kindred stood and followed Marquand. In a few minutes they approached a two-story brick building with a playground in the back.

"Retarded kids," Kindred observed. "Every single one of them."

A dozen or so youngsters were playing.

"Matthew, case histories show that in many instances they are retarded because their mothers drank liquor or took drugs or both prior to their births. Virtually all could have been living 'normal' lives today otherwise."

"What a tragedy!"

"Oh, it is certainly. But I have witnessed scenes profoundly worse, believe me. I have seen soldiers from more than one war so scarred emotionally by their experiences that they have regressed into a state approaching retardation. What they underwent was so invidious that they couldn't cope on one level, and they withdrew to another that seemed to offer solace. And then there were the others who became in a sense 'retarded' due to physical injury.

"Matthew, believe me when I say that these men are the ones to be pitied. Most have families. They have known what it is to be blessed with all their faculties, to communicate fully with the world around. I don't know if I could survive the kind of frustration that will be part and parcel of the rest of their lives.

"But you know what, Matthew? These youngsters have some advantages over even normal folk like you and me. They really don't know what has happened to them. And from everything we can perceive about them, they are beyond Satan's grasp."

...beyond Satan's grasp.

The thought grabbed ahold of Kindred and shook him.

"Can those who are moderately or severely retarded sin?" he mused out loud.

"You're the theologian, Matthew. But it would seem to me that sin is basically in what we choose to do or not to do. More than likely none of them will ever sin sexually, for example, because they literally don't know what it is all about. Will they sin by murdering anyone? Will they sin by robbing? Will they sin by lying? I know beyond doubt that they are embarrassed by and turn away from X-rated movies. Some sociologists feel that those retarded below a certain level of comprehension will never *learn* to lie; they seem *incapable* of anything but the truth."

"So where is the sin?"

"Precisely, my friend. What it amounts to is that while they may physically reach the so-called age of accountability, they never will do so spiritually or intellectually, frozen at a stage of development that, along with little babies and very young children, may make them the only true innocents since before Adam and Eve were cast out of the Garden of Eden."

As he was rubbing the head of one of the children, Marquand went on to say, "These kids have no choice, no control over their lives. But you and I do, Matthew.

You and I determine the direction in which we go. God will open up heaven to the retarded, indeed He will. And that is as it should be. But I wonder: Is it richer and more fulfilling to enter into His presence because we never had to make a choice or to consciously accept Christ into our lives, accept His gift of forgiveness, and turn our backs on Satan in the process?"

Marquand wiped his eyes with a handkerchief.

"If in all this world there were only the innocent retarded, would Christ have had to die?" he asked, musingly, of no one in particular. "But there *are* more than these youngsters on this planet, Matthew. There are geniuses as well as average people, and those in between. They can accept Christ or they can reject Him. *You* made that choice a long time ago. But that's only *half* of the picture, I guess you could say. The other half is that gift I mentioned: His forgiveness."

Marquand's eyes widened, and there seemed almost to be a glow coming from within them.

"Matthew, Matthew, praise the Lord for what just popped into this military mind of mine. God forgives you, whether you accept that gift or not. In a sense you have no other *choice* apart from the original one of receiving Christ into your life or keeping Him out. Once you decided to open that door to your soul, all the rest was *automatic* and otherwise *unconditional!*"

Marquand's gaze met Kindred's.

"That *is* the only answer I can offer you for your dilemma, Matthew. It is all I have, my friend."

Some time later, after they had played a game or two with the youngsters, they decided to return to Kindred's room, Marquand again glancing at his watch.

Suddenly a scream shattered the relative quiet. A second or two passed, and a young nurse came running out of the brick building.

"In the basement!" she shouted. "One of them, one of *them!*"

Other nurses seemed terrified, but not their charges, who glanced up briefly and then went on with their games.

"I'm going down there," Kindred said.

"I don't think that's wise," Marquand protested. "You're—"

"—not fully recovered yet? Is that it? Maybe this is what I need, to confront it all starkly, once and for all."

Marquand was unhappy but knew he couldn't stop his friend.

Kindred found the man in charge, a Dr. Douglas Saville. Around forty years old, the man was roughly five feet eight inches in height, bald, with a rather large stomach, his manner authoritarian.

"No, sir," he started to say, "I don't care who you are. Only the military—"

Marquand walked up to the two of them.

"I *am* the military," he said crisply. "Kindred here is cleared, I assure you."

Marquand's manner left no doubt about his status. Kindred hurried on past a nonplussed Dr. Saville.

One of the nurses showed Kindred to the door leading to the basement.

"Father, be with me, be with us, dear Lord," he prayed, just before opening it and walking down a short flight of stairs.

The basement was extensive, running the entire length and width of the building. Stored there were medical equipment, chairs, piles of books and magazines, toys, more.

And huddling in a far corner was an aging, frightened Dweller not far from a hole he had managed to dig through a wall of plaster over wood beams.

Kindred approached slowly.

The Dweller looked up. He was one of the oldest Kindred had seen to date, hair nearly as white as the skin, eyes bloodshot, lips pale, thin.

"Matthew Kindred!"

This Dweller knew him!

"I am Karuth. All that screaming. Someone threw something at me, hit me right here."

Karuth pointed to a gash in his left side.

"How did you know my name?" asked Kindred, his tone almost awe-filled.

"All of us know. Every single one. You are...famous."

Kindred sat down in front of Karuth.

"Will you let me help you, please?" he asked kindly.

"Can you really help any of us, Matthew Kindred? Are we not doomed?"

There was no anger in his voice, seemingly no bitterness, just a resignation to whatever would befall him next.

"How old are you, Karuth?"

The Dweller's manner turned slightly coy.

"Is that important to you?"

"If you don't want to tell me, that's fine."

"I will, Matthew Kindred, I will."

He took in a deep breath.

"The day I was born, your President Lincoln was delivering his famous Gettysburg Address."

Almost a hundred and thirty years old!

It hadn't occurred to Kindred to think about the life span of each Dweller. Many seemed old, true, but many more were not.

"I have seen the Industrial Age born. I have seen the effects of the Great Depression. I..."

Emotion took hold of Karuth.

"...but I will never see another century."

Kindred spoke slowly, with utmost care.

"Yet you *will* experience eternity."

"But by then I may be the only one left," Karuth continued as though not hearing. "Or I might be like some rat in a laboratory experiment."

"No, no," Kindred hastened to say. "All of that was stopped some time ago. It won't happen again."

Karuth's expression at that point was unfathomable. Kindred wished he could read its meaning.

"Didn't you hear me, Karuth?" Kindred persisted.

"Hear you?"

"Yes. You will live forever. You are—"

Karuth put the fingers of his left hand to Kindred's lips.

"I love you for saying that, Matthew Kindred, but false hope is—"

"It isn't false. You are human! You can be given all the rewards of having faith in Christ as your redeemer."

Karuth shook his head.

"No more, please. I cannot cope with it."

Karuth refused to let the truth cut through the age-old blindness under which Satan had been successful in putting the Dwellers.

"But, Karuth!"

"Enough, Matthew Kindred. Please take me upstairs now."

As they were about to leave the basement, Karuth said, in trembling voice, "I.. I don't know if I'm ready to face their loathing."

Kindred stopped at the top step before opening the door to the ground floor.

"Perhaps more easily than the loathing you hold for yourself," he said sharply

"Your words are angry. They cut me deeply. Have you no pity?"

"I may not. You seem to want all of that yourself!"

Karuth reached out to slap him but had no strength to do so.

"See, Matthew Kindred! I can't even defend myself, with actions or words."

"You would never need to do that, Karuth, if you just opened yourself up to—

Karuth, struggling to get away from him, tripped and started to fall down the stairs But Kindred was able to grab him in time.

205

"You took my hand then," the minister said. "Take my words now, I beg you."

Karuth examined him for a few seconds.

"You are not offering idle platitudes, *are* you?" he asked.

"No, I am not. Sit down. I will tell you quickly what happened."

When he finished, Karuth was crying.

"My God, my God, You have not forsaken me after all!"

He reached out to embrace Kindred.

"I do not have to fear the abyss any longer, do I?" he said.

"For you it doesn't exist."

He helped the ancient one to stand, and they walked out onto the first floor. Nurses and doctors were hovering around, some of them gasping at the sight of the Dweller.

"Why do they react so?" Karuth whispered.

"Because it is part of human nature to react often negatively to anyone who is significantly different from them. That has been a device of Satan's from the beginning of civilization."

"I see that they have two natures also."

"The sin nature, the flesh, as the Bible says; and a spiritual nature—one constantly warring against the other."

When they appeared in the doorway leading outside, another set of gasps and whispers could be heard.

And then Karuth saw the retarded youngsters.

He stopped walking and stared at them. Remarkably they sensed his presence and turned in his direction.

"Oh my...."

Karuth seemed to gather greater strength from somewhere within himself and pulled away from Kindred to go toward the children. One of the doctors stepped in front of him, trying to block his way. But Karuth's expression of love and patience was so non-threatening that the doctor stepped aside just as quickly.

Karuth didn't have to walk very far. The children flocked to him. He seemed to gain even more strength from their attention. Kindred saw him reach into a pocket of the animal-skin garb common to all Dwellers and bring out a leather bag, dispensing the contents to the children.

The pills! More of the pills!

Kindred hurried over to Karuth.

"Please, save a couple of them, would you?"

"I will, my friend, I will. But I can show you where there are many of these."

"Many?"

"We were isolated from the warriors, not in agreement with them at all and too old to do anything to stop them. So we spent our time trying to duplicate the pills ingredient by ingredient. We succeeded to a degree.''

"To a degree? What do you mean?''

Karuth didn't answer but continued to give the pills to the retarded ones gathered around him.

When all but a few of the pills were gone, he told Kindred that he was very tired indeed and needed to rest. Marquand had already arranged for an army VIP trailer to be sent in; it would be arriving shortly.

Marquand glanced at his watch again.

"Matthew, we must go back now,'' he said.

"Go, good human friend,'' Karuth remarked, overhearing this. "I will be fine.''

The Dweller smiled.

"And so will most of them,'' he said, indicating the youngsters.

The general and the minister walked leisurely back to the main building and then to Kindred's room. Neither spoke again until they were inside and sitting down, stunned by what they had witnessed but even more by the implications of what Karuth had said and done.

"I wonder what Karuth meant when he said that they had succeeded in duplicating the pills but only to a degree.''

"I have a suspicion, Matthew. It's not a pleasant one.''

"What is it?''

"That they can help others but not themselves.''

"You mean that the pills won't work on the Dwellers?''

"As originally formulated perhaps. But who can say? I have never fancied myself a prophet.''

"You know,'' Kindred said finally, "Klatu and the others were nothing more than Satan's pawns, as soldiers are pawns in any war—his kind destined to live and die and leave nothing of worth, nothing of permanence. They were marginally alive, yes, while underground, but then as soon as they emerged above ground, they sealed their own doom.''

"There are many pawns on this planet, Matthew, in government, in the military. As you've just said, the sort of wickedness in high places that we read about in—''

He stopped himself.

"What's wrong?'' Kindred asked.

"I meant it when I said that I...I...can't discuss it just now."

It was clear that Marquand could not go on in that vein. It was also quite clear that, in even the deepest of friendships, there were still buried sectors of thought and feeling that could never be totally brought to the surface.

"Are you OK?" Kindred asked, noticing that Marquand's manner had changed, a hint of dark and troubled thoughts below the strong-looking exterior.

Marquand brushed aside the question. "It is more important just now for me to ask if *you* are going to be OK, Matthew?"

"You have helped me more than I thought I could be helped. None of us waves a magic wand around and, presto, it's all sunlight and roses. But—"

There was a knock on the closed door of his room.

"Come in," Kindred said.

"There's the rest of your reason for victory in your life," Marquand said, smiling.

Kindred turned, his eyes widening.

David! Looking up from his wheelchair, tears starting to flow.

"Hello, Dad...."

Marquand stayed with them for a couple of days and then left, sensing that they needed to be alone.

"I like him," David commented as the general was driven off in a military vehicle.

"So do I," Kindred acknowledged. "But when it all started, I couldn't have predicted the way it is now between the two of us."

They were sitting in a gazebo that had been placed on the front lawn of the institution.

"Tell me about it, Dad."

Tell me...Dad.

Kindred found those words indescribably joyous; he had been in the midst of an emotional desert, and David's very presence was a fresh supply of water, quenching a thirst that on occasion threatened to destroy him.

When he had finished, David was looking up at his father with an expression bordering on awe.

"You could write a book, maybe two," the boy said.

"I've thought about it, son."

"Would you write about me?"

"A big part would be about you."

"Really?"

"Really."

David seemed immensely pleased.

"And Mom, too?"

Kindred hesitated, half-trying to avoid talking about Mary for as long as possible. Being with David would enable him at least to attempt to deal with that part of his guilt. But as far as Mary was concerned, such an opportunity would never be realized.

"David?"

"Yes, Dad?"

"Are you bitter?"

"About what happened, with Mom and me?"

"Yes."

"I've never thought about it like that. I never hated you or anything, even when I hung up on you that time. But I do miss Mom very, very much."

The two of them burst into tears then. Kindred leaned over and hugged his son.

"So much has changed," Kindred sobbed. "So much can never be returned to the way it was. You don't know how that has eaten at me over the past year or so, David."

"But it's over now. Mom's not in pain. And, Dad, I'll have a new body someday, better than this body ever was. Isn't that what the Bible promises?"

Isn't that what the Bible promises....

Those words were repeated a hundred times in Kindred's mind over the days and weeks to follow.

Not all of the guilt that had corroded his sense of self-worth and forced his flight evaporated overnight. It hung on with appalling tenacity, like a leech gorging itself on blood.

Then, one afternoon, David came to his room from the institution's library.

"Dad, listen to this," he said, holding a slim little volume in his hand. "It's so beautiful."

Kindred looked up from the edge of the bed where he had been sitting, lost momentarily in recollection.

Love isn't like a reservoir. You'll never drain it dry. It's much more like a natural spring. The longer and the farther it flows, the stronger and the deeper and the clearer it becomes.

"And here's another—it's really something."

David handed his father the book, indicating the passage he wanted him to read.

Love is not a possession but a growth. The heart is a lamp with just oil enough to burn for an hour, and if there be no oil to put in again, its light will go out. God's grace is the oil that fills the lamp of love.

Kindred closed the book and looked at his son. David smiled pleasantly at him.

"Dad, God's love kept filling us even when we thought that, by our actions, we deserved His condemnation. And that love is endless. Nothing can change that; it will only get stronger and deeper and clearer."

Kindred examined his son. During the year they had been apart, something had happened to the boy. Tragedy had not broken his spirit but amplified it, strengthened it; at a point when his earthly father had deserted him, he came to realize that his heavenly Father never would. A maturity descended upon him that hadn't been there before, a wisdom almost unnerving.

David noticed the expression on his dad's face.

"I dream a lot these days, Dad," he said. "Oh, I don't hold to visions and that sort of thing the way some do. You taught me to be careful, that dreams and emotions can be manipulated by Satan."

"What have the dreams seemed to say, David?"

"That the Lord has something special in store for me and...."

David paused.

"And what, son?"

"Someone else along with me—we're going to be a team someday."

Kindred wasn't sure what to say.

"It sounds puzzling, I admit. Have you any sense of it yourself, David?"

"I don't. It's both scary and exciting."

A moment of silence between them.

"Am I that other person?" Kindred asked.

"Could be, Dad. I just don't know."

They both lapsed into silence, feeling a shared sense of destiny that rested very heavily on them just then.

They went outside after lunch and "did the grounds," going from one end to another. They saw others whose traumas had proved far too exhausting, who were little more than empty husks waiting for death to take them.

"It's so sad," David remarked in a whispery tone. "They could have everything if they just filled that emptiness with the oil of God's love."

Just ahead they suddenly saw someone running toward them.

"Go, good human friend," Karuth remarked. *"I will be fine."*

The Dweller smiled.

"And so will most of them," he said, *indicating the youngsters.*

The boy approached the two of them, his expression joyous.

"You were with Karuth, weren't you?" the teenager asked Kindred.

"I was. Have you heard from him?"

"You don't know, sir?"

"I'm not sure what you mean."

211

"He's still here. That general arranged it so he could stay with us for awhile."

"That's wonderful."

"You bet it is. Won't you follow me? You gotta see this, sir."

The two of them nodded in agreement.

As the boy went on slightly ahead of them, David whispered to his father, "He has the look of a Downs Syndrome person, Dad. But he doesn't seem to talk and act like one."

"I know," Kindred agreed, not able to say anything more just then.

Not all of the youngsters were substantially improved.

A nurse explained why.

"As far as we can tell, the ingredients in the pills work to change the chemical and other imbalances that are at the root of much of what we call retardation."

"There is nothing metaphysical about it then?" Kindred asked.

"Not at all. Nothing that would cause alarm even with a clergyman such as yourself."

She nodded toward a group of the children to her left.

"They will never be much different. Oh, there may be some improvement, I suppose. But, you see, along with the conditions within their brains there has been the malformation of the skull cavity in which those brains rest. It has caused extensive damage to the muscles."

"Can some be operated on to change the bone structure a bit?"

"Not with enough hope of success to justify the risk factor in nearly all the instances."

The nurse smiled as she similarly indicated a second group.

"They, however, are quite another story. The improvement in a matter of days has been astounding. There is no other word appropriate to describe their progress. Astounding! Those somewhat mildly retarded are now virtually whole, with no evidence whatsoever that they had such a condition."

"What about the Downs Syndrome children?" David asked.

"The one who brought you here has had the most startling improvement. He is probably 70 to 80 percent improved. Others may be only 20 to 40 percent better. But even that is unbelievable. It can mean the difference between spending the rest of their lives in an institution such as this one or going out into the world and making a better life for themselves."

"Where is Karuth?" Kindred inquired.

"Around the north side of the building. May I take you to him?"

Both nodded assent.

They saw the Dweller on a swing, one of the youngsters pushing him forward each time. He turned for a second and noticed them, then waved them over.

"Is this David?" Karuth asked, after he had been helped off the swing.

"I am," David said in response, awed by the presence of the aging creature standing in front of him.

The nurse left them, as did the youngster who had been with Karuth, and the three of them sat on the grass, enjoying one another's company.

David peppered Karuth with questions. When they got to the Council of Many, the boy became particularly interested.

"Inherited memories?" David repeated. "Nothing to do with reincarnation?"

"As I understand reincarnation, no. Are many deceived by that sort of thing in your world, David?"

"Yes, sir, many. Books promote it. Speakers praise it. Movies and television shows try to convince people that nothing's wrong with it."

"How foolish...," Karuth said, his voice trailing off.

"Karuth?" David asked.

"Yes, my young friend?"

"Have you ever experienced dreams that were in any way prophetic?"

"Yes."

"You have?"

Karuth turned to David.

"As you have, David Kindred."

"You know?"

Karuth would only smile.

A frown creased David's forehead.

"Karuth, you *must*—"

"I will say only this, David Kindred. It is a dream you share in its totality with only one other person in this whole world, someone young like yourself."

David was about to probe further, but his father placed a hand on his shoulder, stopping him.

"He needs to rest," Kindred whispered into his son's ear.

"I do, I'm afraid," Karuth said, overhearing. "A lifetime thus far of 130 years is a long, long period for this body."

Karuth summoned another nurse by waving at one he had glimpsed a second or two previously.

But before he went off, he turned to David and said, "I'll be looking forward to our reunion in heaven, David Kindred."

Then he excused himself and, leaning on the nurse, walked away.

213

When Karuth was no longer within earshot, David turned to his father and said, "He's that old?"

"That's what he claims."

"Wow!"

They both fell into silence briefly.

To have lived much more than a century, Kindred thought, *governed by a mind-set that was a mirror image of nihilism, and always with no expectation of things ever changing. How could Karuth have kept his sanity unless...*

David was the first to speak afterward.

"Dad?"

"Yes, David?"

"He said that he was looking forward to our reunion in heaven. He's just an animal. Is that some kind of fantasy he's been having?"

"No, David, it's true."

"But how?"

Kindred told his son what had happened.

"That's wonderful! That's *real* wonderful," the boy replied. "I've been reading a lot about them, trying to learn all I could. There'll be Dwellers in heaven, wow!"

"Lots of them, I suspect."

They started walking back toward the other building.

"Dad?"

"Yes, David?"

"How could he have known about my dreams?"

"I am as much in the dark as you are, son."

An early evening chill had settled upon them.

"Dad...I'm a little scared. I know the Holy Spirit is with me, that He will be my Comforter no matter what, but I'm just a kid still. I look at the future as I used to look at the darkness in my bedroom: no reason to be afraid, of course, and still the darkness seemed threatening in those days. When I think about the next month, the next year, maybe further ahead than that...you know, it's like that darkness is back but ten times worse. Dad, don't ever leave me. Promise me that, will you?"

"As though I were promising Christ Himself."

"Dad?

"Bend down so I can kiss you."

Kindred did as his son wanted.

"I love you very much," David whispered afterward into his ear.

Kindred knew then that nothing except death itself would ever separate them again, and then only for awhile.

FORTY-ONE

DAVID KINDRED WAS ALLOWED TO STAY AT THE
institution until his father's release.

Marquand had arranged quite a surprise that final day there. A military band greeted them as they went outside. And Kindred was awarded a special medal for helping to end the warfare between humans and Dwellers. Not only that, Kindred was put on the government payroll as a "special consultant": no actual work involved, but he was paid something loosely referred to as a "pension."

They decided to visit Nocales, which was nearby. The community had been built up quite a bit over the last year or so, the growth fueled in part by tourist interest in the spot where Klatu had been first spotted, a marker placed in front of the springs.

Soon after arriving, the two of them stood beside it. Only a handful of tourists remained in the springs.

"You were very close when it happened, Dad?" David whispered.

"Just a few miles away," Kindred replied.

He recalled that first meeting, Klatu's body against his own, a stranger fighting for his life as, a short while later, he would fight for Klatu's as well.

"Dad, you're crying," David said.

"Oh, yes, son. With these memories it could not be otherwise. And now Klatu's probably buried under tons of rock."

Suddenly they both heard another voice, quite loud.

"I thought it was you!"

The tall, distinguished black man who approached them had been standing on the other side of the marker at first.

"Forgive me, but I don't know what you're talking about," Kindred told him honestly.

"You do," the man insisted. "You do indeed!"

"But I don't."

"I owned a Dweller, you know. I bought him at a shopping mall, paid a lot of money."

Kindred was beginning to realize what it was all about.

"What happened, sir?"

"He committed suicide, which I have heard is an unusual act in itself for a Dweller...took a knife and plunged it into his chest. I arrived at the house before he died. I held him in my arms and he bled all over me."

Several seconds passed as he stood there, shaking with a sudden display of guilt.

"I've thought a hundred times since Nuran died," he said, "how convenient it was to have him around. He helped my wife and me with everything—cleaning the house, doing the gardening, emptying the litter trays of our cats, day in, day out, never a complaint from him. If he felt, for an instant, that somehow he hadn't pleased us, he would work twice as hard. I suspect I may even have taken advantage of that by occasionally feigning displeasure so that he would get even more done for us.

"And all during his time with us, his will to live must have been shriveling up and dying. How little I paid attention to *his* needs, apart from the obvious ones—having enough food to eat, time to sleep, the rest. How little interest I showed in the intimate thoughts of what must have been that remarkable mind of his."

He stopped for a second or two, holding his head at a slight angle, as though mentally chewing on some profound and troublesome reality.

"What *he* thought? Isn't that amazing, now when it is too late to help him? Nuran thought, analyzed, worried about the future. He had the potential of at least a measure of *humanity*, yet we treated him like an obedient, subservient pet. Oh, Rev. Kindred, he was capable of so much more.

"He had fallen one day in the cellar, broken his leg, and couldn't get back up the stairs. Nuran decided the only thing he could do was not simply wait there but crawl out a side door to our neighbors. They said that despite his pain, while he was waiting for the paramedics, he sat in front of them, humming a melody.

"There isn't anything he wouldn't have done for us. He would have sacrificed his life to save ours, if that had ever been necessary."

He started sobbing.

"Can you see what that would have meant for him? Rushing headlong into oblivion to spare us! But how much would we have been willing to give up for—"

His words choked into his throat.

"How can I ever live with that?" he just barely managed to add. "How can I?"
Kindred bent down beside him.

"You don't know why he took his own life. Can we *ever* hope to look inside and truly, truly understand the minds of any of the Dwellers, minds so much like ours, and yet so very different?"

"But *not* knowing is what tears me up inside. Did I, in some unaware moment, send a signal of indifference? Did he sense my self-centeredness?"

"I don't mean to sound simplistic, sir, but the answer is that you must cast all this upon *Christ's* shoulders. He has *promised* to take our burdens as His own yoke and to carry them in our stead."

"If only I could accept that," he said. "If only I could believe that God would treat me any better than the Dwellers."

"You must start by learning not to let this haunt you," Kindred added, looking at David out of the corner of his eye. "Truth can liberate you, or it can bury you. The choice is yours. Sir, I *know*. There was a time when I couldn't stand what I saw in the mirror each morning. It is only by God's grace that I am here today."

Later, after they had talked further, and Kindred got some sense of having helped him at least to a degree, the man left that spot. Then father and son lingered for a bit longer.

David was looking up toward the stars.

"Dad, why didn't you tell him that Nuran was actually human?"

"Because then his guilt would have been worse."

"I...I don't see what you mean."

"Because nothing he said proved to me whether or not he and Nuran *would* spend eternity together in heaven."

Kindred was sitting on the sand beside David.

"Klatu did so many wicked things, Dad. It's hard to think of his being anywhere but in hell. I mean, he killed maybe hundreds of folks. He ordered the killing of lots more than that."

"If Hitler had accepted Christ five minutes before he died, he would have gone to heaven despite the atrocities he generated."

"Stalin, too?"

"As difficult as that is to comprehend, based upon the Bible's record of divine promises, the answer has to be yes."

David was silent then.

Finally they started back toward their car.

"Dad," David said, after his father had helped him into the front seat, "how could someone who lost an entire family in a concentration camp ever accept a chance that they might meet Hitler in heaven?"

"I never said Hitler or any other evil monster like him is in heaven. But look at it like this. If a repentant Hitler were to be kept out of heaven, it would be necessary to deny you and me entrance as well."

"I don't understand, Dad."

"Because Christ's death would have been without purpose. Deny salvation to one individual out of countless millions, and you call God a liar."

David spoke little after they left Nocales. It was only after they checked into a motel on the way home that he told his father what was bothering him.

"Dad," David said as he sat up in bed, "I have trouble with what you said earlier."

Kindred was sitting on the edge of the bed.

"You mean about Hitler?"

"I know what he did was awful, Dad; yet I wasn't alive when he was murdering people. But kids my age have lost parents, brothers, sisters, friends because of the Dwellers; a few who died were *my* friends. How can God forgive all that?"

"I don't know, David."

"Dad, I gotta ask you this: If Klatu had been responsible for murdering Mom, would you have felt the same way?"

At first Kindred could not answer his son. In the back of his mind, gnawing at him, the same question had surfaced, and he had hoped not to have to deal with it.

"You're not answering me, Dad."

Finally Kindred leaned forward, taking his son's hands in his own.

"The sin nature part of me might tempt me to grab justice away from the courts, take a rifle, track him down and blow his brains out."

"But you said God forgives."

"I'm not God, David. I have the weakness of my sin nature. Murdering Klatu—"

"Not murder! You would have been executing him *for* murder!"

"It's murder, son, murder plain and simple. We mustn't play games with words. The unsaved world does that all the time."

"The unsaved world kills its criminals."

"And, David, that means *I* would have to die."

"You?"

"Because I would have skirted the *law* by going my own way. No judicial system could afford to look the other way."

218

Suddenly David was signaling his exasperation with that conversation.

"I don't agree, Dad. I could never forgive anyone who killed—"

Kindred's eyes filled with tears.

"Then, David, that means you never really have forgiven *me* after all."

"Dad, you didn't *murder* her. It was an accident."

His cheeks moist, words nearly choking in his throat, Kindred managed to say, "Klatu's life was an accident, son. He should never have been born. He should never have lost his own beloved wife. He—"

His face became red, sweaty. The room started to spin in his vision.

"Dad, Dad, please, you're going to make yourself sick, you—"

"*Listen to me!* Klatu should never have been by my side, saving my life. He should never have been driven nearly mad by *imagining* that he was an animal, with no immortal spirit."

Kindred's eyes became glassy from the emotional strain of the past months.

"Dad, I understand. Please, I do."

He struggled a bit to reach his father on the bed; when he did, David put his arms around him and hugged him very, very tightly.

"Forgive me, forgive me, forgive me."

"Oh, David, it was so *awful* at first in that cavern. And then so beautiful. To learn the truth. And now we have to somehow figure out a way to take that to a disbelieving world."

"I know, and I love you, and we'll get through it all."

"I feel so ashamed. Even now I still am weak and...and I can't give you all the answers you obviously need."

"Answers don't matter right now; I see that. If we're meant to have them, the Lord will show us."

David cupped his father's head in his hands.

"I love you," he said.

"And I love you. I could never feel otherwise, son. You're truly all I have. The greatest miracle the Lord has ever given to me is bringing you back, even though I deserve so little of His grace. David, David, I pray to God we never lose one another again."

They stayed up for hours after that. There were other nights when they would talk things over, when they would clean out any remaining wounds. But none was like that one; none came even close.

FORTY-TWO

THE PRESIDENT OF THE UNITED STATES DELIV-
ered perhaps the most startling nationally televised address in the history of the republic,
and it was relayed to dozens of countries around the world.

"Ladies and gentlemen," he said as he sat at his desk in the Oval Office, "some
most remarkable truths have been presented to me recently. I will get right to the
point, my fellow Americans. For what I will tell you is tantamount to a national
shame, but one that belongs to the rest of the world community as well."

He cleared his throat, then continued:

"Governments everywhere have been sanctioning, even participating in, wholesale
murder. We rightly recoil at the atrocities perpetrated by the Adolf Hitlers of history,
because he knew what he was doing, while it can be said that our recent crimes have
been out of ignorance and, therefore, far more excusable.

"But the end product of ignorance is still devastation, the devastation of an entire
branch of the human race!"

The president paused, letting those words sink in.

"The so-called Dwellers are not animals," he continued, altering his tone. "They
indeed are as human as the rest of us."

Nothing had leaked out apparently, for even the network TV cameramen could
be heard gasping in shock.

"Their bodies have been piled in mass graves everywhere, the stench of which now
becomes a collective accusing finger pointing at each and every one of us in government, in the armed services, on the streets of every town and city in this nation,
and in country after country around the world.

"Those who feel guilt share something with this elected leader. I go to my bed each night praying that God in His mercy will forgive us and not abandon us to the shame that we have brought upon ourselves.

"My friends, it is clear now that what we were doing to the Dwellers would have to be judged ghastly, even if we had not discovered the fact of their humanity, and they had indeed been the animals all of us originally supposed. But we told ourselves that because they were different in appearance, because they didn't *seem* human, therefore they *weren't* human, and animals were, after all, fully expendable.

"I have ordered the proper agencies to investigate the use of animal experimentation by private industries that are doing business with them. This government will no longer put money in the pockets of companies whose profits are carried on the backs of helpless creatures.

"Every inhumane act decreases our own humanity. Every teenager who finds it fun to set a cat or a dog on fire becomes more and more like the animal for which he or she has so little regard. Every woman who sanctions the use of fur cut from defenseless seals is no longer completely human, having given up a part of herself on the death-streaked ice of the Arctic wilderness.

"Animals were a gift from God. Each time we destroy one for so-called science or at the cosmetic labs to satisfy the endless vanity of insensitive millions, we throw their bloody, ravaged carcasses back in His face in an act of appalling blasphemy.

"I will leave you now, to your consciences, to those moments when you must look in the mirror, as I did this morning, and pray from a stricken soul, 'Father, Father, cleanse me, I beg Thee.'

"Good night, ladies and gentlemen...."

During the weeks after that address, attitudes and events began to change dramatically. Peace was established at last between humans and Dwellers.

The church service in New Jersey was going along nicely until a group of Dwellers entered and stood at the back just as a hymn was being sung. They were noticed immediately. A murmur broke out among the other worshippers.

Kindred slammed his palm down on the podium.

"I know you're uncomfortable," he said. "You've heard me preach about the Dwellers but you've never been this close to a group of them and under the same roof."

He could feel the disgust of the members of his congregation, could feel their loathing in almost palpable waves.

"Let us continue lifting our voices in song to our God," he said.

Haltingly they continued.

And then something remarkable happened. The hymn was four verses long. Kindred had the congregation sing only two. But after the organ had stopped and the others finished, there were yet some voices singing.

Everyone turned and looked at the Dwellers.

The group of a dozen or so continued with the remaining two verses, each word correct, the melody perfect.

Something else was remarkable.

Their faces.

"They seem so happy," someone whispered.

Finally an elderly man, using a cane to help him walk, stepped out into the aisle and walked toward the Dwellers.

He stood before them, reached out his hand and took the hand of one member of the group. Then they walked back down the aisle.

In a few seconds others did the same thing.

The final member of the congregation to do so was David Kindred, rolling his wheelchair up the aisle and returning to his seat with a new friend by his side.

Nevertheless, in the midst of slowly growing tranquility for humans and Dwellers alike, it became apparent that after so many centuries of survival these creatures were to be doomed by the events of just a few decades. The underground atomic and nuclear testing and the increased water and air pollution caused initially by the fallout and later by industrial wastes above ground were to prove genetic death blows beyond the curative power of the pills that were having wondrous effects within the larger human community on planet Earth. One by one, Dwellers started dying, unable to endure such human-made assaults.

Official statements through spokesmen in country after country claimed that Dweller numbers had decreased precipitously. Eventually only a handful apparently remained.

And then...but one.

FORTY-THREE

WHEN THE KINDREDS HAD RETURNED TO THE small town in New Jersey where they had lived together until Mary Kindred's death, Matthew Kindred had found that his old church had never signed on a permanent replacement for him but had been going through one interim pastor after another. The congregation didn't even have to vote him back in but simply listed him as away on extended leave of absence.

With startling normalcy, life came together for Kindred and his son, and they were able to come to grips with the death of a woman they both loved very deeply. Furthermore, the board of deacons had started a special fund designed to help finance spreading the truth about the Dwellers before they all perished.

Two years later....

Matthew and David Kindred were set to meet the last of the Dwellers. David had seen only Karuth and was excited about meeting another.

"Dad, are we really going to walk right up to him?" the boy asked, after the two of them landed at Tucson, Arizona, and were driving off toward a destination four hours ahead.

"We are," Kindred replied. "His name is Geran."

"That's a funny one, Dad."

Kindred was silent for a bit as he sat behind the steering wheel, the memories returning in a wave, flooding the synapses of his brain.

I'm dying....

Take this pill, Matthew Kindred, take it immediately.

The air was clean, pure, the feeling of it entering the lungs exhilarating, so much so that the group of three just stood there, momentarily, inhaling deeply, their eyes closed, their hearts beating faster....

A voice came from the darkness, quite gentle, quite old, of almost unfathomable wisdom, like that of a dozen Solomons....

They passed the hours during the drive in retrospection, alternating with the fellowship both had come to treasure. Their talks were a source of understandable blessing to Matthew Kindred, because David proved to be intelligent, sensitive and deeply loving.

Finally, in an isolated desert community, they approached a house with a high stuccoed wall around it and a wrought-iron gate at the front. The two of them got out of the car and went up to the gate. Kindred rang the bell recessed into the wall. A few seconds later, an Hispanic woman in her early thirties came out.

Kindred stood for a moment, looking at her, recognizing the woman almost immediately, amazed.

"My name is Rosita Alvarez...yes, the same one," she said. "It is amazing how the Lord works."

She smiled as she added, "Now my whole life is being spent tending to the last of their kind...after wanting all of them dead. And after I was almost killed myself."

She went on to tell them about being nursed back to health and how grateful she was that no charges were pressed.

"You told them that, if you survived, you wanted no charges against me," Rosita commented. "That kind of forgiveness forced a change in my life."

She smiled as she reached out and embraced Kindred warmly.

Then they all went inside the ranch-style house. The odor of cedarwood was apparent.

"After so many years living in caves, smelling nothing but damp old rock," Rosita explained, "Geran found the scent of cedar appealing. Soon after he opened his mouth with the request, the carpenters and others were being hired."

She paused, a frown on her forehead, and then: "Be patient, I must ask you gently. His mind is going, you know. He becomes frustrated very easily. He wants so much to be human and yet he never will. When he was younger and death didn't seem so near, he was better able to cope. But now...."

She shrugged her shoulders, a gesture of regret, then went to get Geran.

Kindred glanced about the room in which they were standing.

The style was unquestionably Western, with distressed wood beams across the ceiling, Indian-designed rugs on the floor, the furniture saddle leather, and numerous pieces of Western pottery and other knickknacks in evidence. The walls were paneled with thick planks of cedar.

Rosita returned to tell them that Geran was outside in his garden and wondered if they would please join him for a few minutes there.

Geran was bent over a straggly rose bush as they approached. He looked up, smiled, wiping his hands clean with a towel that Rosita handed him.

"I am so pleased to see you, Matthew Kindred, and your David. I meet very few famous ones these days."

"Famous?" Kindred asked, puzzled.

"You are not aware of how well-known you are?"

He hesitated, grappling with the present tense, knowing that all of his kind, except him, were dead.

"How well-known indeed," he continued. "You were from humankind but different. Our kind idolized you, wishing that they could be as you are, human, and yet not like others who hated us merely because we were of another race of beings."

Geran spoke without bitterness or sarcasm.

"Some, I think, became convinced that you were a special messenger sent from God to help us. But then we realized that this was not so, that though we would be able to leave the physical place we thought of as hell, we would never be able to enter the spiritual one called heaven, with or without your help. You lost any fragile hold on divinity very quickly, Matthew Kindred, but you became something else."

"What was that?"

"A friend."

As he had been talking, Geran was fingering one of the rose stems. A thorn pricked his pale skin, and he seemed unaware of this, even after a considerable stream of blood had begun to spurt out.

"Geran, Geran, look at what you have done!" Rosita exclaimed, rushing to his side with a cloth handkerchief she had taken out of a pocket in her dress.

He was quite embarrassed, a red blush all the more pronounced because of his innate paleness.

"Why don't we go inside, all of us, and sit down?" Rosita said, leading her charge back into the house before he could actually answer her.

A few minutes later they were sitting in the main room, sipping ice tea. David was looking at Geran with ill-concealed awe, this albino creature with the tufts of golden hair covering the visible part of his upper torso, wearing a pair of tattered dungarees and looking curiously like some ancient hippie.

"Forgive me if I stand," Geran said. "When I am sitting too long, these old muscles of mine become stiff, cramped. As I awaken each morning, it is, well, very, very difficult for me after spending a long night on my back, unmoving."

A lull. Awkward. No one quite sure of what to say next. Kindred's gaze picked out additional details about the room—little pieces of Dweller pottery and such among the Indian artifacts, a framed photograph of Klatu!

"Geran, how did you and your people regard Klatu?" the minister asked.

"Please, Matthew Kindred, you do not have to use the word *people* in order to be polite. We were never a *people*, not in the midst of our finest moments, whatever those might have been. We were a species perhaps, but not a people."

Geran bit his lower lip as he added, "Forgive the tone. You, above all humans, should never be addressed in that manner."

"But you were correct. It was a clumsy attempt to be—"

"Kind," Geran finished the sentence for him. "And I love you for it, Matthew Kindred."

He walked slowly over to the photo of Klatu.

"Klatu was to have been our deliverer. He was, many thought, our messiah. But then it is so very true that whatever God fashions, Satan endeavors to copy and to use that copy to blaspheme His holy name, to disrupt His divine plan."

Geran sighed, closing his eyes as his head tilted upward.

"He was dashing, aggressive, providing the rude awakening we needed from our naive outlook about life above ground. He wanted to take human society, rend it asunder and then rebuild. Some of us, a minority, toyed with the notion that he might be the Antichrist instead of our redeemer."

He turned to face the three humans sitting in front of him, hushed into silence by what he had said.

"I do not sound like an animal, do I?" he stated. "But the truth of the matter is that I do not *understand* very much of what I have just said. I know the words but so much of what I have learned is, in a way, the act of pronunciation, not perception."

Kindred stood then and walked up to him.

"You are *not* an animal, Geran," he said. "You *are* human. Why have you not accepted that wonderful truth? Your lack of understanding comes not from being an animal but rather from age. Many humans go through just what you are enduring now."

Geran looked at him without comprehension at first. Then he turned suddenly and was glancing out the window that overlooked his little garden.

"I've been very lucky with my roses, you know. Most are really healthy. I spend a great deal of time with them. I can give them life, you know. I can plant the seeds and watch them grow. That is a wonderful feeling for one as old as I am."

He suddenly started hugging himself as though a chill had gripped him with uncommon severity.

"Rosita?"

She stood and walked to his side.

"Rosita, my dear...."

"Yes, Geran?"

226

"Please, Rosita, hold me. I am very, very scared just now."

She patted him gently on the back and led him away to an adjacent room and shut the door behind her. A few minutes passed, and she reappeared.

"He's sleeping now, curled up in bed with a teddy bear," she told them.

"Rosita," Kindred asked in the gentlest tone of voice, "how long will it be?"

"A few weeks—probably not much more than that."

She was obviously fighting back some tears.

"I lost a dog once and I mourned for a long time, and yet there was never any question that I would survive. But now, with Geran, I wonder how I ever will. I love him very much."

She went over to a bookcase and pulled out a Bible.

"I read to him by the hour. He seems to understand—he really does. And yet I feel so useless, watching him die, frustrated that, even if he understood everything I was saying, he could not gain salvation, because he has no soul."

She faced Kindred.

"You were just being kind, weren't you, when you spoke to him like that?"

"To be merely kind in that case would have been telling a lie. And God would never honor that. I told the truth."

Rosita tilted her head slightly.

"I heard the president, as did so many millions of others."

"But you didn't believe him?"

"How many politicians have been truthful over the past ten years? So many want to believe him, I know, but they distrust the government much more today than a generation ago."

Still clutching the red leather-bound Bible in one hand, she wiped her eyes with the other.

"How do I let go, Rev. Kindred? Please tell me. When I lost my mother, then my father and next my husband, I was almost destroyed. But I was able to hold on, because they were Christians, and we could look forward to a reunion in heaven. But when Geran takes his last breath, he is gone forever, if you are mistaken in what you believe. That would mean I...I'd never see him again. How, sir, could I ever survive that?"

She walked up to him and fell, sobbing, into his arms. There was little he could say. Nothing in the history of the Christian church, nothing in the lives of countless millions of clergymen over the years, nothing at all was available to help him— no precedents, no convenient words of wisdom. Over the years so many institutions had shown themselves to be riddled with satanically inspired scandal. It was not difficult to see why various shades of cynicism were running rampant.

He glanced over her shoulder. A sound.

Rosita heard it, too, straightening up, cocking her head.

Abide with me, fast falls the evening tide....

From Geran's room, scarcely audible.

The darkness deepens....

Rosita and Kindred approached as quietly as they knew how.

Hold Thou Thy cross before my closing eyes...

Rosita stifled a sob.

...and point me to the skies.

Rosita opened the door slowly. Geran was still in bed, a teddy bear at his side. His arms were stretched outward, the palms held up. She walked over to his form, which was quite still, and she saw that he was scarcely breathing.

He turned to his friend and said, weakly, "What...does...it...mean when...I hear...the music of...trumpets before...before...I die? Is that...good, Rosita? Can you...tell me if it's...good?"

Before she could try to answer, his head tilted toward Kindred, his left eye winking just once, as a smile crossed his face, and then both eyes closed, his arms still reaching upward.

Rosita turned to Kindred.

"Is he...gone? Please tell me if he's gone."

Kindred leaned over Geran's body, lifting first one arm and pressing it gently back against the bed, followed by the other.

Kindred nodded reluctantly, tears streaming down his own cheeks.

Rosita bent down and kissed Geran on the forehead, noticing how cold he had become so quickly.

"Good-bye," she said, her voice shaky. "Good-bye, dear, dear...friend."

She turned to Kindred.

"The angels were welcoming him, weren't they?" she whispered. "Oh, God, I believe You now. I believe You—praise Jesus, I do!"

GERAN WAS TO BE BURIED IN AN UNDISCLOSED spot on the outskirts of Washington, D.C.

As Kindred sat beside his son on the jetliner taking them to the capital, he thought of the past couple of years. These had begun as a part of the continuing nightmare that had engulfed his life but was now close to termination with the winding down of another tragedy, the death of the last Dweller alive anywhere.

Kindred's celebrity status had preceded him. He spoke with a surgeon, another minister, a nurse, others. Some had suffered terribly as a result of the conflict. Amazingly, few were bitter, blaming it on what humankind had done, not the Dwellers.

"They fought back," said a native American named Flowing Stream. "My people did that a century ago and lost. We have had a great deal of empathy for the Dwellers, you know.

"But at least now many of us are prospering. That is what makes the story of the Dwellers all the more tragic. They are gone, Rev. Kindred. There can never be an opportunity for redress. The Japanese got it during the late 1980s. The blacks have been getting it for a long time. Chavez crusaded for the Latinos and won step-by-step. Even then his victories may have been used for propaganda by the wrong political viewpoints. My people have made enormous strides. But not so for the Dwellers. That is sad, sir, very, very sad indeed."

Kindred could not disagree.

The plane landed at Dulles International. Reporters and photographers were waiting at the gate. Kindred answered their questions, and then David and he were whisked away to a hotel in the center of Washington, D.C.

They spent the next several hours talking about the life they had together finally.

GENERAL MARQUAND'S VOICE WAS CRISP-sounding over the telephone line.

"Tonight," he said. "The route is a closely guarded secret."

"Then I don't want to know," Kindred offered.

"I didn't intend to tell you. It's got to be a total blackout—no exceptions."

...a total blackout.

Kindred turned, looked at David.

"You could stay behind, son," he said.

"I've stayed behind too long now, Dad," David replied. "After that time with Geran, I want to be by your side when we say good-bye."

...when we say good-bye.

He had been saying good-bye more than he cared to acknowledge: Miath, Klatu, Geran. Creatures who had come into his life and by whom he had been deeply touched. And now, after this one, they all would be gone, as though they had never existed, because there was nothing left to signify that they ever had.

The ancient Greeks had their legacy in the Parthenon and other buildings and in their sculpture and writings. The Mayans, Aztecs and Incas left their jungle-shrouded ruins. Others left various scattered pieces of what once had been vibrant civilizations.

But not the Dwellers. They built no colossal structures with pillars and high ceilings, sweeping and majestic; they left no road system, no bridges, no ancient tombs taking twenty years and thousands of workers to build. Their homes were caverns; their local roads were tunnels; their long-distance highways were a vast network through the oceans of the world; their libraries had been living groups of selected members of their kind, with no scrolls nor leather-bound volumes.

Within an hour a black sedan had pulled up in front of the hotel. The Kindreds were waiting in the lobby when the plainclothes FBI agent approached them.

"Rev. Matthew Kindred?" the man asked. "And David Kindred?"

Both nodded.

"Follow me, please."

David's wheelchair was folded up and put in the trunk after he was helped into the back seat of the car.

Seconds later they were whisked off, and within minutes they had pulled down an alley next to a nondescript two-story building on a side street in the midst of the capital. A single light above a door in the back provided illumination.

David's eyes widened as he was wheeled inside.

On the doors leading to offices on the first floor were the names of different departments in what appeared to be a secret FBI enclave: Domestic Terrorist Activities, Drug Interdiction, a number of others.

Geran's body was in the morgue section in the basement. They took the only elevator in the building and then went down a long corridor to a room at the end.

Inside were file-cabinet-like bins, only much wider and deeper. One of the agents accompanying them pulled out a particular bin. Geran seemed even more pale than usual. Kindred went up to the metal drawer in which his body rested. He reached out and touched the left shoulder, pulling back a bit but then scolding himself for doing so since he had presided over so many funerals in the past. Yet this body, this funeral, this farewell was different from all the others, including Mary's, distinctive by its sheer, gaping extinction of an entire race.

...a total blackout.

Everyone around Matthew and David Kindred seemed uptight, furtiveness apparent in the tone of their voices, the language of their bodies.

From what the television news programs had indicated, terrorist activity in the United States had increased dramatically during the time of turmoil involving the Dwellers, with different groups seizing the opportunities offered by the widespread chaos. More common than ever were the acts of train sabotage, arson, bombings, and perhaps the most insidious of all, contamination of drug supplies, with addicts dying at an accelerating rate.

Then in came Marquand, with the president of the United States and several Secret Service agents. Kindred gulped several times, and David's mouth dropped open before he quickly closed it in embarrassment.

"I am here," the president spoke, anticipating the questions of those surprised by his presence, "because I wasn't involved early enough in the Dwellers' tragedy to make a difference. And I will carry that guilt to my own grave. But here, despite

231

the element of danger, or perhaps because of it, I can make a statement."

...despite the element of danger.

Kindred was aware of the need for secrecy, but the president's manner made everything seem more chilling. He fought the sudden compulsion to have David sent back to the hotel.

In a moment of almost inexplicable suddenness, they were hurried out of the morgue. Geran's body was to be put into a van followed by the car carrying the president, Marquand, Matthew and David Kindred, and a Secret Service agent besides the one who was the driver. Another unmarked sedan followed, this one filled with five agents. In addition to all that, the police were alerted and were roving the vicinity in greater numbers than usual.

The ride through the capital, though shrouded by night, was nevertheless an eye-opener for the Kindreds. Store windows had been shattered virtually in every block. Several cars obviously had been ablaze, their husks dark and twisted. One building had been partially destroyed, perhaps by grenades. And much more— the after-effects of terrorist activity. Everywhere there were army trucks, police cars, men in uniform.

"It is a pity," commented the president, "that human nature makes all this caution mandatory."

Kindred agreed.

"We may be upset," the minister said, "but if we dig deep into the Bible, we aren't going to be surprised."

The president was sitting to the right of Kindred with David in the middle. Kindred studied him briefly.

A tall man, he was in his mid-sixties but looked older. The past year or so was enough to rob even the strongest individual of vitality, putting a decade of wear and tear on the body and showing up on the face with increased wrinkles, heavy circles under the eyes, a certain paleness to the skin, a weariness of countenance.

"What are you afraid could happen?" Kindred finally asked.

"We have two groups that hate the Dwellers. One is a white supremist organization that views them as even worse than blacks. The other is an Islamic fundamentalist faction convinced that the Dwellers are scientifically mutated secret agents of a satanic Western world, a biologically generated fifth-column creation that will be used against them all over the world. They don't believe that Geran is dead, and they don't think he's the last of his kind."

The president turned to Kindred.

"But that isn't all, Rev. Kindred. A secret Soviet saboteur cadre was sent to the

232

United States during the worst of the Dwellers' turmoil. They never proved very effective at the time. However, we have reason to suspect that to save face they would try to take advantage of any 'war' involving the other two; indeed, they would attempt to precipitate one.''

"But how?"

"By getting double agents involved with both. Once that happens, the rest is fairly easy. The fanatics become chess pieces, moved about at the whim of Moscow.''

...and He turned them over to a reprobate mind.

Kindred thought the depravity of humanity would never take him by surprise, especially after the past couple of years. But he found it truly startling that hatred toward the Dwellers would continue, becoming just another part of the game being played between white supremists, Islamic fundamentalists and Soviet saboteur-spies!

"Where have you decided to bury Geran?" Kindred asked.

The president didn't answer at first. Then he said: "You deserve to know despite the blackout.''

"Thank you, Mr. President.''

"We are not going to bury him.''

"*What?*"

"This Geran, the last of the Dwellers, is not dead.''

Geran...is not dead.

"But, Mr. President—"

"I know what you are going to say: that you saw him die yourself. And then, as the rest of us, you viewed his body in a secret morgue somewhere in the nation's capital.''

"That's right. I—"

"And your next question is why? Why this elaborate hoax?"

Kindred was so stunned by then that he had run out of words and could only nod.

"Because Geran *isn't* the only remaining Dweller. The Muslims are correct, you see. But it is only a *suspicion* on their part. They're not sure. So they're looking for signs. We've been doing everything we can to convince them that Geran is gone and that his race is extinct. Your emotional statements to the media were convincing, because what you were saying you believed to be quite true.''

"This charade taking place at present," interpolated Marquand, "is to show them that Geran is being buried in an isolated spot under the strictest secrecy—let me rephrase that, under what they *perceive* to be the strictest secrecy. It has sprung just one small leak, a leak to both groups to convince them that they are really quite clever, clever enough to crack our intelligence operations! And to observe the burial for themselves!"

"But I saw him die!"

"You saw him *appear* to die," Marquand corrected the minister. "That is the effect we wanted."

"How many other Dwellers are there, General Marquand?"

"Only a small colony."

"Where, sir?"

"That *is* the problem."

"How do you mean?"

Marquand cleared his throat nervously. "Right here on the outskirts of Washington, D.C.—the most spy-infested, bugged, scrutinized city in the nation!"

Kindred understood fully why there was such a big "production" for what at first seemed a relatively small matter.

"We will 'bury' Geran in an historic old cemetery...located over a series of tunnels leading deep within the earth."

"So you will be digging not only his grave but also—"

"—a direct connection to that tunnel network."

"But how did you know?"

"Geran told us. That's why we had to hurry you out of the morgue. He regained consciousness just two or three minutes later."

Kindred lapsed into silence.

A colony of the Dwellers yet alive!

Kindred glanced at his son. What heavy revelations for a young boy to over-hear!

Several more minutes passed. They had left the boundaries of the capital and were now out in the countryside.

"My hope," stated the president, breaking the silence, "is that some day all this subterfuge will be unnecessary and that we can coexist with the Dwellers and maybe learn from one another."

"We coexist even with animals, Mr. President," Kindred agreed. "Jane Goodall proved that with the apes. The Adamsons did so with lions. And these are just so-called brute beasts. The Dwellers are human like the rest of us and more so than some. We can teach one another a great deal if, ironically, *our* human nature doesn't get in the way."

"But could it be, Rev. Kindred, that due to their beginnings they will never cease to have just that little bit of Satan within them? My only worry, despite my hope to the contrary, is that they will always be a time bomb, waiting there beneath the surface of the earth, ready to explode again when they have sufficiently replenished their numbers."

Kindred had no answer. He sank back into reverie, fragments of memories surfacing.

The creature's head, tiny in relation to her body but large by any other yardstick, poked up through the water, and she let out a low sound that was a combination of pig's grunt and cat's purr....

Kindred smiled at the recollection. But there were other snatches, moments coming to the surface of his mind.

The air was cool, pure, the feeling of it entering their lungs exhilarating, so much so that the group of three just stood there momentarily, inhaling deeply, their eyes closed, their hearts beating faster and faster as the air's effects radiated through their bodies, nerves atingle with the joy of it, even the ecstasy, leaving them without words, only the sensations mattering....

Klatu and Miath were both gone, Kindred reminded himself sadly, victims of the rampant spirit of the age and pawns in the awful designs perpetrated by their own....

...an indispensable link with the past...in a kind of ancestral chain...imbued with a whole chunk of history, one volume in a living encyclopedia of past generations.

Still wrapped in thoughts of those days when the next few hours seemed always to promise yet another intriguing discovery, Kindred at first was only dimly aware that they were pulling up in front of the old cemetery.

Everything would be conducted to foster the illusion of a secretive burial service, including the eulogy, a farewell prayer, heads bowed, the rest. Watching eyes and listening ears had to believe in the *authenticity* of what was happening.

As the casket was being carried to the gravesite, Kindred noticed just how old the place was, with markers from as far back as 1710! And none more recent than 1859.

Kindred delivered the eulogy.

"Often those who love their pet dogs or cats or birds or other animals are criticized for paying too much attention to the process of letting go when that pet dies. *He was only an animal.* Those are well-worn words of rebuke. And while physically and certainly spiritually that dog, that cat, that bird was indeed nothing more than an animal, the emotional links go far deeper. A beloved pet is truly part of any family, a genuine member, albeit not human. When he dies, since the loss is permanent, and not guaranteed the Christian's hope of restoration, that pet's loss is deeply, deeply felt.

"How much more tragic it seemed at one point for those who grew close to any of the Dwellers! They were really the offshoots of a satanic experiment gone amok. Yet we all are creatures of God and the devil, our sin natures torn between two masters."

"Until recently the Dwellers never gave in to satanic domination. They fought against Lucifer all through the many, many, many centuries since that first creation. It is ironic that we, as human beings created directly by almighty God, became Satan's instruments in his attempt to redirect the instincts of the Dwellers! Our actions were his weapons.

"And now we bury Geran, who is the last remaining—"

Kindred stopped in mid-sentence. To say that Geran was the last of the Dwellers would be a lie. How could he, a minister—or for that matter, any Christian—lie?

Seconds passed....

Marquand took him to one side.

"What is wrong?"

Kindred told him.

"Matthew, I understand your concern, but if we have those who are looking at this rite for some evidence that Geran really is being buried, anything we do out of the ordinary can only make them suspicious."

"But God forbids lying."

"Yet doesn't He forgive our sins?"

"Yes, but—"

"Then please sin just this one time and later beg Him for forgiveness."

Marquand wasn't being flippant. What he said had some logic. And yet—

The exploding grenade rendered all such considerations moot. It landed only a foot or two from Geran's casket. The blast tore open the wood and spilled the body onto the grass. Geran was injured but alive.

A shout from a small forest of trees nearby was followed by a dozen men running, firing with machine guns at the group in the cemetery. Secret Service agents pulled their own weapons and returned the shots.

The president was hit in the shoulder. One of the attackers took a direct aim at Kindred. David, seeing this, put his wheelchair into high gear and entered the line of fire. The burst meant for his father caught David instead, flinging him out of the wheelchair and rolling him over and over down an embankment at the edge of the gravesite, the chair following him.

Kindred screamed madly, racing toward the man who had shot his son.

"Fall down!" shouted Marquand.

Kindred did this instinctively. Out of the corner of his eye he saw Marquand mow the attacker down with a machine gun.

Less than two minutes after chaos had broken loose, it was over.

Eight of the attackers were dead. Four had fled. Three Secret Service agents were dead. The president's wound was not serious.

"David!" Kindred screamed as he got to his feet.

He raced to the embankment and over the edge. The wheelchair was lying on its side, wheels still revolving.

In the background he heard a flurry of words....

"Attacks have commenced in the capital itself."

"We're cut off."

"Which group is responsible?"

"Can't tell as yet. Right now let's say they all are."

"But how do we get back?"

"They're sending an army helicopter."

David was lying on his side, moaning.

"Son, son," Kindred said as he sank down on the grass and held his son's body in his arms.

"Dad...I...do...love...you," David said in gasps.

"You never have to prove that. God knows you don't."

David's eyes widened.

"Dad—look!"

Kindred turned and saw Geran standing over them, blood trickling down his right shoulder.

"Give me your son," the Dweller said, already bending down to take David's body.

"No!" Kindred protested frantically. "I need to get him to a hospital. You can't—"

"Give me your son!"

Geran was picking up David, despite his own wound. Without saying anything further, he carried the body down the rest of the embankment and approached something that Kindred at first couldn't quite discern in the darkness. Then, squinting his eyes, he thought he picked out the outlines of a small cave entrance, largely covered by undergrowth.

Kindred raised his eyes to the dark sky and shouted, "Oh, Lord, what have I done!"

Out of the corner of his right eye, he saw a Secret Service agent take aim; before Kindred could stop him, the agent had shot Geran in the back. Amazingly, dying as he undoubtedly was then, he was still able to take David into the cave.

Kindred ran quickly up to the mouth; only a few seconds had passed, but by then Geran and David had already disappeared into the thick darkness inside.

"I only saw that thing abducting your son," the agent said as Kindred emerged outside. "What was I to do?"

"But why do you think I wasn't running after them?"

"You'd trust that...that creature with your son's life?"

"More than I trust a great many humans at this point."

"I would never have done that, sir."

"But you were supposed to protect Geran."

"Only if he seemed non-threatening. For Pete's sake, I saw him grab your son and—"

Kindred walked away in disgust, standing a dozen or so yards to one side, his body shaking with anger and apprehension and other emotions, underlined by a chilly foreboding that drenched him in heavy beads of perspiration.

The corruption of a city! A people!

He jumped as a hand rested on his shoulder.

Marquand.

"The helicopter's here. We must go back now."

"But my son, David, I've got to wait and—"

"We must go *immediately*. All of us. I cannot simply leave you here. I happen to be responsible for your survival."

Kindred understood and reluctantly joined the others.

As the helicopter approached Washington, he could see fires here and there, other split-second bursts of white or yellowish light that probably came from hand-held Stinger-type missile launchers.

Suddenly, at the Washington monument, there was an explosion so severe that the force of it shook the helicopter as though it had been grabbed by an unexpected tornado. The monument ripped loose from its base and toppled over into hundreds of pieces, shaking the earth beneath.

"And they worry about nuclear war!" Kindred heard one of the Secret Service agents exclaim.

"But how could this have come about?" Kindred asked out loud of no one in particular.

"You mean, how could we be prepared for an attack from without, with our missiles trained on Moscow, and yet be so vulnerable from within?"

The voice was Marquand's.

"Yes, sir, that's what I mean," Kindred responded.

"Because we just aren't as smart, as well-organized, as vigilant as we think we are."

Kindred was about to say something else when he spotted a burst of light, then a cylinder-shape coming through the darkness, headed directly for the helicopter.

"Attack! Attack!" the pilot screamed.

He launched a dummy missile from the belly of the copter, a device designed not to counterattack but to act as a heated decoy to fool the oncoming missile. But there hadn't been enough warning; the decoy only partially succeeded. The missile exploded some distance away from the copter as it hit the decoy, but the explosion damaged the rotor blades. The copter was heading straight for the ground. Its fall was cushioned a bit as it hit some trees near the Potomac. But it still landed with devastating impact.

Kindred was thrown from the copter onto his left arm, breaking it. Two of the Secret Service agents helped the president out. As Marquand disembarked, the copter burst into flames, and his clothes caught fire. Taking off his street jacket, one of the agents dashed over to Marquand, beating out the flames.

Kindred painfully stumbled over to the general and sat down on the grass next to him.

"Matthew, my dear friend," Marquand said. "The world is going mad around us."

He coughed up some blood.

"I have to tell you something. I have to tell you that we discovered a shadow government within the federal bureaucracy."

"What was their purpose?" Kindred asked.

"To continue the experiments on the Dwellers."

"What?"

"Yes, Matthew, it's true."

His eyes were rolling from side to side.

"Klatu and the others were just striking back in self-defense," Marquand added, "though going overboard in the process."

His voice was nearly gone.

"Go, my friend," Marquand said, "and survive as best you can."

Kindred took his hand, held it for a moment, then placed it gently back on the grass. Then he left that spot as quickly as he could, wandering into the city.

Chaos had spread throughout Washington.

People were battling hand-to-hand in the streets.

I let my son be taken from me without a whimper, Kindred thought, his temple pounding. *And I don't even know where they are keeping him. I wander through this hell, and he is nowhere around. I can do nothing. I just gave him up. And now I am alone, alone, alone.*

Looters were taking stereos and computers and other appliances.

His arm was hurting more and more. He could barely stand because of the pain. But his mind was so very clear, a sense of seeing less and less through a glass darkly.

Corruption indeed was everywhere, inside and outside of government. It wasn't being unpatriotic to recognize that if so many of those at the top were guilty of various crimes, the signals thus sent to every business, every school, every home had to have the most negative of ramifications.

He suddenly felt as dirty inside as many of those running past him looked on the outside.

America—the pilgrim's pride!

But more than just in the United States, human nature was hooked on works of darkness everywhere—abortion, homosexuality, rape, drugs—all came out of the same hellish imaginations, the reprobate minds foretold in God's Word.

Kindred was very weary indeed. He sank down on the bare asphalt of a street he could not name in a city gone mad.

Oh, Lord, bring some sanity back to all this. Give me some reason to go on living....

And then he lost consciousness.

There was no way of knowing, when he awoke, exactly how much time had passed. It must have been several hours, for he could see the first hints of dawn. But beyond that....

He stood and continued walking, stumbling, picking himself up, numbly turning a corner, down one street, then another, overhead helicopters, spotlights transfixing this running man or that banded group.

"Matthew Kindred! Stop!"

The copter was directly above the minister, catching him in its beam.

He did not stop but ducked painfully to one side.

At first he didn't notice the manhole cover a few feet away, didn't notice it moving, noticed nothing, in fact, but the turmoil inside himself, the ache of fear.

Then he saw it, saw the white, golden-hair-covered hand push the round piece of metal to one side. A Dweller poked his head above the level of the street, noticing the minister immediately.

"Matthew Kindred! We have been searching everywhere. Matthew Kindred...your son."

David showed himself then.

"Dad! Dad! Those pills. Other things. They healed my wound. I still can't walk, but I'm alive!"

Kindred left the shadows, ignoring the copter, and raced to his son. A shot rang out. Kindred felt a terrible jolt of pain through his entire body. He fell against the asphalt.

"He's not dead, Abdul," said one of the two men in the copter.

"He will be now," added his comrade.

"Hurry. Use your American weapon. Make everyone think the Americans themselves committed the crime."

"And then we get out of here—fast!"

Three Dwellers had emerged from the manhole and were pulling Kindred's body along with them, the minister drifting in and out of consciousness.

"Now, Abdul, now!"

Suddenly the copter lurched to one side and burst into flame, slamming into an apartment building. Kindred and the Dwellers were thrown to the ground. Seconds before a wave of blackness claimed him, Kindred saw a fourth Dweller drop the rocket launcher he had found abandoned on the street and used an instant earlier against the copter.

ONCE AGAIN MATTHEW KINDRED FOUND HIM-
self in Dweller hands fighting for his life. This time his son also sat by his side, tears
streaming down his cheeks.

"God won't let you die," David kept saying over and over again. "God won't
let you die."

Days were to pass, he was told later. Once two bullets had been dug out of him,
and Dweller pills had been stuffed into him, and lotions applied to the wounds, he
came in and out of a feverish state, mumbling mostly incoherently. He reached for
his son's hand, found it and held it as though it had become a life raft. Floating
as he was on an open sea of great turbulence, that hand, that raft, was all that he
had left. Without it there was nothing.

But finally the journey ended. He had gone to the edge of death but not quite
over, and he opened his eyes and could see without delusion.

"David," he spoke weakly, "my son."

"Dad," the boy hugged him gently, mindful of his father's state. "I love you
so very much."

Kindred could see that they were no longer in the sewer area but back in an
underground cavern.

"How many are left?" he would ask later of the Dweller who identified himself
as Zurth.

"A handful, Matthew Kindred," came the reply. "And all are males. We will
never be able to extend our race."

Kindred was introduced to the half-dozen other Dwellers. All were quite old. It
had been an ordeal for them to climb to the surface and try to find him there in

242

Washington, then to go back down again, taking his unconscious body with them.

"But we love you," Zurth said. "We love you, because you do not hate or fear us."

In that one instant Zurth seemed not so much Dweller, but a more customary, everyday sort of creature befriended in kindness by a man and attempting to show its gratitude, as a cat would rub against his leg or a dog leap up and lick him on the face.

What Zurth did was reach out and hug him. One by one the other Dwellers did the same thing.

A few days later, after fully recovering, Kindred was approached by Zurth.

"My friend," the Dweller said, "I have something to show you. Do you feel like walking a bit?"

Kindred nodded.

So they walked together down one of the natural tunnels and into a small alcove.

Kindred stopped short.

Someone was sitting there, his back to them, his head bowed.

Kindred walked up to him, touched his shoulder.

The figure turned around.

"Clark!"

Marquand had changed, though: his face haggard-looking, his clothes hanging on a tired and bony frame.

"They rescued me, Matthew," he said. "I didn't want to see you until you were back on your feet, until I could clear my own head and talk with you."

Kindred sat next to his friend on a long, flat rock. Zurth discreetly left the alcove.

"I gave you some startling information not so very long ago," Marquand began. "Not all of it made sense, I suspect. There were gaps. I thought I was dying. Everything came in a rush."

"It doesn't matter now, Clark. I'm grateful to God that you're alive."

"Thank you for that, Matthew. But I think it is necessary that you know that the president and I were, for the longest period, *unaware* of what was going on. It might seem hard to believe that the most powerful man on earth can have the wool pulled over his eyes. But it's true; it's very true.

"When we found out, we discovered that the influence of those using the Dwellers in their experiments had spread so far and so deeply that exorcising it completely would have been quite impossible."

"You couldn't know with certainty whom you could trust!"

"That's right. But finding out that they existed and what their motives were turned out to be only part of the shocking truth we uncovered. Matthew, did you ever, ever realize how many practicing satanists are entrenched within the U.S. government?"

"I read reports at one time. These came at a point in my life when—"

"I understand, my friend," Marquand interrupted politely. "Well, those reports were true. Hundreds of them, at every level. The devil's puppets working like spiritual termites at the foundation of our nation. Matthew, he never gives up. While the Lord will be victorious in the end, I can say that the next few years will literally be hell for the United States and the rest of the world."

He had started trembling a bit and then stopped talking momentarily, as he steadied himself.

"But what caused that attack on us? Those guys were supposed to be tricked into thinking that the burial was for real."

"It began, I suppose, not to smell right to them, as the expression goes. They could sense something wrong, something very wrong."

Suddenly Marquand, once the hardened military professional, became quite distraught as memories assaulted him.

He saw someone he had known, someone he thought he could trust, someone who had appeared altogether human. He saw that man performing an act with one of the Dwellers, an act so ghastly, so unnatural, so evil, that he would never forget it, would never be able to carve it from his mind and throw it away.

"It wasn't intercourse, Matthew. It went far beyond that. It was an attempt to transfer consciousness, to transfer an entire *self* from one body to another."

The Dweller, partially conscious, was screaming, its cries ripping through Marquand's brain like a buzz saw. Other "humans" were standing around, watching, hoping that the experiment would move that much closer to success.

"I had them all executed, Matthew," Marquand said, his eyes wild. "I told my men to open fire, and they did, and one by one those monsters cloaked in human skin fell, cursing us. One of them stumbled toward me, Matthew, hatred in his eyes, hissing sounds coming from between his lips. He dropped at my feet and reached out and grabbed my ankle. I had to shoot him again and again. It wasn't murder, Matthew, God knows it wasn't murder. I...I...."

He went over to the side of the Dweller, who was still alive.

"Please, please forgive me," he said, cradling the old head in his lap.

The Dweller looked up at him.

"No, no," the creature said earnestly. "Please forgive us. Please forgive us for being born."

The Dweller died then, but not violently, the head turned toward him, one hand reaching up partway to his own face and then dropping back to the floor, motionless.

"I knew we had to do everything possible to take as many Dwellers as we could out of their hands and to prevent the capture of others. Geran became a symbol of all that we were trying to do."

"So the fact that he was supposed to be the last Dweller—even that was a charade?"

"No, we honestly thought that was true, at least in the United States. We had no idea others were still alive, still here in their age-old home."

Marquand leaned forward.

"Matthew, if those in the shadow government find out that there are other Dwellers yet alive, these...these poor people will be hunted down mercilessly and subjected to a fate exceeded in grotesqueness only by damnation itself."

Marquand became animated then, his attitude distinctly changing.

"But that is where I can help perhaps a little, perhaps more than that."

"What do you mean, Clark?" Kindred asked, though he really did guess what his friend was about to say.

"More than thirty years in the military, Matthew! On the battlefields of Korea and Vietnam. At the Pentagon. I *could* help. And..."

He spoke a bit more conspiratorily.

"...I know others who would join me."

He smiled slightly then.

"There's something else, Matthew."

"What's that?"

"I think I'll be able to find Klatu."

Kindred swallowed quickly several times.

"Where do you think he is, Clark?"

"With a group of nuns, Matthew...*with a group of nuns!*"

The smile became broader.

"They're somewhere in South America, near some tributary of the Amazon. The nuns have been so isolated from the world that little of the chaos has affected them. From what I hear, Klatu told them virtually everything. He and they are not only working with the natives, a group linked genetically to the Aucas, but a number of other Dwellers have been adopted into the tribe!"

Kindred sat back, taking it all in.

Klatu wasn't killed underground after all. That fragile hope of his hadn't been so foolish.

"Matthew?" Marquand's voice cut into his momentary thoughts.

"Yes?"

"Mother Veronica is, I hear, with them as well."

Klatu survived. So did that dear, dear lady!

"I pray that we meet up someday," Kindred sighed.

"I feel certain they wish the same."

In the weeks and months to follow, Marquand would recruit others to help, those who were fleeing the government and the onrushing takeover by the satanists and their puppets. But they would not remain in the Washington area. Dwellers were to be found elsewhere. The few who stayed did so because of age and health, not able to make any long journeys. One by one they died....

Kindred and his son would spend their time traveling the tunnel system, David transported easily by a stretcher-like contraption that allowed the boy to be pulled along after his father.

David was never able to meet Nessie; the Dwellers heard rumors that the ancient creature had finally died of pollution, its mammoth carcass rotting away somewhere on the ocean bottom.

Eventually the Dwellers underground in the Washington area were gone. Standing before each body, each time, Kindred said a brief eulogy and then buried the pathetic creature.

Zurth was the last to go.

"Would...you...do...one...favor for me, Matthew...Kindred?"

"Of course, my friend, my dear friend."

"Take me up...there and let...me sniff...the clear air...one more time."

Kindred nodded, unable to speak.

"And bury me under the heavens...please."

They happened to be not far from the surface at that point. And Zurth's weight had dropped to under a hundred pounds—not much to carry. First Kindred took David up and sat him on a soft pile of moss, and then he came for Zurth.

They were in a clearing in the midst of a forest.

"Listen to those hooting sounds," Zurth remarked. "Birds, aren't they?"

"Yes," Kindred told him. "Two or three owls, I suspect."

"I've never before heard the sound of an owl, Matthew Kindred. How strangely beautiful...."

It was night. Zurth could look up at the stars so plentiful in the clear, clear sky.

"It is suddenly so cold. The moon sheds no warmth."

He turned to Kindred.

"Please, will you lift me up a bit?"

Kindred took Zurth gently in his arms and did what the Dweller had asked.

"No, I want to stand as straight as bent old bones will allow. Please help me stand fully."

And that Kindred did.

"To stand like a man...to die like an animal," Zurth mused.

Then a final bit of strength returned to Zurth for one fleeting moment. His body straightened, his shoulders arched back, and he lifted both hands to the heavens.

"I cannot give back to You a spirit that I do not possess. But, please, O God, please take from me, now in this final moment, the shame of a life that was so very wrong."

He turned his head and his cheek touched Kindred's own.

"Those reports about us being human after all. How wonderful it *would* be to believe them. But I cannot, beloved Matthew Kindred."

"Zurth, you *are* human. You *can* believe what you've heard. On my honor, Zurth, on my honor."

Suddenly Zurth's eyes widened, his mouth dropping open; and he was gone an instant later, his body dropping to the soft moss beneath him, on his back, his head turned to one side.

Kindred buried Zurth less than half an hour later. He and his son joined hands by the gravesite, and then they were gone from that place.

In the days to follow, they did little more than talk, as much about the past as the future. They ate as best they could, knowing that it would take a long, long time for them to become proficient at surviving in such a basic state.

It was about a week later, at camp beside a lake filled with fish, a ready source of food for as long as they wanted, that they noticed someone else in the vicinity, glimpsing him in the afternoon that day as they had prepared a fire and were cooking some bass.

The figure was on the opposite shore of the lake.

"Dad, look!" David said. "He's young, not much older than I am maybe."

Kindred squinted his eyes, then agreed.

"He's just looking at us," David added.

As he said that, the other boy pulled out something that had had a cover of underbrush hiding it.

"Dad, a raft of some sort!"

And that it was. The boy dragged it to the edge of the water and managed to push it far enough out that it floated free. He climbed onto it, and using makeshift oars fashioned out of bark, rowed across the clear waters toward them.

"Are we in danger, Dad?" David asked logically.

"Somehow, son, I don't think so."

Only a short while later the other boy had made it across and had shoved the raft onto the shore.

"I thought I was alone," he said. "Praise God that I'm not."

He was in his early teens, tall, blonde, well-muscled, exuding health and strength. It was obvious that the life he had been leading outdoors was invigorating.

The three of them were soon sitting around the fire, eating.

"My parents are dead," he told them. "They were trying to stop the slaughter of a group of those Dwellers. They caught some of the bullets."

He wiped his mouth with the back of his hand.

"The Lord knows we'll be together again someday," he said unself-consciously, "but I still miss Mom and Dad all the time."

David and he began a kind of special dialogue, one peculiar to young people.

"Do you dream sometimes?" David asked.

"I try not to."

"You try not to? I...I don't understand."

"That's when Satan often is successful in prying into our subconscious and bringing out all sorts of things."

David described the dreams he had been having.

The teenager looked at him strangely.

"What's wrong?" David asked, uncomfortable under the other's gaze.

"I have dreamed exactly as you have."

"Exactly?"

"Exactly."

"The fact that the Lord has something special in store?"

"The same with me, David."

"What could it be?"

"I can't tell except that we will be called upon to serve Him in a way that no one else ever has."

"Wow!"

Then something occurred to David.

"But you said that dreams are often manipulated by Satan? How could that be with ours?"

"The two natures within us. At night our defenses are down, and our dreams become a battleground between the Lord and Lucifer. What it means, in our case, is that Satan will try to discourage us, to get us not to listen to the Lord."

"I never thought of it that way."

"I didn't either at first."

He smiled a bit.

"You and I are young by any standards. But we have seen more over the past few years than whole generations before us."

David nodded agreement.

"Makes a guy wonder what's ahead, doesn't it?" he added.

"Sure does."

The two boys and Kindred talked for a bit longer. It was nearly dark when they stopped, at least for that day.

"Getting late," David remarked casually to his new friend.

"Yeah," the other boy agreed as he got to his feet.

He told them that he had built a little shelter nearby.

"It's not much," he said. "But we can share it if you like. It's a mess now though."

Kindred said that didn't matter; they were pleased just to have some fellowship.

"Really," the boy said, "I want it to be right, especially now that it's the two of you."

"What do you mean?" Kindred asked.

"Give me half an hour," he said, pointedly ignoring the question. "I do want to make it a little more presentable. OK?"

They nodded.

"Thanks, Rev. Kindred, and David."

Kindred realized that they had been so caught up with one another, each surprised about the existence of the other, that they hadn't exchanged names before then.

"How did you know?" he asked, not sure whether to be alarmed or pleased.

Once again, without answering, and with a manner that suggested he was enjoying the moment immensely, the boy jumped back onto the raft.

"Hey, what's *your* name?" David asked.

He turned and smiled broadly at them.

"Jonathan."

"WHAT IS THE SENSE OF IT ALL?" THE AGING
theologian named Felix asked rhetorically, as he sat at the chessboard before starting
the next game.

"Who can say but God?" his younger fellow theologian friend named Rolf mused.

"Yes, but what did we learn from all that?" Felix questioned again. "It is not
an easy matter, I know."

"Perhaps we have learned in a cataclysmic fashion, and what a pity it took such
to teach us, that there are very few of God's creatures that are not worthy of respect,"
Rolf offered. "Rattlesnakes may qualify as exceptions, I suspect. And I can't think
of those slugs I find in my garbage from time to time as particularly inspiring, shall
we say. Doubtless there are others."

"Killer bees!" Felix exclaimed. "Yes, indeed, they surely are not included."

"But the list of creatures we must not harm for reasons of vanity or whatever,
that list is truly gigantic, dear friend. Take baby seals; those cute little minks and
foxes and other animals like them—harm one, rip off its fur to aid and abet the
egocentricities of those whose pitiable insecurities demand such temporary solace,
and we add some kind of corrosive moral cancer to *all* of society. Put any to death,
and we run risks of which we may not immediately be aware."

Rolf cleared his throat, eager to add another bit of insight, as though proving himself
to the older man.

"It may be akin," he went on, "to what Scripture says about entertaining an angel
unaware. The reverse may be just as powerful a truth: Do not abuse, do not cause
pain needlessly to any creature, no matter how lowly it seems, because—"

"I see where you are heading," Felix replied. "Couldn't we also say this, that

251

our sin natures place us under the spirit of delusion, from which we do not always extricate ourselves? Thus, to the Germans, the 'Final Solution' seemed perfectly acceptable, even the essence of true morality. But when the Jews were slaughtered during the Holocaust, all of us suffered, even those completely innocent of genocide.

"Indeed, Felix. So it was, Rolf, when Adam and Eve sinned thousands of years earlier, that we were born with their disease, and it became ours."

Rolf pushed himself away momentarily from the table, the thought captivating him.

"A man in Chicago releases some aerosol pollutant into the air, and it joins others, and distant Calcutta becomes a victim."

"Precisely!" Felix exclaimed, happy that his friend had made the connection.

"But is that all?" Rolf asked. "Is there no more to be gleaned from everything that has happened?"

"There may be, Rolf—there may be indeed. But we are looking at so much even now as through a glass darkly, my friend. We do not have such clear focus as we shall enjoy after He has taken us unto Himself. To be content with what we can grasp at this very moment, that is what must surely please our heavenly Father, wouldn't you agree?"

Rolf cleared his throat, then nodded.

" 'When He, the Spirit of truth, is come, He will guide you into all truth!' "

"Yes, Rolf, that sounds very good, very good, to be sure. "Anything else smacks of impatience, of faith based upon the assurance of imminent revelation, rather than the essence of things hoped for but not as yet seen, and with no indication as to when, Felix."

The two very good friends, pleased, began their game.